ENDLESS SKY: OLD BONES

DON JONES

DONJONES.COM

for Christopher,
who believed.

FOREWORD

Endless Sky is perhaps not proper LitRPG. It is much more akin to *Ready Player One,* where being in a fully immersive game is part of the plot. Characters develop in-game to work through that plot, but there's a lot less focus on grinding, leveling up, and other video game elements than you'll find in most LitRPG novels.

I don't disparage the true LitRPG, because fans of that genre do indeed love it, and I've found a couple of series I do enjoy (The Completionist Chronicles is one). Instead, this is simply a note that I'm not writing what some genre fans would consider a "true" LitRPG.

That said, according to LitRPG Reads (https://litrpgreads.com/blog/what-makes-a-good-litrpg-book#1-7-signs-of-a-great-litrpg), *Endless Sky* ticks all the criteria for a "good LitRPG book," so opinions may vary!

This novel may in fact be closer to the GameLit genre, although I definitely borrow elements from LitRPG, such as showing in-game messages, carefully tracking characters' stat sheets, and so on. But the internet seems *super* confused on what GameLit is supposed to mean, so I dunno.

Regardless, I have tried to create an enjoyable, compelling, and engaging story, strong characters, and a plot that hopefully keeps you hooked the whole way through.

I hope you think it's fun!

Don Jones

Las Vegas, 2023

DonJones.com

Endless Apocalypse™

Fight to survive, *Mad Max* style

EndlessApocalypseGame.com

Endless Deep™

Experience the wonders below the ocean's surface

EndlessDeepGame.com

Endless Frontier™

Shoot it out in the Wild, Wild West

EndlessFrontierGame.com

Endless Jungle™

Mysterious jungles and dangerous rivers

EndlessJungleGame.com

Endless Toons™

Reach into your hammerspace and pull out some fun

EndlessToonsGame.com

Endless Heroes™

Will you work to save the city . . . or destroy it?

EndlessHeroesGame.com

Endless Night™

Battle—and become—vampires, werewolves, and other creatures
of the night

EndlessNightGame.com

Endless Paradise™

Relax at our infinite beachside resort

EndlessParadiseGame.com

Ready to move beyond playing just eight hours a day? Contact us about settling into an Endless Play™ immersion pod—with all costs fully covered by most rental and meal subsidies!

Also check out:

- *Endless Duty™*
- *Endless Desert™*
- *Endless Empire™*
- *Endless Kawaii™*
- *Endless Safari™*
- *Endless Crusade™*

Whoever you are, whoever you want to be—there's an Endless Domains™ world for you!

1 / DUNGEON CRAWL

"Armor on the port side is at fifty percent," Stroman said in his deep, even voice. "Lad, keep that side away as best you can. Frank, looks like they're massing."

"Aye," our pilot said calmly, their hands dancing across *Princess'* helm console.

"I see them," I said, my voice a bit tighter than I'd intended. We'd taken a pummeling to this point, and we only had a half-dozen of the little bastards to take out. "Still down to one laser?"

"Until the auto-repair has a minute to repair the linkages from reactor two, yeah," Stroman said. "I'm pushing a lot of power from reactor one to the armor."

"Sure wish we had an engineer," I muttered.

"She's sitting pretty in a calming white respawn room," Mi-Cha said, a bit more bite in her tone than usual.

"Firing missiles," I said, punching the console as the enemy ships wheeled back toward us, incidentally forming a bit of a cluster as they did so. "Firing railguns. Firing dorsal laser."

‹Starship Weapons: Critical Success›

I howled with joy, likely startling my crewmates, as my skill roll maxed out. Our laser punched through two of the six enemy ships, impossibly heavy railgun slugs pierced two more, and my missile salvo managed to take out the remaining two.

"That's what I'm talking about" Stroman crowed. This his console cheeped. "Another signature. Only one. Probably the dungeon boss."

"Gods, I hope so," Mi-Cha muttered. "Tactical, give me a sitrep."

Stroman rattled through the numbers quickly. "We've got half our missiles, but reactor two's linkages are still fried. Without a human engineer down there, the 'bots will need a lot more time to fix those. Armor is at seventy percent overall, fifty on the port side specifically. I'm using power to hold it together, and the repair systems are already shuttling nano-stock as fast as they can. Speaking of which, we're down to thirty percent nano-stock. Reactor one is in good condition. Engineering is a mess—even if we had people down there, the systems are at twenty percent. They'd be at a massive skill disadvantage. Med bay is toast—"

"—along with the doc—" I grumbled.

"—and there are questions about life support in the hab ring. Oh wait, contact is resolving, stand—holy mother of hell in a kilt."

My weapons station more or less mirrored what Stroman was seeing, and I whistled. "That's a big 'un."

An understatement, to be sure, and definitely the dungeon boss. The ship picked up many of the cosmetic details of the smaller ones we'd see in the previous *eight* waves: smooth, rounded lines of dark, oily-looking metal, highlighted with red accents. But this was clearly the Poppa Bear of the lot: It was a flat disc at least two hundred meters across, "standing" on one edge so the face of the disc was facing us. The middle of the disc—probably thirty meters or so, although our scanners weren't at full capacity at the moment —was a raging maw of inward-pointing spikes and roiling orange plasma.

"It's going to try and eat us," Lad breathed, sounding almost delighted. They never managed to get wrought up about anything.

"Scanning," Stroman said, his voice finally tense. "Readout on your consoles."

It wasn't great news.

[Target Identification: Beholder Monarch]
[Target Identification: Level 20]

"We're in over our heads," Mi-Cha growled. "But we've come this far."

Our ship, *Pretty, Pretty Princess* was technically classified as Level 19, although we'd equipped her more like a Level 30. Problem was, a lot of that equipment was on the fritz, as running the ship required a full complement of crew, and we'd lost all but the four of us in the previous attack waves. Almost without thinking, my own character sheet header scrolled before my eyes:

Frank Kozina
Class: Truthsayer (hidden)
Class: Business Manager
Account: 482,819 Credits
Party funds: 7,389,246,766 Credits
Level 16

I'd managed to grind up four levels in the past year or so, but I knew we were *all*—save maybe for Mi-Cha, who was always kept her character sheet close to the vest—in over our heads.

"It'll be worth it for the quantum sequencer," Las said happily. "It seems to be waiting for us. Do we engage?"

But it wasn't waiting for us.

Without so much as a preamble, a twenty meter-wide column of plasma launched itself from the enemy ship's—middle? mouth? orifice? whatever—and blasted across the kilometers between us far faster than Newtonian physics or Einstein's laws should have allowed. Lad squawked, slamming their console and managing to turn *Princess* maybe a meter or two before the star-hot blast struck us.

Pretty, Pretty Princess was built like a brick. Literally: the ship was brick-shaped. The majority of that exterior hull was nano-armor, capable of re-forming and repairing itself, given enough power and nano-stock from our interior storage containers. The flat nose of the ship was especially armored, with multiple meters of nano-armor tightly woven together in a dense crystalline matrix. The bow of the ship could, and had, taken a beating that would have crumpled most other ships in her class, all thanks to that armor.

The Beholder Monarch's plasma blast tore it away like so much tissue paper.

A stupid, giggly part of my mind expressed admiration for the accuracy of the Endless Sky sim as nano-armor flashed to vapor, turning Lad's last-second veer into a full-on spin.

"We're blind in the front," Stroman barked unnecessarily. A full third of the ship's tactical sensors had been layered on top of the nano-armor in a fine mesh, all of which had boiled away into space.

"Fortunately, we're not facing it with the bow anymore," Lad snapped back, finally leaning into the gravity of the situation. "Frank?"

"Not with us spinning like this," I said. "Even the missiles are locked out. I need you to slow us down."

The flat voice of the ship's computer chimed in: "Hull Integrity Alert."

No kidding. The bridge's artificial horizon was a stuttery pulse of blue and red, the ship's nose dragging us into a sickening tumble. My stomach flopped in realtime (Sim accuracy! Amazing!). The Monarch didn't chase; it held position, another sun-bright tongue gathering at its center.

Mi-Cha was shouting, soundtracking the chaos: "Stroman! Cut gravity! Gimme zero-gee before it shears the ring! Power to integrity systems!"

"On it, Captain," Stroman gritted, voice like a grinding servo. He slammed the override and all the blood rushed to my temples. My hands fumbled over the weapons console, and I saw Lad's knuckles flash white on the helm, eyes hard and flat.

"Second volley, incoming," Stroman called, and Lad's jaw flexed.

"Brace for impact," Mi-Cha snapped. But there wasn't time. The Monarch's beam punched the *Princess* midships. The whole hull quivered like a violated tuning fork and the status HUD bled crimson.

> [Emergency: Multiple Hull Breaches. Habitat
> Ring Compromised.]

The bridge lights flicked to blacklight mode as the system rerouted, and I could see the inside of my faceplate reflected in the screen. It looked pale, scared, but I was too busy to notice.

"Stroman, weapons grid—" I started.

"I'm already patching aux to the dorsal battery. You get one shot, Frank. One." His tone was final.

Mi-Cha's hand crushed my shoulder. "Frank," she hissed, "make it count."

I watched the Monarch through the aft display, the only camera still feeding. It was lumbering closer now, maw opening and closing in rhythmic anticipation, a church bell of hunger. Its forward array glowed, and the radial plasma spikes were flexing, flexing—

I scanned for a weak point. There was nothing. No classic boss-glow, no highlighted panel. But just as its third attack began to spool, I saw a flicker. A paler segment, like a thin glass ring at the equator of its disc. Not a proper vulnerability, but a seam.

"Stroman," I said, voice dry, "ready the railgun. I need five seconds to calibrate. I'm going to need two shots, rapid-fire." I was already rerouting every last watt from the dying hull into the forward capacitor.

Lad, to their credit, kept *Princess* in a tight, ugly spiral, never presenting a flat target. But the Monarch was too big to miss.

A message flashed in my vision:

> ‹Starship Weapons: Final Shot. Railgun
> Overclocked. Chance of Catastrophic Failure:
> 86%.›

Not ideal.

But my world had narrowed to a single icon: the glass seam. The Beholder Monarch's charging plasma painted the world in optical white. Time dilated, every sense stretched out to infinity. I could feel Mi-Cha's breath on my neck as she leaned forward in her captain's chair. I tapped the trigger.

‹Starship Weapons: Critical Success›

The shot was so bright it blinded the bridge, pixelating my retinas into static. I felt the hull shudder at the double recoil, then a long, trembling silence.

"Reactor one's near critical," Stroman said. "Two is offline, linkages are scrap."

The Monarch's glass ring blossomed open, shattering, and its whole disc flexed, convulsed, and then the plasma at its core detonated outward in a gory, beautiful nova.

I yelled, not with triumph but in animal relief. The HUD blinked into clarity, the Monarch now a dissipating cloud of debris.

"Did it," Lad panted, slumping over their console. "We did it."

Stroman let out a whoop exactly once, then let himself slump. "Hull integrity... well. We're alive."

Mi-Cha whooped too, which she never did. Then, with her usual steel: "Frank, double-check. Confirm that thing is dead."

"On it," I said, running a sweep. The wreckage read as inert, no radiation spikes, no system pings. The sim, or the AI behind it, lingered a beat, as if respecting our right to paranoia—then spat up a crisp notification:

‹System Notification: Dungeon Cleared! XP
Gained: 1,200,000›

We all sat there, the four of us, letting the battered bridge fill with the glow of it. The numbers ticked up, console lights shifting back to normal. All the wounds, the stupidity, the near-suicides— instantly justified.

Mi-Cha finally broke the silence: "Inventory check. Did we get the quantum sequencer?"

Everyone was quiet. "No loot drop," Stroman said, his voice uneasy.

"But it says we cleared the—" Mi-Cha began, her own tone confused.

Another message glowed inside our eyeballs.

> ‹System Notification: You have cleared Dungeon Abraxis XVII. You have opened the way to the Pit of Bones.›
>
> ‹Dungeon Entrance: Pit of Bones›
>
> ‹Pit of Bones is a Level 30 Dungeon›
>
> ‹Not Recommended for your party at this time›
>
> ‹Rewards: Minimum 2,000,000 XP, Quantum Sequencer›
>
> ‹Available Title: Bane of the Beholders›

"What," Mi-Cha growled, "the actual fuck?"

"We've been baited and switched!" Stroman complained.

> ‹You have one hour to proceed or turn back the way you came.›
>
> ‹59:59:58›

The countdown timer dimmed slightly and shrunk into a corner of my vision.

"This is bullshit," Lad said succinctly.

"We've known some of the upper-level dungeons were nested," I countered. "This is just the first we've seen."

"Yeah, but level thirty?" Mi-Cha said. "Are there even any level thirty parties in the game?"

"Not that anyone has admitted to," Stroman said.

"We're turning back, right?" I asked quietly. "I mean, the ship is not in good shape."

Mi-Cha's voice was like steel. "Frank, an entire *world* of people have been doing the research grind on this transporter technology *for a year*. They've managed to identify two of the ten components we'll need."

"I know, the quantum scanner and the quantum sequencer. We got the first one last week."

"And we're getting this one," she said flatly. "Stroman, what can we do in the next fifty minutes?"

"Not damn much," our XO said, his eyes flicking over his console. "That bow armor is more than triple our nano-stocks at full, and we're nowhere near full. I can maybe get reactor two rolling to half capacity. Missile stocks are good, both battle lasers are online. Every RFLAM is offline."

My gut tightened. The Rapid-Fire Laser, Anti-Missile emplacements were our only defense against incoming missiles, and the last dungeon had flung *thousands* at us. "Guys, we can't—"

"I'm in," Lad said with a shrug. "Beats sitting around Nexus watching medieval re-enactors go hunting for space dragons or whatever."

"Frank's not wrong, though," Stroman pointed out. "We're in bad shape, and like I said, it's not going to get much better."

"So we respawn like everyone else," Mi-Cha said.

I almost gasped at her casual use of the term. "We lose the *ship* if that happens. *And* the loot. *And* a shitload of XP. *And*—"

"So we earn it back, Frank," Mi-Cha snapped.

I ground my teeth and tapped at my console, pulling together as full a tactical readout as I could.

‹Starship Battle Tactics: Success›

Numbers don't like. "Stroman, you've got to be seeing the same thing I'm seeing."

He hesitated. "I failed my tactics roll."

"Well, I didn't. We have a *less than one percent chance* of surviving *the same dungeon we just cleared* if we continue. And that was ten levels below this Pit of Bones. Guys, we know where this thing is. We can put a battle cruiser out here to keep anyone else out. We can level-up and come back for the quantum sequencer. This makes *no—*"

"I'm calling the vote," Mi-Cha said.

A chill ran down my spine. (*Amazing sensory accuracy in this sim!*)

"In," Lad repeated.

"In," Mi-Cha added.

"Out," I said loudly.

"Stroman?" our captain demanded.

Still, he hesitated. "I made my roll, man," I said softly. "The numbers don't add up."

His voice was... soft. Almost distracted. "Yeah, Frank. But isn't this why we picked this game instead of *Endless Paradise* or something?"

"Jesus, Stroman, you can't—"

"In," he said.

"Shit," I muttered.

"You know the agreement, Frank. When we—"

"I'm in, Captain," I said heatedly. "You'll get my best. And an 'I told you so' when we're back on Nexus *sans* a ship."

"Take us in, Lad." I knew she wasn't ignoring me, but it sure damn felt like it.

Pretty, Pretty Princess, still shedding dying nano-armor particles, eased forward.

‹Dungeon Commences: Pit of Bones›

We barely even had time to get our bearings. *Princess'* battered hull shuddered, and the HUD vomited new contacts all around us, a sphere of death closing like a fist. Dozens—no, scores—of the Monarch's bastard offspring, each a different flavor of nightmare, arrayed in a perfect formation. The system named them: Skullspawn, Haemovores, Bonecutters, all Level 18 or higher.

And this was just the first wave.

They didn't hesitate, didn't monologue, didn't even issue a challenge. The guns opened up.

The world became noise and red.

Lad's voice: "Evasive!"

I was already on the triggers, not even waiting for them to finish the word. Every battery we had left barked, spat, or shrieked. Missiles howled away in a double ripple, railguns spat depleted uranium like a spitting cobra with a grudge. Lasers—one ventral, one dorsal, and a third of the mesh offline—slashed the black between us and the enemy.

It wasn't enough.

The first salvo from the Skullspawn lanced through the half-melted armor on our port side and carved the habitat ring in half. Stroman cursed, then started barking compartment status, but I already knew: the hull was venting atmo and the hab section was a charnel house. The sim was good enough to keep the grav down, but I felt the sucking void through the soles of my boots.

I kept firing.

"Lad, in the pipe—" I started.

"Already on it," they snapped, and the Princess tumbled, rolled, then slipped through a gap in the enemy formation that only existed for a microsecond. Sensors painted streaks of angry blue plasma as we slipped the needle, but our shields were a joke and two more hull sections went bright red.

[Emergency: Hull Integrity 12%]

"Stroman, can you extend the heat sinks?"

"I can. Might give us five seconds. They'll be vulnerable"

"It won't matter. Do it."

He did.

The heat sinks were supposed to radiate away waste heat over minutes, maybe hours. We dumped it in an instant, a spiky, radioactive cloud that glared so bright even the sim's filters couldn't quite keep it out of my eyes. Four of the Bonecutters were blinded, spun off, and one hit its friend head-on, both detonating in a spectacular spray of neon wreckage.

I let myself feel hope. Just for a second.

Then the Haemovores launched. Their spike-jets stitched across our hull in a ripple, and I watched as the main battery went dark. The bridge shook so hard that my teeth cut my lip, and all the displays froze, then rebooted in panic mode.

"Frank," Mi-Cha said, her voice weirdly calm, "can you still fire?"

"I can do railgun, but not much else. Lasers are dust. Missiles are out. I—" I tried to reroute from the main bus and got a message that wasn't even in English. "It's all jury-rigged from here."

"Give me your best shot," she said.

Princess bucked as the next volley hit, and every warning klaxon I'd ever heard screamed at once. I aimed the railgun at the biggest thing I could see—the bone-white flagship at the center of the formation, a chimeric thing with a jaw like a buzzsaw and a crown of burning metal.

"Firing," I said, but the words were drowned in full-body vibration as the gun went off.

I saw it hit. The round punched into the flagship and for a second, just a second, it looked like victory. The enemy's core went nova, flaring out ionized gas and bone fragments. All the little ships paused, as if their puppetmaster had sneezed.

"Lad, now!" Mi-Cha barked.

Lad kicked *Princess* into a death spiral, diving straight through the debris cloud. The sim's physics were lovingly cruel: every chunk that hit us ripped away another layer of hull, but for half a breath, the enemy couldn't see us.

Then we were out—and *Princess* was in pieces.

"Warning: Bridge integrity at critical."

No kidding.

The hull gave way. The bridge shuddered and, with a wet, metallic screech, sheared off from the rest of the ship. I heard every bone in my body vibrate; I tasted blood.

"Auto-eject sequence initiated," the computer said, like it was reading a bedtime story.

The last thing I saw before the viewports opaqued was *Princess*, my *Princess*, the fucking tank-brick of the galaxy, blossom in a brief, beautiful explosion. She took a dozen enemies with her in a final, spiteful act of physics.

Then the escape module was tumbling, and I was strapped to my chair, Mi-Cha screaming orders, Stroman running damage control, Lad trying to hotwire a navigation override into what was basically a steel coffin. We thumped and skipped across the void, a ragged marble in a cosmic alley.

For a second, it was just us and the void.

Then the surviving enemy ships pivoted, their attention laser-focused. They ringed us, and I realized with a cold spike of horror that the sim was going to make us experience all of this.

We couldn't even fire back.

We could only watch as the biggest of the brutes lined up, wound up, and punched a hole straight through the center of the bridge module.

The world went white.

‹You Have Died›

For a moment, I thought that was it. That the sim would disengage, that the fail-state would boot us back to Nexus. But my screen blinked, throbbed, and then resolved into a blank, white void.

I was naked. Not physically—in the sim, I still wore my battered, blood-slick flight suit—but the sense of exposure was real. I turned, saw the others: Mi-Cha with her hair wild, Lad still perched like a gargoyle, Stroman standing, arms folded, already glaring at the world like it owed him money.

A prompt appeared, floating, mocking:

‹You have failed Dungeon: Pit of Bones.›

2 / NEXUS

I sat in the command station's upper gallery, a ring of glass and brushed steel overlooking a mall of identical consoles, identical faces, and identical navy-blue jumpsuits. The station clock blinked seventeen seconds behind schedule. I flagged it, just because I could, then immediately flagged my own flag for being petty and unnecessary. My skill in Bureaucracy had just leveled up and even the act of reporting myself for abuse of the reporting system got me another fractional percent toward the next level.

That was the kind of day I was having.

Down below, Kira traced her usual circuit between the traffic board and the comms pit, back stiff and arms tucked at her sides as if she were performing a kata. Kira didn't walk, she skimmed, and every so often a corner of her lips quirked in silent pleasure at catching the rest of us slumping into entropy.

I yawned. Openly. The sim's mouth-feel was exact, even the slight dryness at the back of my throat. No one noticed. Everyone here was either too new or too self-involved to pay me any mind. The old crew had scattered, Mi-Cha to the citadels of Endless Kingdom to "work on my melee skills," Lad grinding piloting contracts in some asteroid belt, and Stroman's name popped up in the logs once as a "consulting discipline officer," but even that could be a joke or a bug.

The world, as of this morning, was not a world. It was a twelve-kilometer-wide ring station orbiting nothing, run by a skeleton crew of players and an army of glass-eyed, angelic-faced "staff." There were, last I checked, forty-seven real people on station and some high-four-digit count of NPC "ghosts" doing the rest.

I clicked into my character sheet, mostly for the nostalgic pain of it.

> Frank Kozina
> Class: Truthsayer (hidden)
> Class: Business Manager
> Level 14 (-2)
> Account: 182,993 Credits
> Party funds: 7,389,247 Credits†
> †Party dissolution and escrow pending dispute. See Form 2274-B.
> Bureaucracy: 14 (-2; Expert)
> Leadership: 9 (Disputed, see HR)
> Starship Tactics: 12
> Truthsayer: [DATA BLOCKED]
> Engineering: 3 (Unlicensed)

I did not need another reminder that the party funds were in limbo until the new ship build was certified. That new ship, last I checked, was fourth in the construction queue at the drydock above the Lunar Mare, and unless one of the parties ahead of us suffered a catastrophic accident, "jumping the line" would require ten times the funds we had left.

A flicker on the upper display told me Kira had finally decided to acknowledge me. Her face, compressed to an ovoid on my wristband, said only: "You flagged the clock again."

"And I flagged myself for it," I said, not bothering to hide the annoyance. "I'm growing as a person."

"Correction," Kira said, "you're only growing in Bureaucracy. Your Humanity stat is stable at two, trending down."

I grunted, then ran a hand through my hair, which was still as black and uninteresting as when I'd created this avatar. Kira, of course, had gone full platinum and cyber-sleek, which was half-ironic considering her background was in ancient navigation and logistics, not post-human fashion. She strode into the gallery without knocking, holding a glassy tablet at a perfectly neutral angle.

"Morning," she said. "Or whatever you call it at zero-two-hundred."

"Nightmare," I said. "The hour of ghosts."

"More ghosts than humans these days," Kira replied. She waited, then tilted her head. "You want the report?"

"Thrill me," I said.

She set the tablet down and scrolled through a series of colored blocks with a flick of her pinky.

"Arrivals from Endless Kingdom in the green, minimal incidents. Next up, we have a special cohort from Endless Frontier—three A-classes and a D, all requesting permission to bypass customs and proceed directly to housing. They're threatening to file a dispute."

"They always have a dispute," I said. "And never a ticket to show for it."

Kira ignored this. "Endless Industry shuttle is inbound at 0347. Five passengers, two listed as 'Free Agents' and three under sealed assignment. I ran the names against the Nexus Manifest and none came up as flagged." She shrugged. "Guess they're clean."

"Guess so," I said, already bored.

Kira paged to the next screen. "Departures are on schedule. Endless Jungle first—note, two passengers seem intent on bringing back souvenirs that are flagged as 'active containment risk.' I logged the anomaly with Quarantine, but..."

I waved a hand. "We'll just have another stampede through the commons if they get loose. Noted."

"Next, Endless Desert—only three travelers, one of whom is, and I quote, 'carrying a lifetime grudge against you.'"

"Is that the Luminari again?"

Kira nodded. "She says she'll duel you at the earliest opportunity."

"That's every Tuesday, then."

She didn't crack a smile, but her eyes sparkled with silent delight. "Last, Endless Night."

I shivered, for effect. "Anything from there is bad news. Do we know why anyone would want to go?"

"Speculation in the queue: they're there for the artifacts. There are persistent rumors that certain items only persist through a true character death in Endless Night, and then only under specific conditions." She squinted. "It's a longshot, but the data miners seem sure of it."

I let that hang for a minute. The hum of the station returned, a background whine like a mouthful of cold wind and recycled oxygen. I tried not to think about the fact that, statistically, three quarters of those who entered Endless Night never returned, and of those who did, half came back glitched in one way or another.

"Let me guess," I said. "Most of these are just going to rotate through and end up back here with a grievance."

Kira lifted the tablet, tapped the next field. "Ninety-three percent, last cycle. The rest vanish into the system or 'retire to a quiet life of service.'" She made air quotes. "Which just means they got bored and left their avatars parked somewhere scenic."

I scanned the deck below. The comms pit was quiet, just a pair of maintenance ghosts with hollow eyes trading lines of code in between actual calls. The ops center, lit in deep blue, flickered with the afterglow of a dozen half-finished arguments. I spotted a security ghost herding a pair of rowdy pilots toward the disciplinary zone; they struggled, but the ghost's arms were like vices.

"If I ask you to take a walk with me through the ring, will you say yes or no?" I asked, mostly out of desperation.

Kira considered, then tucked the tablet under her arm. "I will say yes, provided it's not a walk but a full inspection."

"Done."

She led the way, her gait a bit more relaxed now that she'd scored a win. Down the steps, into the main concourse—a wide, open cylinder rimmed with storefronts and kiosks, each staffed by ghosts running on various settings of "friendly" and "eager to serve." The lights in here were calibrated for maximum daylight illusion, and as a result, the people who worked the nightshift always looked a little jaundiced and sickly.

"Remind me," I said, "did you ever work a ground station, or was it always the ship?"

She shrugged. "Did a stint as dockmaster at New Sydney. ConFed. Hated every minute. Too many tourists combined with too much bureaucracy."

"What's the worst tourist crime?"

"Refusing to learn basic vacuum protocol," she said, without hesitation. "Or the ones who thought smuggling drugs would matter in a system that manufactures most of them."

I snorted. "What's the point of crime if there's no scarcity?"

Kira didn't answer, but the curve of her mouth suggested she'd asked herself that one a few times.

The ring's "sky" was an LCD-matte projection of bright blue, with fake clouds drifting through at a mathematically optimized pace. I had them turn off the sun. The population of the ring at this hour was thin—just a handful of human-looking avatars, a few post-humans with data auras, and the odd, impossibly bland faces of the NPC staff. I recognized maybe two real players; the rest were either simulation stock or passers-through.

I said, "Let's check the shipyards. Maybe some idiot crashed their freighter and we're bumped up the line."

She veered left, toward the nearest viewport. The simulated night beyond was absolute black, but at the far edge of the ring, drydock lights blinked in blue and white, harsh and stark against the void. I dialed the zoom to full.

Fourth in the queue, right where we'd been yesterday, and the day before. The three ships ahead of ours were massive, labor-intensive projects. One looked like it had been fused together from a hodgepodge of naval dreadnoughts and sports yachts. The other two were just classic, uninspired brick-ships with missile banks big enough to flatten a moon. Unflattering copies of *Princess,* basically.

"Still fourth," Kira said, echoing my thought. "Estimated time, thirty-three days."

"Thirty-three days?" I almost choked. "Last week it was twenty."

"Labor dispute," she said. "Someone is trying to unionize the NPCs."

That broke me. I laughed, for real this time, so loud that a passing security ghost side-eyed me like I was about to start trouble. "Do they even know what unions are?"

"Probably not," Kira said. "But they know how to file a grievance."

We stood in silence, watching the shipyards blink and churn. I tried to imagine what it would feel like, to sit at the helm of my own ship again, to have a crew that wasn't pieced together from ghosts and simulants.

It didn't help.

A couple minutes passed. Kira, efficient as always, checked the time and recalibrated her stance. "We should keep moving. The main shuttle port is cycling arrivals every fifteen minutes right now, and there's a rumor that one of the Endless Industry parties wants to hack the airlocks for a prank."

I was tempted to ask how she even heard about it, but with Kira there was always an answer, and usually it was "I read the logs." So I just nodded and let her lead.

On the way, a flight of stairs led down into the food court—a garish, overbright cluster of bars, diners, and replicator kiosks. A few real players huddled in groups, quietly eating, drinking, or watching the news feeds. On the overhead, a looping ad for "Live the Adventure: Endless Sky" stuttered and glitched, then resolved into a promo for Endless Kingdom, all jousts and dragons and swooping camera shots.

A memory flashed: Me, sitting at a table with the rest of *Princess's* crew, splitting up the loot and the drama, arguing over upgrades. It seemed like a million years ago, and maybe it was.

I felt the ache in my teeth before I realized I was clenching my jaw.

"Lost in thought," Kira observed, not a question.

"Lost in something," I said. "Do you ever miss the ship?"

She considered. "I was only on it for that one mission. And hey, the ship is gone, but the mission isn't. As long as there's a destination, I don't care if it's a junker or a palace."

"Must be nice," I muttered, but I think she heard.

At the port, the incoming shuttle from Endless Industry had already started debarking. The five passengers looked like every stereotype of steampunk ever built: top hats and goggles and even a goddamn brass monocle. I almost rolled my eyes, but then remembered that I used to wear a custom flightsuit with a logo on the back. Not much better.

The crew chief was a pale young man with a face like a knife and a habit of glaring at every surface as if it owed him money. He marched straight up to Kira and me, holding out a digital passport.

"Permission to enter Nexus proper?" he said, eyes hard.

Kira took the passport, did a perfunctory scan, then handed it back. "Standard quarantine applies. Any biological artifacts need to be declared and processed."

He scowled. "We're not bringing in anything organic. Just here to see the sights and maybe run a few—experiments."

"Define 'experiment,'" I said.

He grinned, a real, oily thing. "Wouldn't want to spoil the surprise."

Kira tensed, but only a little. I made a show of stepping between them. "I'll be watching the logs, and if anything gets weird, you'll be on the next shuttle to Endless Night."

The man's grin never faltered. "Understood, sir."

He gathered his party and vanished into the corridor.

Kira said, "You handled that well."

"Don't patronize me," I said. "My skill in Bureaucracy is already at Expert."

She almost smiled. Almost.

We made the rounds, logging each handoff, each report, each petty little dispute. My head felt like it was made of bees, but I kept at it, because the only thing worse than doing this job was doing it badly.

After two hours, Kira peeled off for a break, promising to check in before the next shuttle. I lingered in the gallery, watching the slow pulse of station activity and wondering, not for the first time, if this was my actual afterlife.

I hoped not. But I was beginning to suspect.

————

AFTER THE SHIFT, I WALKED THE EMPTY CORRIDORS BACK TO what passed for civilization: a three-level atrium, all glass and bone-white columns, dotted with "cafes" and the Central Bar, which was required by law (I checked) to stay open all hours of all days.

A simulation can do a lot with a beer. They'd tuned the weight of the glass, the faint note of bitter at the end of the sip, the way the cold bloomed down your throat. I ordered the usual and let myself slide into a booth.

Around me, the late crowd was thin: a merchant from Endless Jungle, his feathers dusty and his eyes on his wrist-comm; two maintenance ghosts sitting side-by-side at the counter, not talking, not moving; a lone suit from the desert world, gold-threaded and chewing what I prayed was not simulated raw meat.

I took a sip, and then, just for the hell of it, ordered another. The system glitched and brought me two at once. Progress.

There were times—before all this—when I'd been other things. I'd been a mid-level majordomo on an Aa'an cityship, pulling in six-figure commissions and running a team of twenty. I'd been a contract assassin for the Guild, back when the Guild had standards and the murder wasn't the point. I'd even once, very briefly, run a delivery service on the outskirts of the Core, ferrying fake data cubes to fake criminals in a city built out of hallucination.

Now? Paperwork. I did the paperwork, and, worse, I did it well.

"Where did I go wrong?" I muttered, and the glass offered no answer.

I was halfway through the first beer when a voice, fresh and unmodulated, cut through the room: "Is this seat open?"

He looked seventeen, maybe, with a mop of blue hair and the kind of skin that came only from the highest-end avatar design. He wore a full sleeve of mechanical tattoos—little filigrees of gold circuit and glass, running up his arm and into the side of his neck. His boots were matte-black, his jacket the same. If there was a way to telegraph "I'm from the cyberpunk world," he'd used it.

I waved at the seat, and he sat.

"Frank Kozina, right?" he said, pronouncing it the way my mother would have: "Kozeena."

I wanted to say no, but I just nodded.

He grinned. "Man, I can't believe I'm sitting here. I saw your old stats, back in the leaderboard days. Didn't you run the central ops for *Princess*?"

The memory was like a splinter under my tongue. "And weapons. For a while."

He slumped forward, fingers twined. "Sorry, is that... too soon?"

I shook my head. "It's always too soon."

"I'm Jay. Jay Eleven, if you want the full tag, but that's embarrassing. From Endless Industry. Just got in."

Endless Industry was a favorite of the old theorycraft forums: it was adjacent to Sky in the sim architecture, but ran on a completely different economic model, with high dependence on resource flow, sabotage, and a cutthroat "market." Basically, it was Wall Street with lasers.

Jay's eyes scanned me for a reaction. I offered nothing.

He leaned in. "So, I gotta ask. Is it really true that the game worlds are all, like, connected now? Not just by shuttle but at the base code?"

I felt myself smile, despite everything. "It's true. You can run a macro in Kingdom and, if you're lucky, it'll propagate to Jungle or even Industry. The first ones to figure it out got some good press. Now it's old hat."

Jay's jaw dropped. "Do you ever think about what that means?"

I did, all the time, but I doubted we were thinking the same thing.

Jay said, "It means the whole system is just a single sim, right? Like, one big backend, all stitched together."

"That's right," I said, not unkindly.

He looked like he'd just solved a math problem no one else could. "So the old rules don't matter. If I get a mod to work here, I can get it to work back home. Maybe even in Kingdom."

I shrugged. "Try it. If you break the simulation, they'll just restart you in Endless Night."

Jay blinked. "Is it true that nobody comes back from that?"

"Some do," I said. "But not as temselves."

He shuddered, then, and reached for the nearest glass. I let him have it. He took a swallow and made a face. "Not bad. Not real, but not bad."

"Nothing here is real," I said.

Jay looked at me for a long second, and I could see the question coming before he asked it. "Why are you still here?"

I didn't have an answer. Or maybe I did, but it was too long and too boring to say aloud.

He said, "I mean, you're a legend. You could run any station, anywhere. Why stick it out in Nexus? Is it, like, a debt thing? Or are you playing the long game?"

"Neither," I said, but he didn't believe me.

He smiled, wide and reckless. "I'm going to try something. A hack I built in Industry. If it works, you'll be the first to know."

"Try not to get caught," I said, only half a joke.

Jay slid out of the booth and vanished into the corridor, boots making no sound at all.

I looked at my hands, at the glass, at the fake condensation sweating down the sides. There was a time, not long ago, when I would have killed to be the one running the hacks, pushing the boundaries. Instead I was the guy warning the kids about the Night.

I left the bar unfinished, the second beer untouched.

On the way back to my quarters, the ring corridor was even emptier than before. Above, the simulated stars burned steady and unblinking, and somewhere far below, the shuttles shuttled, the ghosts ghosted, and the whole system churned on.

I wondered what it would be like, to just walk out, like the others did. To find a world, maybe even Endless Night, and see what happened when the rules were really gone.

I should have known better than to try to cut through the concourse when the day's first shuttle from Endless Kingdom was due. The arrivals lobby was an atrium of high arches and stained-glass projections, a half-hearted attempt to impress knights and nobles used to cathedrals. It mostly smelled of ozone, cleaning solution, and virtual sweat.

A man in full plate intercepted me mid-stride, sword clanging at his hip. "Sir Kozina!" he boomed, which was both accurate and extremely annoying.

"Can I help you?" I asked.

He planted himself before me and struck a pose of noble outrage. "There is grave error in the system. Last evening, while attempting to hoist a cask of ale, I found myself—" he hesitated, as if the admission itself was sacrilege—"unable to move the cask. Not by so much as an inch! I demand recourse."

I recognized him: Sir Charles of Endless Kingdom, top-tier paladin, former habitue of the PvP leaderboards, and, unless he'd been wiped, a notorious griefer. He had a reputation for getting into fights with ghosts and winning.

"Sir Charles," I said, keeping my voice professional, "I'm afraid that Nexus runs on baseline physics. There's no heroic multiplier here. If you want to perform feats of strength, you need to return to Kingdom."

His eyes widened, the horror real. "So I am but a man?"

I shrugged. "We're all just people here."

He deflated by at least two centimeters. "This is unacceptable. I shall file a formal grievance with the Chancery."

I smiled. "Form 118-B, available at any kiosk."

He nodded, clanked away, and was replaced by the next in the impromptu queue: a woman in a harlequin's mask, hands jittering, mouth a too-wide crescent.

She said, "Sir! Sir! I have a physics complaint!"

"Go on."

She twitched. "I am a licensed user of Toonspace. My inventory is infinite. Last shift, I reached into my pocket for my mallet and—" she mimed an empty pocket—"there was only lint. What's going on?"

"Did you try rebooting?" I deadpanned.

She nodded, then paused. "It hurt. Is that normal?"

I made a note to ask Kira if the updates were filtering over to the Toons. "Hammer space doesn't translate outside of Toon. You're limited to standard carry capacity in Nexus. Try the hat next time, but be prepared for disappointment."

Her eyes filled with tears. Real ones, big and cartoon-perfect. She sagged, then—against every law of anatomy—flattened herself to the floor and oozed away.

I checked my wrist-band: two disputes, two resolved. The system dinged a point to my Diplomacy score.

Third in line was a merchant, arguing with himself over the cost of a synthetic spice. Fourth, a player who claimed the ghosts were plotting against him. Fifth, a woman in desert silks, trying to sell me on a pyramid scheme (literally, it was for virtual pyramids).

It went like this for another twenty minutes. Each problem, petty and dumb. Each solution, marginally less so. My brain was sliding into wallpaper mode when I saw Kira, lurking behind the rail at the far end of the hall. She raised a hand in silent salute.

I cut through the queue and joined her.

She said, "You're trending."

I groaned. "Which board?"

"Damage control."

I allowed myself a chuckle. "That's better than nothing."

She watched the hall with me, eyes scanning every interaction. "You know, it won't always be like this. There's talk of a new patch. Maybe even a world merge."

I snorted. "Yeah. Maybe they'll even patch out griefers."

She smiled, which on Kira was a tectonic event. "You'd be out of a job."

"Maybe that's for the best," I said, only half-joking.

We stood there for a while, saying nothing, watching the world through the glass.

When I finally made it to my quarters, the room was exactly as I'd left it: neat, impersonal, a faint overlay of simulated home. I poured myself a water, sat at the edge of the bunk, and stared at the wall.

If this was what the rest of my days looked like, it was at least better than being dead. Probably.

Outside, the stars didn't move. Not even a little.

3 / CHAMPIONS ON THE RUN

I woke to a whine in my ears, the sound of the station lights cycling to morning mode. Same as always: the fake day's first photons painted the inside of my eyelids pale blue, a color not found in any natural sunrise. My first thought was that someone had left a console diagnostic running in the admin gallery, but when I checked the logs, there was nothing out of place. The hum was just my brain, rebooting.

The clock on the wall, analog for maximum irony, ticked exactly seventeen seconds ahead of schedule. I logged it. I flagged my own logging for unnecessary pettiness, then flagged that as recursive pettiness and filed a duplicate dispute. This was my new morning ritual, a way to remind myself that there were still things in the universe more pointless than my job.

I showered, dressed, and ate the identical "nutrient loaf" that arrived at my quarters at precisely 0700. The taste was equal parts cardboard and remorse, but it filled the gap. I checked the comms: nothing from Mi-Cha, Stroman, or Lad, which meant they were either deep in a world or pointedly ignoring me. If I'd been them, I'd have done the same.

Nexus Station, as always, ran on inertia. The ghosts—hundreds of them—handled ninety-nine percent of the actual work. My role was to catch the exceptions: the things the ghosts couldn't process, or that had escalated past the point of sensible resolution. Or, more often, the tasks that required a Real Person's signature so no one could claim the system was run by machines alone.

Today's queue was twenty-three items long. The most urgent, according to the color-coded system Kira had built (before she'd left for better jobs in higher rings), was a supply order from the luxury deck. I opened it and sighed.

> [URGENT: Out of Champagne. Guests
> demanding restitution.]

I did the sensible thing and passed it down to Food & Beverage, adding a note that if the guests didn't calm down, they should be referred to Quarantine for "observation." My next most urgent task was a tourism dispute: a party from Endless Kingdom had tried to import a live wyvern as an "emotional support animal," only for it to eat three other guests' pets and then crash through the glass dome of the arboretum.

> [Resolution Required: Reimburse pet owners,
> assign punitive damages to offending party,
> repair dome.]

I rubber-stamped the refund requests, debited the Kingdom party's account, and tagged the dome as a low-priority maintenance issue. Let the guests enjoy a breeze for once. The final step was to send a sympathy bouquet to the pet owners. The sim let me select from the "Sympathy" menu: lilies, white roses, or the ever-popular "muted wildflower" option. I picked lilies, knowing the recipient would immediately leave a negative review about being reminded of funerals.

By 0900, the only non-ghost in the ops gallery was me. I pinged the admin comms. Nothing. I tried Mi-Cha again, just in case. Still nothing, not even a bounce. I told myself that she was in the middle of a campaign, maybe even the one she'd been grinding for since last cycle. Lad and Stroman were probably running escort missions in the asteroid fields, racking up cash for the next round of upgrades. No one needed me. That used to bother me. Now it just felt like fact.

I checked the incident logs. The overnight shift had flagged six "Code Violet" events: three fistfights, two attempted hacks, and one "unruly display of affection" in the food court. The latter required escalation to human review, so I opened the video.

It was a man and a woman, both flagged as "transit guests" from Endless Jungle. The woman had scales, the man wore an exosuit lined with white fur. They were making out, loudly, and the simulation had gone to great lengths to reproduce the sound effects in high fidelity. I skipped ahead, saw that they'd tried (and failed) to copulate on top of a vending kiosk, then wandered off to find a hotel room. I filed the review as "resolved, no further action," and docked the ghosts for overreacting.

By 1030, I'd run out of meaningful tasks. I walked the ring, checking each concourse for anything out of the ordinary. There was nothing. The sky, still blue and false, glared down at the world with the perfect indifference of a screen saver. The shops were open, the bars were open, the gyms were open, but the only customers were ghosts and the handful of real people who bothered to log in this early. No sign of Kira. No sign of anyone I used to know.

In the lower levels, I found the maintenance chief—another ghost —standing at parade rest by the main recycler. I asked if there were any issues.

She said, "No issues, Station Manager Kozina. All systems optimal."

"Are you sure?" I asked.

A micro-pause, then: "There is a minor blockage in Waste Duct 7-B, but I have assigned a team."

"Good work," I said, and tried to smile.

She did not smile. She waited until I left, then returned to her subroutines.

I wandered up to the upper gallery, the ring's best view, and stared through the viewport at the drydock. Our ship was still fourth in line, still little more than a wireframe in the construction hangar. I watched the drones crawl over its surface, adding bits and pieces of armor, then stripping them off and trying again, as if they couldn't decide what shape it was supposed to be. Maybe they couldn't. Maybe there was no one left on the build team who knew what "Frank's Ship" was meant to look like.

I pulled up the message queue. Not a single new ping from the old crew. Mi-Cha's inbox bounced with a polite "User not accepting messages." Lad's was full. Stroman's was blank, but that didn't mean anything. He'd never been much for words.

I considered writing a long, passive-aggressive message, then thought better of it. Instead, I drafted a supply order for the bar. The new shipment of beer was "not up to prior standards," according to three anonymous complaints. I flagged the supplier, issued a request for discount, and scheduled a tasting event for any real human who wanted to attend. I set the theme as "beer summit." Maybe someone would show.

I checked the clock: 1135. Still too early to start drinking, unless I was actively trying to get demoted. As if there was anyone who could.

I sat at my desk and watched the logs scroll. This was the part of the job that hurt the most: the waiting, the nothing. The ghosts didn't even bother to look busy. They drifted, perfect mannequins of efficiency, and the station just kept turning. My stats crawled up by fractional percentages—Bureaucracy, 0.01; Leadership, 0.02; Starship Tactics, nothing at all. I would have traded a point of Bureaucracy for a single hour of crisis.

The next time something happened, it was a "guest" from Endless Paradise, a retirement sim that billed itself as "The Beach That Never Ends." He showed up at my office door with a sunburn and an attitude.

"Hey, pal," he said, without knocking. "I got a problem."

I gestured for him to sit. He didn't. Instead he leaned over my desk, arms covered in peeling skin, and glared.

"The pool on Level 7 is closed. You know how many credits I paid to use that pool?"

I didn't, but the system did. I pulled up his file. "I see you're a Sapphire-level guest, with full amenities. The pool's closed for routine cleaning, but there's a secondary on Level 3—"

"No," he said, "I want Level 7. It's got the big windows. My doctor says I need real sunlight for my condition."

I pointed at the ceiling. "It's all simulated. There's no difference in the UV output."

He smirked. "That's what they said in the last sim, too. Then I found out I was dying for nothing. If you don't open the pool, I'll file a class action."

"I'll log your complaint," I said, and did. I also flagged his account for "potential disruptive behavior," which would get him a visit from Security if he pulled this again. "Is there anything else?"

He stormed out, muttering about lawyers and the ozone layer.

By noon, I was already behind on paperwork. Half the forms were pointless, but they needed a wet-ware signature, so I did them. I authorized two transfers, approved a med-evac for a ghost with "irreversible memory fragmentation," and denied a request to fire the janitorial staff for "being too clean." (That last one came from a group of Endless Jungle survivalists who preferred to "hunt and gather" their own food from the corridor planters.) I sent them a case of live mealworms as a compromise.

At 1400, I tried Mi-Cha again. No answer, just the same bounce. I sent a message to Lad: "If you're not dead, please respond." The system confirmed delivery, but that was it.

By 1500, I started to feel it—the static behind my eyes, the numb exhaustion that came from too much repetition and not enough sense of purpose. I thought about the old days, when every hour was a scramble to keep the ship from blowing up, every day a fresh argument over upgrades or loot. I used to think that the endless grind of

Nexus would be a vacation. Now I'd have given anything for a single minute of chaos.

The only relief came at the end of my shift. I watched the blue sky fade to a soft gray as the station dimmed for "night." The ghosts, tireless as ever, didn't even acknowledge the change. I sat at my desk, drank the not-quite-beer, and stared at my own reflection in the viewport.

It looked tired. It looked bored. It looked, if I was honest, like someone who had lost the thread.

I tried the old hack: swapped out the wall display for a projection of the ship in drydock. I watched it for an hour, hoping the drones would finally get it right, finally settle on a design. They didn't.

At 2300, I shut down the display and walked the ring one last time. I nodded at the ghosts, who nodded back, empty-eyed and perfect. I passed the bar, still open, and saw that the beer summit was a bust. No one had come. Not even the bartender, who was a ghost.

I made it back to my quarters, ate another loaf, and lay down. The hum in my head was louder now, an ache behind the eyes.

Outside, the stars didn't move. Not even a little.

My bed was a slab of memory foam and regret. I lay on it, staring at the seams in the ceiling, a detail so lovingly rendered it made me want to file a complaint just for the sake of it. There was no proper darkness on the station, only a kind of synthetic dusk—shadows cast by a hidden algorithm instead of a real moon.

When I couldn't stand the stillness any longer, I sat up, pulled the old bathrobe over my shoulders, and padded barefoot across the room to my "trophy wall." There were no actual trophies, just a holomap control: a simple black band, inscribed with a logo, which responded to the brush of my thumb. I pressed it and let the map bloom to life.

The Endless Worlds.

I had renamed it that, as a joke, the first week I got this assignment. Most people called it "the domain map," or just "the system." To me, it was a parade of everything I'd ever wanted and lost.

The first world was Endless Sky, my origin point. I zoomed in on the old sector map, watched the familiar swirls of ships and stations and wars, each one a drama unfolding without me. Our last ship—Pretty, Pretty Princess, may she rest in vacuum—was rendered as a tiny blue triangle, barely visible among the asteroid debris. I wondered if there would ever be a new ship, or if it was all just a joke now, the entire idea of crews and voyages and purpose.

I panned over to Endless Paradise, the tropical world where my mother had "retired." I used to think this was literal: she had gone to Endless Paradise, built a house on the sand, and spent her days collecting seashells. I later found out she mostly played cards with other retirees and occasionally started a pyramid scheme. She never answered my messages, so I zoomed in on her island instead. A neat rectangle of beach, with an improbable blue lagoon. Empty, at this hour.

Next came Endless Jungle, billed as the "True-Life Adventure" world. It was mostly big trees, big bugs, and the kind of people who thought they were the first to discover fire. I didn't know anyone there, but I'd once dated a woman who claimed to have "walked every river on the map." When I checked her stats, it turned out she'd never left the starting zone, and her main hobby was picking fights in the world forums.

I cycled through the rest: Endless Kingdom (Mi-Cha's latest haunt, if she was still out there), Endless Night (no thanks), and the other minor domains, each with their own flavor of simulated pain.

Then I landed on a world I'd never visited.

Endless Champions.

I squinted at the display. Endless Champions had been added after my physical body had been recycled, a superhero-themed domain that, as far as I knew, almost nobody actually played. The promo video still ran on a loop: capes, powers, musclebound heroes punching each other through buildings. If there was a player base, it was tiny.

What struck me was the total lack of shuttle traffic between

Champions and the rest of the system. Usually, there'd be at least a blip of movement—a tourist party, a returning contractor, someone on a bender. But here, the log was blank. No arrivals, no departures, no messages. I poked the log, just for fun.

> [Note: Shuttle 77x-CH inbound to Nexus.
> Scheduled arrival: 0700 next cycle. Manifest:
> 2 passengers, transfer from Endless
> Champions to Nexus.]

I made a note of the shuttle ID. The passengers were Endless Sky players, so maybe someone had decided to go on a bender after all. Endless Champions probably had some bananas modifiers on the base physics parameters. Probably a lot of fun. I flagged it, not because I cared, but because it might be the only interesting thing to happen all month.

I powered down the holomap, stretched my arms, and considered pouring a glass of whiskey. Instead I stood by the viewport and let my eyes unfocus, watching the stars fail to move.

What did I want? Not a new ship, not another crew—though I missed them all, in a way that was hard to admit. I wanted to start over, to be someone who hadn't already failed at every previous thing.

I didn't want to be Station Manager Kozina, Lord of Paperwork, Master of Petty Disputes.

I wanted to be, for lack of a better word, new.

With that thought, I climbed back into bed and let the fake dusk roll me under.

————

THE STATION CLOCK TICKED 0645, WHICH MEANT I HAD fifteen minutes to kill before the shuttle from Endless Champions hit the arrivals bay. I killed it the same way I killed every morning: by drinking the coffee simulacrum that passed for real in the admin lounge, and by watching security feeds for anything that looked out of place.

Today, that was everything.

There were ghosts in the corridors, but they moved with a jittery energy, as if the system was running ten percent too fast. The tourists loitering in the main ring looked up, saw the blue "sky," and visibly flinched. Even the janitorial staff—the only avatars allowed to appear bored—moved with a kind of nervous purpose. Maybe they felt it, too: the sense that something was about to break.

I got to the port early, so I had time to watch the shuttle dock. It came in hot, clanging against the mag-locks hard enough to make the glass vibrate. If there was any doubt about who was on board, it vanished when the hatch hissed open and a wave of bodies surged out.

The manifest had listed two, but there were at least forty: men and women in costumes, some ripped, some pristine, all with a kind of secondhand dignity. A few looked like straight cosplayers, but the rest were the genuine article—"supers," in the Endless Champions vernacular. The first two out were capes: one in red, the other in electric blue, both looking like they'd been dragged through a blender. Next came a woman in a bronze exoskeleton, then a guy in a suit made entirely of black silk, his eyes glowing the color of a drowned screen.

It went like that for five minutes. The last one off the shuttle was a hulking mass of rock, slabs of granite knitted together with cables of something that looked suspiciously like rebar. His seams glowed orange, as if there was magma just under the surface.

I cut through the crowd, ignoring the "oohs" and "holy craps" from the onlookers, and planted myself in front of the rock-thing. He was at least a head taller than me, and his voice sounded like a trash compactor full of gravel.

"You in charge?" he asked.

"Define 'in charge,'" I said.

He grinned, a dry fissure opening across his jaw. "Doesn't matter. Got a problem."

"Let me guess," I said. "You're not supposed to be here."

He nodded. "We hijacked the shuttle. Had to. Place was overrun."

I waited. He seemed to want permission.

"Overrun by what?" I said.

He looked over his shoulder, at the crowd of ex-supers clustered together. They all looked at him, then at me. "The Roknid," he said. "The mechanical spiders. We thought they were just a plotline, but... they don't stop. Not even when the world ends."

I knew the Roknid. Everyone from Endless Sky did—they were the nuclear option, the final boss, the enemy the AI threw at a party when you were out of ideas and wanted to end a campaign with a bang. But they were supposed to be restricted to the Sky, locked in as a narrative device. They weren't supposed to jump domains.

"You sure?" I said. "Maybe it was a knock-off."

"No." The Dark Thing shook his head, spraying a little grit. "We watched them eat three cities. After the first day, we stopped trying to fight."

I looked at the rest of the crowd. They were shivering, despite the fact that the station kept the temperature a perfect 22C. Some were bloodied, most were covered in ash, and all of them carried the look of people who'd left something behind.

"You got a name?" I asked.

He hesitated, like he hadn't had to think about it in a while. "They called me Obsidian, but I like 'Dark Thing' better. It's funnier."

I conspicuously didn't roll my eyes. "Okay, Dark Thing. I'm Frank. I run this place."

He let out a deep, rumbling laugh. "Hell of a place to run."

"Is there anyone else coming?"

He shook his head. "This was everyone. The rest either didn't make it to the port, or..." He trailed off, the granite plates shifting in something like a shrug. "Doesn't matter."

I did a quick calculation. With two per room and a little creative accounting, I could house all the refugees in the unused guest block. "You need anything? Food, beds, medical?"

He looked at the others. "They could use showers. And time."

I nodded. "We'll get you set up. Just don't break anything. These walls are a lot softer than you."

He grinned again, the crack deepening. "No promises."

The crowd was already breaking up, some drifting toward the food court, others clustering in knots to whisper and stare at the station's sky. A few, I noticed, wandered off alone. I dispatched two ghosts—Security and Medical—and told them to handle everything. For once, the ghosts didn't argue.

As I turned to leave, the shuttle pilot caught my eye. He was slumped against the bulkhead, face pale, hands shaking. I knelt next to him.

"Hey," I said. "You alright?"

He swallowed, then managed a shaky laugh. "Never thought I'd get out of there. They told me to expect two. I got fifty."

"Could've been worse," I said.

He nodded. "Yeah. Could've been me left behind."

I stood, patted his shoulder, and left him to recover.

On the walk back to admin, I messaged Facilities to expect guests, messaged Security to expect trouble, and messaged Medical to expect trauma. Then, for the hell of it, I messaged Mi-Cha again.

Nothing. The silence was starting to feel like a habit.

Back in the gallery, I watched the logs scroll. The supers had scattered through the ring, but none had caused trouble yet. A few had taken up residence in the observation lounge, staring out at the drydock as if waiting for something to rise from the void. The Dark Thing sat alone at the bar, drinking a pint of orange juice one thimble at a time. He looked, for the first time, like he didn't have a role to play.

I sat at my desk and tried to process. The Roknid, in Endless Champions? It wasn't supposed to happen. Either the code had glitched, or something worse was going on.

I checked the shuttle schedule, just in case. Next arrival: Endless Jungle, then Endless Paradise. After that, a resupply from the old homeworld. No mention of the Sky, or any of the other domains. No word from Mi-Cha, Lad, or Stroman.

I found the two tourists from the shuttle in the station's health clinic, arguing with a medical ghost about the difference between "mandatory quarantine" and "medical observation." Both wore the pale blue and white jumpsuits of Endless Sky, civilian model. Neither looked like a hero, or even someone who would choose to vacation in a superhero hellscape.

I flashed my admin badge and the ghost vanished, freeing them for my interrogation.

The taller of the two was a man with a thinning patch of hair and a face set in permanent skepticism. He clutched a protein bar and ate in tiny, suspicious bites. The woman had the look of a former office manager who'd once had a sense of humor but was now deeply, unambiguously pissed off.

"You the station manager?" she said. "You look like a station manager."

I shrugged. "You look like you just survived a mass-casualty event."

She snorted, then nodded. "Yeah. Name's Anna. He's Bex."

Bex offered a micro-wave, then crammed the last of the bar in his mouth.

"I need to ask you about what happened on Endless Champions," I said. "Just a quick debrief."

Anna leaned forward, elbows on knees. "Is this... is this a thing that happens often? Whole worlds going off the rails?"

"No," I said. "Not unless there's a code push that goes really, really wrong. But nothing's been updated in months."

Bex wiped his mouth. "They told us it was a special event. We thought, cool, maybe some extra loot or an achievement. Then the spiders showed up, and..." He shook his head.

"They just kept coming," Anna said. "Not like in Sky, where there's a spawn cap or a cooldown. They filled the city. Ate the city. You'd kill one, and the rest would just... adapt. And then they started using the environment."

She shuddered, genuine. "At first it was just buildings and trees getting consumed, but then we started to notice that even the sky wasn't right. It went all... low-res. I haven't seen that since alpha builds."

I tried to picture it: a city being eaten, not just overrun but erased from the system itself.

"You said the sky looked weird?"

Anna nodded. "Like the render distance had been dialed down to zero. The horizon would disappear, then the buildings, then the ground. We kept moving toward the edge, but there was always less and less behind us. Not just blank space—actual deletion."

Bex chimed in. "We made for the transit ring, but there were already people waiting. When the spiders hit, everyone panicked. They trampled each other. The ring started to—" He mimed a rippling, flickering motion. "It was like it was going to crash."

I said, "So you made it out just in time."

Anna shrugged. "If you can call it that. I had friends who didn't make it. They were just... gone. Not dead, just like they never existed. Their names got replaced by placeholders in the party list."

That wasn't supposed to happen. Even in full character death, the system left you a ghost. Real death could happen, but there was always a recored. Being erased—no record, no tag—meant the world itself was breaking.

"Did anyone mention a cause?" I said. "A virus, or a hacker?"

Anna snorted. "They always blame hackers. But no. The only thing anyone said was that the Roknid were acting off-script. Smarter, faster, and like they had an objective."

I nodded, half to them, half to myself. "You two did the right thing, getting out."

Bex rolled his eyes. "We just wanted to see the superhero world. Pick up some artifacts. Maybe beat up a villain or two. Instead we spent thirty hours hiding in an abandoned sewer while the world got eaten."

Anna's hand trembled, only a little, but I saw it. "Can we go home now? Or are we stuck here until someone says it's safe?"

I said, "You can go back to your quarters, but I'd advise you not to leave the ring until we know what's going on."

She laughed, sharp and brittle. "Yeah, I'm not going anywhere for a while."

I left them with the medical ghost, who resumed scanning them for trauma. Out in the corridor, I let myself feel the first real dread of the day. The Roknid had always been bad, but this—this was different. It was like the code itself was eating the world, and the only warning was a blurry sky and a horizon that shrank with every minute.

It made me want to check the rest of the worlds, to see if the same thing was happening elsewhere.

I pinged the system, pulled up the holomap, and checked the status of the other domains. Sky: stable. Jungle: fine. Paradise: a blip, but nothing serious. Endless Night was the only one offline, but it had always been that way.

I pinged Kira's old number, even though I knew it was a waste. Then I messaged Facilities, told them to beef up security on the transit ring, and set a flag for any incoming traffic from Champions. If there was any.

For a long minute, I stood in the empty corridor, hands on the cold rail, and waited for a sign.

Nothing came.

———

THE CENTRAL BAR WAS HALF-EMPTY AT BEST, THE GHOSTS outnumbering humans by an order of magnitude. The lighting was set to "evening melancholy," which meant a slow pulse of purple and gold along the ceiling and a playlist full of music that sounded like the inside of a submarine. I spotted the shuttle pilot at the far end, hunched over the bar with both hands wrapped around a cup of something opaque.

I slid onto the stool next to him and waited until he noticed me.

"You the boss?" he said, not looking up.

"More like the custodian," I said. "You holding up?"

He shrugged, then tossed back a shot of the blue stuff. "I've flown evac for years. I've seen panic, stampedes, even a couple of riots. This was different."

"How so?"

He fished a toothpick out of a jar and stuck it between his teeth. "Those things weren't supposed to be there. I mean, sure, I've run into the Roknid before—who hasn't, right? But they were always... contained. They only cared about ships. Maybe a station, if it was on the wrong side of the board. Never seen them go after a planet, let alone a whole world."

I nodded. "You're from Endless Sky?"

He looked at me, finally. "Born and bred. My first real gig was flying mop-up after the Second Expansion. I logged more hours dodging Roknid than most people spend in a whole campaign."

We exchanged the look: the mutual respect and mutual weariness of people who'd both survived the same old war.

He said, "Used to be, they'd hit a ship, strip it for parts, and move on. You lose a few crew, maybe a cargo run, and that's the price. This was... different. It was like they were angry."

"Angry?" I echoed.

He stared into his glass. "I know, it sounds dumb. But they didn't just tear the place up. They erased it. Like they wanted to make sure nothing was left. Even the data—" He hesitated. "I saw them eat the logs. Not just kill the black box, but burn out the whole record. It's like they were erasing the story."

I tried to picture it, but my mind kept going back to Anna's line about "placeholders in the party list." You didn't have to be a code-wizard to know how wrong that was.

"Any idea why?" I said.

He snorted. "If I could think like a Roknid, I'd have a better job."

We sat in silence for a minute, sipping our drinks.

"Remember when they introduced the Roknid?" he said, out of nowhere. "All the big forums lost their minds. Half thought it was a bug, the other half thought it was the AI trying to punish powergamers."

"I was on *Princess,*" I said. "We ran from the first one they dropped. Barely made it out."

He grinned. "Bet you made a fortune on the salvage, though."

"Not enough," I said, but the memory felt good. "You think they're going to come here?"

He hesitated, then nodded. "If they're in the code, yeah. They don't stop. It's what makes them fun, I guess. Until they come for you."

He drained his glass and gestured for another. The ghost behind the bar obliged, polite and silent.

"I heard a rumor," he said. "Maybe you can confirm. Is it true that if the Roknid eat a world, it's gone? Like, no respawn, no backups?"

I thought about it. No official word, but the fact that Endless Champions was now just a blank on the map told me everything I needed.

"Yeah," I said. "It's gone."

He laughed, but there was no joy in it. "Well, shit. Guess I'll keep the engines warm, in case anyone needs a lift."

I stood. "Take care of yourself."

He saluted with the toothpick. "See you in the next life, Station Manager."

Outside, the ring was even quieter than usual. The sky was set to "dusk," but the algorithms couldn't quite simulate the way a real horizon bled into darkness. It looked more like a screensaver than a world, and maybe that was all it ever was.

I walked the ring in silence. The ghosts gave way for me, all polite and glassy-eyed, as if they knew something I didn't.

For the first time since the day I lost Princess, I felt the old itch: the need to act, to do more than just patch up the world while it fell apart around me.

I checked the holomap, watched the other domains orbit in their little patches of simulated space. If the Roknid could cross over, nothing was safe. Not even Nexus.

I made a mental list of what needed doing. Security. Firewalls. Maybe a quarantine protocol, if the system would let me. I'd have to check the logs for anomalies, cross-reference every incident with the Sky's old campaign data, and find out if any other bugs or monsters had gone off-script.

Maybe it was a waste of time. Maybe it was already too late.

But as I circled back to the admin gallery, I felt something I hadn't felt in months.

It wasn't hope, exactly. But it was close.

4 / RECONNAISSANCE

IT TOOK EXACTLY THREE MINUTES OF HOVERING MY HAND OVER the call interface before I committed to hailing Mi-Cha. In that time, I composed and deleted half a dozen drafts of what I'd say, none of which survived my own scrutiny. There's no dignity in pinging an ex-captain at 0200 hours station time, but the message from the prior day—the one about the Roknid eating a whole world—ate at me.

I thumbed the comms pad. The system gave a half-second chirp, then projected her face on the far end of my desk, a ghostly flicker over the lacquered surface. Mi-Cha was exactly as I remembered: jawline sharp enough to strip wire, hair tied back in a regulation ponytail, eyes locked in a perpetual thousand-meter stare. She wore a casual suit of some martial fashion: dark, rigid, with a single band of crimson down one shoulder. The effect was "Generalissimo on Casual Friday," and it somehow worked for her.

She saw my face, didn't blink. "Frank. Is this a social call?"

"Only if you count existential dread as a hobby," I said. "Am I catching you in the middle of a campaign?"

"I'm always in the middle of something," she replied, but her tone had the crispness of someone who'd expected to be called. "Let me guess: this is about the incursion in Champions? Word's spread quickly."

"Yeah," I said. "I just spent my night rehoming a crowd of superheroes who bailed on a dying sim, and not a single one of them seemed to think it would end there."

Mi-Cha's lips twitched at the edges, then smoothed back to neutral. "It won't. But the AI knows what it's doing. There are failsafes."

"You believe that?"

She considered. "Doesn't matter if I do. I'm not paid to patch code, just to survive what happens after it's patched."

"You're not paid at all anymore," I said.

She shrugged. "Fine. My point stands."

I glanced off-screen, debating whether to change tack. Instead, I let the silence sit until it calcified. "Have you heard from Stroman?"

She raised one eyebrow, a silent fuck-you to my attempt at subtlety. "Not since last cycle. He's busy grinding up his gunnery stat. Apparently, he's got money on the new world record."

"Gunnery's capped at 32, isn't it?"

She smiled, a flash of teeth. "Not if you do the Kestrel Route on Endless Frontier. The modifiers stack, and the leaderboard resets every seven days."

"God, that's so like him."

"Like us, once upon a time." Mi-Cha's gaze drifted, just for a heartbeat, to something off-cam.

I jumped at the opening. "You don't think this is serious, do you?"

"I think," she said, "that the system will do what it always does: log the losses, spin up a memorial, and get back to selling hats and skins." She leaned forward. "Is that what this is about, Frank? You want me to commiserate about the death of a digital city?"

I bit the inside of my cheek, unwilling to admit that this was exactly what I wanted. "People died. Real ones, maybe. Or as real as it gets now."

She looked at me as if seeing a particularly old, particularly brittle statue. "So?"

"So, I guess I just wanted to know if you cared."

Mi-Cha exhaled. "Frank. You're not the captain anymore. It's not your job to care."

"I'm not sure that's true," I said, but it sounded weak even to me.

We let the silence breathe. On the far side of the call, I heard the faint echo of a training sim: metallic groans, distant shouts, a synthetic war cry that sounded more digital than human. Mi-Cha's hands were moving just out of frame, probably cycling through weapons, or typing, or both.

"Do you want to talk to Stroman?" she asked, tone dry.

"If he's not busy."

"He's always busy."

She pinged him on a secondary line, and the three-way connection populated in my visual field. Stroman's feed was classic Stroman: no face, just a third-person capture of his avatar mid-battle, streaks of tracer fire etching a night sky over some endless plain. His comms module superimposed a grayscale bust over the action, which made him look like a bust carved by a sleep-deprived stonemason.

"Hey, Frank," said the bust. "What's up?"

"Just checking in," I said, not even trying to hide the lie.

"Mi-Cha, you in on this too?" Stroman's bust pivoted to a simulated side-glance.

"She's monitoring," I said, "but you're free to shit-talk me as usual."

He let out a rusty chuckle. "That's more like it. What's the crisis?"

"Roknid on the loose," I said. "They ate a whole game world. Endless Champions is a blank patch on the map now."

Stroman's face flickered, then reset. "Shit. They ever patch that exploit from the *Princess* days? The one where you could build a killbox with phased shields and trick the Roknid into deleting themselves?"

"Doubt it," I said. "If anything, they've evolved."

He shrugged, a big, fluid motion that made his avatar's shoulders ripple with artificial mass. "Well, fuck. Better them than me, I guess."

I wanted to be angry at him, but it was hard; he'd always been this way. His emotional range was one degree wider than an avalanche.

"I suppose this isn't your actual problem, then," I said. "You've got a new grind, a new crew, a new—"

"—wait, Frank. You know they're rebuilding *Princess*, right?" Stroman cut in.

I blinked. "No, I didn't know that."

He laughed. "She's at the drydock above Lunar Mare. Some post-grad in Industry is doing a historical restoration. Supposed to be flyable in six months. They're even putting the old livery on her."

"Who's funding it?" I asked.

He made a noise. "I think it's crowd-sourced. Maybe some rich kid with nostalgia for the old board."

I digested this. Mi-Cha's eyes flicked to me, then away.

"So you're saying if I want to get the band back together, I should just wait for the launch party?" I said, more sarcasm than I meant.

Stroman's bust grinned. "Hell, yeah. Or maybe come run a sim with me in the meantime. I could use a partner who doesn't eat paste and crash at the first sign of live fire."

"I'm not a gunner anymore," I said. "I run a station."

"Station's not a ship, Frank. We both know that."

"Do we?" I said, and the line went silent.

I wanted to yell, or laugh, or throw the comms pad through the viewport, but instead I let the dead air drag out.

Finally, Mi-Cha said, "Frank. You don't have to be responsible for everyone anymore. Let the admins handle the mess."

"I know," I said, and hated how much it sounded like a lie.

"Maybe you should take a vacation," said Stroman. "Come play a real sim for a change. I hear there's a new breed of ganker in Jungle—worse than the old bandits."

I almost said yes, just to end the conversation.

Instead: "Keep your head down, both of you."

Stroman winked his grayscale bust. Mi-Cha gave a micro-nod. Then the line cut, leaving me with my own face, ghosted in the glass.

I powered down the comms pad, resisting the urge to file a grievance about the whole conversation. Instead, I leaned back and watched the station lights cycle, blue fading to white as the system declared a new morning.

Maybe they were right. Maybe I should just let it go.

But the noise behind my eyes wouldn't let me.

————

THE STATION CLOCK BLINKED 0545 AND I WAS ALREADY AWAKE, staring at the ceiling as if there'd be a change. Instead, just the usual blue-lit hexagons, perfectly tessellated and wholly indifferent to my nerves.

I had time to walk the ring, and did, passing the closed storefronts and the shivering ghosts who pretended to mop the floors. Every other step, I tried to think of a reason not to go see Kira in person—then ran out of ring and had to double back.

She was at her usual perch in the admin gallery, seated at the traffic control deck with her feet up, a tablet balanced on her knees. She'd swapped out her hair for a straight shock of jet black, and her jumpsuit was a model I'd never seen before: cream with navy blue accents, all the little touches of a real pilot, though I knew she hadn't flown in years.

"You're early," she said without looking up.

"Couldn't sleep," I replied. I picked a seat at the next console over, letting the chill from the metal keep me alert. The admin gallery was nearly empty, the only noise a faint, distant hum of the station's drive pumps. I suspected Kira had turned off the background music on purpose.

She kept her eyes on the screen. "How did the reunion go?"

"About as well as an interstellar HR complaint," I said. "Stroman's turned into a grind monkey and Mi-Cha might be a war criminal now."

"I'm not surprised," she said. "You?"

I shrugged, even though I was. "I thought they'd be more bothered about the world being eaten."

Kira put down the tablet, folded her hands, and fixed me with a look that had all the warmth of a laser scalpel. "You're not worried about the world being eaten, Frank. You're worried about being left behind by it."

I made a noise in my throat. "That's... melodramatic."

She leaned forward. "You spent two hours last night reading through old logs of the Roknid Wars and another hour searching for a crew to take you on a one-way salvage mission. If you're going to lie to me, at least try harder."

I tried to glare at her, but she was right. "I just want to know how it's happening," I said. "Not knowing is worse than dying to it."

Kira looked at me for a long, silent moment. Then, with the deliberate slowness of a conjurer, she reached under her console and produced a battered, three-dimensional holopuck. She set it between us, flicked it on, and let the projection bloom.

It was a ship. A stubby, awkward little thing, shaped like a pillbox with a mesh of antennae and two stubby drive wings. The text under it read: "Slow But Steady."

My chest contracted with a wild, inexplicable nostalgia. "That's—"

"Your old surveyor," Kira said. "One of the ones you guys built to go through the Stargates."

I watched the holo spin, caught off guard by the longing it dredged up. "Wow."

Kira grinned, just for a fraction of a second. "*Slow But Steady* is still on the manifest. She's in storage, bottom of the drydock."

I squinted at her. "You're saying we go see what happened to Champions? In that?"

"It's the only ship on-station other than a shuttle that can fit through the rings," she replied. "None of the mainline models will fit. I checked. And the shuttles don't have sensor suites."

"You don't have to—" I started.

She cut me off. "Frank. You want to know what's on the other side? Fine. Let's find out."

I hesitated, torn between the urge to play it safe and the urge to jump straight into the mouth of the system's latest disaster. The urge to jump won.

"Okay," I said. "But the station is going to need a new manager when the spiders eat my face."

She gave a little shrug. "The ghosts will figure it out."

I reached for the holopuck and toggled the ship's info window. Its last service date was seven cycles ago. Half the systems were flagged "deprecated but functional." The security rating was a flat zero.

I grinned. "How long to get it prepped?"

"It's prepped. I sent a maintenance ghost to wake her up last night."

"You work fast," I said.

She shrugged again, then kicked her feet off the console and stood. "It's just a recon run, right? We see what's left, maybe poke around for survivors or logs, then come home?"

"That's all," I said, but my heart was already pounding.

Kira typed something into the admin console, then slung her bag over her shoulder. "We should take a ghost with us. I recommend the janitorial type—they're less likely to mutiny."

I laughed. It felt like a crime to laugh. "No way. I'll be the janitor."

She led the way, moving through the empty corridors at a brisk walk. I caught up, and for the first time in a year, I felt like we were going somewhere that mattered.

We reached the airlock to the storage hangar. The ghost waiting for us was in perfect maintenance blues, face so bland it might have been machine-generated that morning. Kira waved it through the protocols, then handed me a helmet.

"Last chance to back out," she said.

I looked at the helmet, then at her. "And miss the chance to die for a good reason? Not a chance."

She rolled her eyes, but there was a glint in them.

We cycled through the airlock and walked down the gantry. Slow But Steady was even uglier in person: patched hull, mismatched paint, the name stenciled in four different fonts. The docking clamps gave a little shiver as we stepped on board, as if the ship herself was bracing for what came next.

The maintenance ghost ran a systems check, then showed itself out. I settled into the pilot's seat, and Kira took the navigator's spot, fingers flicking over the interface.

"You know we're technically stealing this ship," I said, just to hear it.

Kira smiled. "I left a note. Also, I flagged it as an emergency rescue op, which should keep the insurance happy."

"Good. I'd hate to lose the deposit."

The systems hummed to life. I ran a pre-flight, mostly for nostalgia, then looked over at Kira. "Ready?"

She nodded. "Ready."

I toggled the nav system. It asked for a destination.

"Champions?" I said.

Kira shook her head, pointing at her console. "The transit ring is dead. There's no outbound gate." She tapped something a few times. "Nope. No return signal."

"Crap." I pulled up a copy of my holographic map. "So look. Champions was never a big draw, right? Endless Sky, Endless Kingdom, those were the big ones. Endless Night." My eyes scanned the map. "Paradise was big with the older set. Endless Industry had its fans."

"What are you looking for?"

"Endless Champions is gone. Fine. Like, *gone*-gone, if the ring isn't responding. But there have to be other worlds that meet the same profile."

"Insane modifications to the physics parameters?"

"Good point." My eyes skipped past Endless Jungle and Endless Deep. Nothing crazy there. "Endless Toon?"

"Huge population," Kira said, shaking her head. "Something like ninety percent of the under-sixteen set wound up there. Before I joined, there were ads encouraging parents to check their kids in instead of daycare."

"Jesus."

"Yeah. What's that one?"

I peered closer. "Endless Circus." I tapped its icon, pulling up the game profile. "Physics modifiers aren't *as* bonkers, but they're still pretty esoteric. Under a hundred thousand players. Pretty niche."

"So as close to Champions as you're going to get, if that's what you're looking for."

"Yeah."

She was already tapping her console. "It's about five minutes clockwise."

I hesitated, then gave myself a mental slap. "Do it."

The engines hummed.

The moment we hit the far side, a message flashed in my vision.

<New Skill: Starship Theft (Level 1)>

I started laughing, deep and ugly and perfect.

Kira turned, one eyebrow up. "What's funny?"

I held up the notification. "I think I just became a pirate."

She shook her head. "You always were, Frank. You just never got paid for it."

For the first time in months, I felt like I was back in my element.

Kira let the maintenance ghost handle the piloting while she ran diagnostics from the nav console. I took the left seat and set the viewport to max transparency, so I could watch the approach to the transit ring.

It was still there, each one same as the next: a circle of stone-white material a hundred meters wide, floating like an ancient monument at the exact edge of the station's gravity well. It wasn't even pretty, just functional, with the signature blue glow where the world's "Stargate" code patchwork had welded itself onto the base sim. Up close, you could see the seams.

Kira keyed the ring's activation code, and the ghost pilot angled us in. As we approached, I watched the ring's light cycle: red, yellow, then a swirling pattern of clashing colors. For all its joke status, Circus's stargate looked better maintained than Champions' ever had.

We slid into the ring's field. This time, there was a reaction: the hull shivered, and for a moment the entire ship flexed as if it was being squeezed through a straw. The viewport rippled, then the world outside was gone.

Just blackness, with a single blue-green dot in the center of the screen.

We'd arrived.

Kira tapped the boards. "Still alive?"

I did a systems check. "All green. Even the coffee maker survived."

She gave me a look. "You can have the first cup. On the house."

Outside, the dot resolved into a ring-shaped world. The details were impossible to parse—shifting, cartoonish shapes, bursts of light, wild blurs of motion. The system tagged it as "Endless Circus," but even the name flickered, cycling through a half-dozen misspellings and joke versions before settling back.

I felt something strange, then. Not dread, not excitement. Just a sense that the rules here were different, and if we weren't careful, we'd be next on the list.

Kira powered up the sensors, and we coasted toward the blue-green madness.

"We're here," she said.

I nodded, set my jaw, and felt the hum behind my eyes return, louder than ever.

5 / ENDLESS CIRCUS

The moment we dropped into normal space, I felt the world trying to vomit me out. *Slow But Steady's* cheap-ass inertia dampers coughed, skipped a cycle, and then started up again, stuttering through the kind of turbulence you only got when the local gravity was a suggestion, not a law. The display screen in front of me went brick red, then cycled through three warning icons:

[Gravitational Shear]
Local Physics: Nonstandard]
[External Mass Deficit]

The only thing missing was a cartoon of a pilot shitting himself.

Kira, of course, didn't even blink. She was already plugged into the nav console, fingers ghosting across a physical keypad and three separate holo-interfaces. For her, this was Tuesday. For me, it was a little too much like the last few seconds before *Princess* exploded, except I could smell the mildew in the seat fabric this time.

The Endless Circus ring world floated ahead of us, exactly as advertised and also absolutely not. The ring was about a hundred kilometers thick and ten thousand across, but something had chewed away a full quarter of it, leaving a jagged crescent hanging in orbit around a blue-white spark of artificial sun. The missing chunk wasn't smooth or even. It looked like someone had thrown a tantrum with a cheese grater, then tried to render the aftermath on a monitor with half the pixels dead. The "shattered" ends of the ring bled off into nothing, the raw edges flickering with pixels, hard-edged and strobing, glitching out in a way that made my teeth hurt. In between, thin arcs of air and water hung in space, refusing to disperse because the local physics had been set to "Do Not Abandon Hope."

I toggled the environmental scan and got back a waterfall of errors, each one less comprehensible than the last.

"Doesn't look good," I said. "How is any of that still holding together?"

Kira's mouth twitched. "The world physics matrix was set up by a masochist," she said. "And the devs copied the settings from an old toon sim, so it's... sticky." She did something to the nav controls and the ship stopped vibrating. The sensors hummed and cycled. "You see the damage to the structure?"

"Hard to miss. Does that mean there's a breach? Like, is the atmosphere venting?"

"No." She shifted the scan to visual spectrum, and the viewport filled with a slow drift of colored streamers, confetti, even furniture— tables and chairs and what looked like a trampoline, just floating free. "If anything, it's thicker than normal. Modifiers are set to keep it inside the event horizon. Nothing escapes."

I made a noise. "So if something breaks off, it just... orbits until it gets eaten?"

"Or until the physics matrix finally crashes," she said. "But that could be days or years. It's not supposed to ever crash."

"Feels like it already has," I said.

She pointed. "Look there."

I peered through the distortion. In the shadowed interior of the ring, whole cityscapes still clung to the surface: a parade of tents, spiraling towers, and immense patches of garish color. Some of it looked like classic circus fare—big tops and Ferris wheels and rollercoaster tracks—some of it was just chaos. But every so often, a segment of the ring would flicker from smooth rendered plastic into pixel soup, then snap back to normal as if nothing had happened.

"Have you ever seen anything like this?" I asked.

She shrugged. "No."

"So how did a quarter of the ring get eaten? Even with the bugs, you shouldn't be able to delete that much real estate. And if you could, why not eat the whole thing?"

Kira's eyes narrowed. "Maybe someone found a way to bypass the admin locks. Or maybe they just set the delete radius to max and let the physics mods handle cleanup." She drummed her fingers, an audible click. "The Roknid shouldn't even be here. Want me to do a sweep for survivors?"

"Do it," I said.

She set up the scan, and the sensors began their work. A web of targeting reticles mapped over the ring, most of them blinking from blue to red and then fading out. Kira clicked her tongue.

"Nothing?" I asked.

"Hold on." She dialed in tighter, adjusted for known life signatures, and let the system do the rest. "There. That's weird."

A single green reticle pulsed on the inside curve of the broken ring. "You've got to be kidding," I said.

"One life sign," Kira confirmed. "Maybe two, but the signal's too erratic to be sure."

"That's not possible. There should be a hundred thousand players in there. At least a few ghosts."

She shook her head. "You wouldn't see any standard NPC signatures with this. So we've got just this one live reading—here." She tapped, and the display isolated a chunk of the ring, a few hundred meters wide, on the shadowed underside.

I leaned in. "What's there?"

She grinned, a dry thing. "We're about to find out. Want to do a pass and ping it direct?"

"Yeah. Let's get as close as we can, then—" I hesitated, remembered the last time I volunteered to make first contact with something that ate worlds. "Actually, let's scan for Roknid activity first."

Kira's smile flickered. "You think they're here?"

"I don't know what else could chew through a world like this," I said. "And if they are, I want to know before we open the hatch."

She dialed in a sweep for the signature of the murder spiders. The system returned a null result, then an error message: **[No Active Hostile Signatures Detected].**

"Clear," she said, but I could hear the doubt. "You want to bring in *Pony?*"

"Yeah. That ring is not stable. If we land, I want something ready to evac us."

She thumbed the comms to the shuttle bay and toggled *Pony* to launch mode. The little can barely qualified as a real ship, but it was quick, and it had better sensors than anything else we owned. Kira punched in the landing vector, and *Pony's* lights winked to life.

"Ready?" she asked.

"Ready," I lied.

She moved to the transfer lock, handed me a helmet, and we both suited up. Her hands were steady, every motion efficient. I fumbled the chin strap, swore under my breath, and cinched it tight.

We cycled through the airlock and dropped into *Pony*. The console lit up, same as ever, though the custom interface skin was clearly an afterthought: big, primary-colored buttons and an icon of a cartoon horse giving a thumbs up. I tapped the launch sequence, and *Pony* detached from the main ship with a soft, chemical pop.

The world outside rushed up: the inside of the ring was vast, but the scale was all wrong, and every landmark looked toy-sized from up here. The "ground" was stitched together from segments of carnival, amphitheater, zoo, and playground, some of it in perfect focus and some of it rendered as flat sheets of placeholder texture. The sky above was the same bright, false blue as the Nexus Station's interior, but here, the illusion was constantly undercut by the ragged, pixelated edge of the broken ring, which bled off atmosphere and color like it was leaking paint into the void.

We dropped fast, no turbulence, just a long, slow glide toward the lit-up chunk of the ring.

Kira watched the nav. "Ten kilometers to target. Still reading a life sign. It's moving now."

I adjusted the scan and tried to filter for any comms traffic. "Nothing," I said. "Either they're not talking, or they don't know we're coming."

She grimaced. "If they're the last one left, I doubt they're in any mood to chat."

I watched the meters tick down. "So what's the plan?"

"We land, make contact, and see if they need an evac," she said. "Then we see if there's anything worth taking back to the main ship."

"And if we run into something?"

"Then we run," she said, as if it was the only answer.

I almost laughed.

At five hundred meters, the sensors started to pick up fine detail. The life sign was under a mesh of crumpled circus tents, not far from what used to be a parade ground. The signature moved in jerky, random lines, like it was pacing or running from something.

I brought *Pony* in slow, angled for a landing on the far side of a debris field. The moment the shuttle touched down, the ground flexed, then snapped back to normal, as if reality had glitched and then caught up with itself.

"Don't like that," I muttered.

Kira was already unclipping. "Let's keep this short."

I nodded, checked my sidearm, then thumbed the hatch release.

As *Pony's* hatch dropped open, a plume of warm, sweet-smelling air flooded in. It was sharp, chemical, and underneath it was the faint whiff of hot plastic and ozone. The carnival ground sprawled ahead: a patchwork of ruined tents, upended carnival rides, and, everywhere, a scatter of glitter, confetti, and small, bright objects that made my head swim to look at them.

Somewhere in that mess, someone was still alive.

"We stick together," I said.

Kira didn't answer. She just drew her own weapon and set out into the mess, shoes crunching on a carpet of broken glass and spilled candy.

We moved through the first fifty meters at a walk, side by side, then slowed as the debris thickened and the ground got weird. I tapped the scanner on my left wrist, forcing the interface to pull a localized map. It rendered the world as a mess of concentric circles, the only thing legible a single green dot about a hundred meters dead ahead.

There was no wind. The tents should've been snapping and billowing, but they hung slack, as if the air was gelatin. The little flags and banners lining the walkways drooped, sagging into puddles of themselves. Confetti stuck to everything: the wreckage, the ground, the backs of my hands. I tried brushing it off, but it clung with a static charge that made the hairs on my arms stand up.

We edged around a toppled "World's Largest Cannon." The barrel, big enough to crawl through, had cracked off its mount and come to rest on a splatter of rainbow-colored mud. I watched for movement, expecting some last-ditch SFX to pop out and startle me, but the barrel was empty.

"Showtime," Kira said, low.

She pointed at the scanner. The life sign had stopped moving, fixed now at a spot inside the biggest tent on the fairgrounds.

I checked the air for sound—anything at all—but the world had gone library-silent. No distant generators, no echo from the broken city segments in the distance, not even the hum of a power line. Just the crunch of my boots in the mess.

"Environmental Scan," I muttered. The system pinged back:

<Skill: Environmental Scan> (Roll: 12/20)

A little pop-up highlighted the air. "Toxic, but not critical. Particulates from the destruction, nothing that'll kill us before we finish the job." I snorted. "Mind you, I got a 12 on that roll, so don't take it as settled fact."

Kira nodded. "No pathogen hits. Still no wireless activity, either." She grinned. "And I got an 18."

"I still don't like it," I said. "If the Roknid are around, they should be putting out noise. They're not lurkers."

She shrugged, kept moving. Kira was always calm when things were weird; I figured it was a personality trait or a bug in the sim.

The closer we got to the tent, the stranger the ground became. The surface shimmered, like it couldn't decide if it was sand, gravel, or something else. Every third step, the world glitched: my foot would sink through a few centimeters, or bounce, or land an inch to the left of where I put it. Kira compensated without breaking stride. I nearly fell twice.

We stopped at the tent's edge. It was red and yellow, with a thick seam of brown gunk melted around the base. The scanner said the life sign was ten meters inside.

"Could be a trap," I said.

"Could be a survivor," she replied.

"Or a very slow bomb."

She gave me a look, then ducked into the tent.

I followed, my sidearm out, safety off. The interior was a mess: broken bleachers on one side, a disintegrating ringmaster's dais at the center, and what looked like the exploded remains of a pie-eating contest on the far wall. The air inside smelled of copper and ozone, mixed with a sickly sweetness that made my tongue numb.

"Where—" I started, then stopped. Something moved in the shadows behind the dais.

A shape darted from cover, straight for the exit on the far side of the tent. I saw a shock of pink hair, legs pumping, arms windmilling with pure panic.

"Hold!" I yelled.

Kira was already moving, vaulting a pile of debris and catching the runner by the collar. The kid—because it was a kid, no older than fifteen—squealed, kicked, then slumped as Kira dragged her into the open.

‹Skill: Environmental Scan› (Roll: 17/20)
‹Skill Up: Environmental Scan 13›

"She's clean," I said, then looked at Kira. "Let go. She's not a threat."

Kira hesitated, then released the girl. The kid stumbled forward, caught herself, and spun to face us, hands up.

"Are you... who are you?" she gasped. Her voice was thin and high.

I holstered the sidearm, forced myself to look harmless. "We are. My name's Frank. This is Kira. We saw your signal. Are you alone?"

The girl nodded, eyes wide and jittering. She wore a battered circus acrobat's unitard, heavy on the stripes and ruffles, but her face was streaked with dirt and the remnants of some kind of face paint. She looked like she hadn't slept in days.

"They're still out there," she whispered. "You need to leave. If you stay, they'll see you, too."

"Who?" Kira said, voice gentle.

The girl pointed at the tent wall, which was vibrating slightly. "The spiders. The little ones. They're inside the glitches. If you get too close—" She made a popping sound with her mouth and a twisting gesture with her hand. "Gone."

I glanced at the scanner. No sign of movement, no sign of anything. But I'd seen enough to believe her.

"We need to get you out of here," I said. "Our shuttle is outside, two hundred meters back. Do you think you can make it?"

The girl's mouth worked, trying to form a word. "If we run," she said, "maybe."

I felt a wave of dread run through me. I'd been in enough last-ditch situations to know how this played out.

"Okay," I said. "We'll go together. On my count."

I watched the tent wall, watched for a break, then nodded to Kira. "Now."

We sprinted, the three of us in a single line, weaving through the maze of debris and failed geometry. My scanner pinged, a sharp burst of red as a patch of ground behind us erupted into a cloud of pixel fragments.

Kira didn't look back. Neither did the girl.

At first I thought the sound was static—a digital tinnitus, the sim running low on audio assets—but as we ran, it intensified, a rising clatter that resolved into thousands of tiny, high-speed impacts. The ground behind us rippled, pixel fragments geysering up and then collapsing into wet, granular heaps. That's when I saw them: a glimmering black tide, spreading over the broken carnival and rolling straight for us.

Not spiders, exactly—spiders were a baseline. These were like the design brief had been "spider, but make it a war crime." Matte-black and chitinous, jointed legs ending in hooks, each one with a single, unblinking red eye at the tip of its snout. Some were the size of a shot glass; others, big enough to pin a child. All of them moved with the same, horrifying intent.

They weren't after us.

They hit the ruined parade ground and turned on each other, swarming over the confetti drifts and puffs of glitter, shredding every scrap of tent, rubber nose, and dropped streamer. The bugs were eating the world—consuming, processing, then excreting perfect black spheres that hovered in midair, vibrating with unreadable code. Every time one of the spiders tore through a patch of low-res geometry, the local reality glitched, flickered, and then popped out of existence. The landscape, the circus, the history—it all vanished in neat, efficient bites.

"Don't stop," I snapped, even as my eyes locked on the horde. "Just keep moving!"

The girl ran like a hare, legs pumping, head down. Kira matched her stride, one hand on the girl's shoulder, and I dragged rear. I risked a glance back and saw the black tide split, a phalanx of the little horrors peeling away and loping after us, not as a mob but in a skirmish line—a thousand-legged advance, coordinated and surgical.

Their red eyes flicked, marking us, but most of the swarm was still deconstructing the world behind. That was almost worse.

We hit the open ground leading to *Pony,* and the world lagged for a heartbeat, then caught up with a vengeance. Three of the spiders leapt for Kira's legs; she stomped one and kicked the other two aside, then spun and fired her sidearm. The shot hit dead-center, and the spider folded like tissue, its shell hypercoloring in a heatmap of orange and red before winking out.

The girl made a rabbit-scream as one of the things latched onto her ankle. I grabbed it by the thorax, wrenched, and threw it as hard and far as I could. It disintegrated in midair, the particles forming a perfect black sphere before being eaten by another spider.

"Is this normal?" the girl shrieked.

"No!" I yelled, and tried not to think about what "normal" even meant.

We reached the shuttle, and Kira palmed the hatch. The spiders were right behind us, but as I turned to lay cover, I saw them peel away at the last instant—spreading out, riming the base of the shuttle's landing gear, then crawling up the sides by the dozens. They weren't attacking us. They were... consuming the shuttle.

Kira grabbed the girl and bodily hurled her up the ramp. I followed, firing three shots into the densest clump of spiders. Each time I hit, the bug glitched out, strobing through a dozen shapes before settling on a black marble and winking away. But for every one I killed, five more took its place, and each was more interested in Pony than in us.

We slammed the hatch. Kira and I dropped into the front seats, the girl curling up and shivering behind us. The external sensors were already half-blinded by the swarm: the view outside warped, jittery, a mosaic of black and blue. *Pony's* warnings went from "mild concern" to "full panic," the data logs flooding with

[Hull Integrity Compromised]

and

[Local System Anomaly]

alerts.

"Can we fly?" I said, snapping on the harness.

Kira's hands flew over the console. "Maybe one shot," she said. "But the spiders are eating the hull. Literally."

"I'll take it," I said. "Launch!"

The engines sputtered, then failed. "Nope," Kira said grimly. "We need to get the hell out."

She bolted for the hatch, which fell open of its own accord, and leapt through. The girl followed with a jump-and-roll that was so acrobatic I almost shook my head in admiration. My own exit was significantly less glamorous as my right foot caught on the back of a Roknid drone, sending me tumbling to the ground.

The spiders' multitude of red eyes swiveled toward us.

"Follow me!" the girl screamed.

We ran.

The kid bolted ahead, feet barely touching the ground, legs piston-fast under her battered unitard. The gap between each stride was a magician's trick: one second she was vaulting a heap of busted popcorn machines, the next she was fifty meters up a ruined midway, a pink streak of desperate motion. Kira and I tried to keep up, but we were out of practice, out of shape, out of whatever cocktail of sim physics that let a person move like they'd removed two-thirds of their bones.

The swarm lost interest in us—mostly—and poured itself over *Pony* like hot tar. The shuttle's hull peeled away in ribbons, the spiders' black spheres gnawing at the alloy and splitting it into glimmering nothing. A thin, rising whine stung my ears as the mass of bugs collapsed the shuttle's landing struts, then burrowed up through the ventral hull, vanishing into the cockpit as if they'd always owned it. They moved with the purpose of a demolition crew, not a predator.

Kira didn't look back, and I didn't, either. We just ran.

The world was a fever dream. Every ten meters the local physics picked a different genre: we'd hit a patch of trampoline ground and go airborne, then land in a drift of knee-deep foam that was equal parts insulation and spun sugar. A warped funhouse tunnel snapped into being around us, mirrors bending our reflections into a kaleidoscope of horror, then the tunnel collapsed behind us, folding itself into a skinny spiral and vanishing down a non-Euclidean drain in the ground.

The girl shrieked directions as she went: "Left! Over the elephant! Under the fence!" Her voice cracked but didn't slow. We zigged when she zigged, juked right when she faked a left, and I realized after the second or third lurch that she wasn't just running—she was leading the spiders, her route a deliberate, practiced chaos. Each obstacle she cleared, the smaller swarm behind us hit a millisecond later, chewing it down to code and dust, never quite catching up.

I took a patchwork fence at a dead sprint, plastic pennants slapping my face, then rolled over a mat of rotting clown dolls. I barely had time to process the sensation—soft, greasy, a dead toyshop smell —before the ground under me evaporated, replaced by a floating bridge of licorice whips and toothpick ladders. I crossed, cavity be damned, and heard Kira's breathing right behind me, low and even. There was a moment, mid-leap, where time stuttered and my vision doubled, and I almost lost it—almost went into a panic freeze—but the kid's voice lasered back:

"Keep moving!"

We did.

A new tent loomed ahead, this one patched with tarps of every color, the edges staked down with what looked like old swords and umbrella poles. The girl ducked under the flap and vanished. Kira and I hesitated, just a second, then followed.

Inside, everything was different.

The air was thick but still. The smell: dust and old sugar, and underneath it, something like caramelized fear. The interior was a maze of old carnival junk—rigged games, ripped-out benches, a dozen battered mascots with cracked faces and hollow eyes. The walls were double-wrapped, heavy with insulation material and sheeting. At the center: a hollow, with a lumpy pile of bedding and a perimeter of broken bottles, each filled with something that glowed faint blue.

The girl skidded to a stop by the bedding and threw herself down, arms clutching a filthy beanbag. She was breathing hard, but her eyes never left the tent's entrance.

Kira crouched, weapon out, covering the flap. I watched the scanner, waiting for the swarm, but the green line on my display pulsed steady. The swarm had stopped. For now.

I turned to the girl, tried to get my own breathing under control. "You did good," I said. "Is this your base?"

She nodded, not taking her face out of the beanbag.

"Why aren't they following?" Kira asked.

The kid sat up, drew a hand across her face, leaving a streak of pink and gray on her cheek. "They don't come in here. I think it's the stuff in the bottles. Or maybe it's the old code. I dunno. I just know they won't."

I checked the nearest bottle: a plastic soda thing, jammed with blue glowsticks and capped with a mess of duct tape and foam. "What is it?"

She shrugged, then shivered. "It just works. At least, it used to."

"Who are you?" I asked, gentler.

She wiped her nose on her sleeve. "Poppy. I was an acrobat. Level Six." She cut herself off, then curled up smaller.

Kira glanced at me, then back at the flap. "How long have you been hiding?"

The girl said, "Days. Weeks? I dunno. Time is weird."

I looked down at my feet, suddenly aware of the garbage and old candy stuck to my shoes. "How did this happen, Poppy?" I said, as soft as I could manage.

She shook her head. "It was normal at first. Like, just another event. Then the sky started eating things. Not even the spiders, just... the world. You'd wake up and a whole chunk of the circus would be gone. Glitched out. If you went near the edge, it would pull you in." She pulled the beanbag tighter. "Most people died right away. If you died, you came back, but closer to the edge. Then nothing."

"Are there any other survivors?" I asked.

Poppy bit her lip. "There were. The Ringmaster lasted the longest. She said she had a plan, but the spiders got her." Poppy's voice faded. "She was in charge. Without her, the world... it doesn't work quite right."

"Our respawn points are still back on Nexus," Kira murmured in my ear.

I shook my head. "We're not leaving her. Poppy, we've got a ship in orbit, but we just lost our way to get to it. Any ideas? Shoot us out of a cannon, maybe?"

"They won't send you that high," the girl said miserably.

"So we're stuck," Kira said.

"Big trampoline?" I persisted. Poppy merely shook her head.

"Frank."

"I know, I know." I lowered myself to a small platform of some kind, probably something an elephant had been trained to put its feet on for a crowd-pleasing pose. "Give me a minute."

The thing was, I *had* the ability to get us out of here. Instantly. I could Truthsay a shuttle into existence—probably, if this world's asset library had such a thing in it. Or Truthsay us all directly to *Slow But Steady*. But I was mindful of Infinitia's caution about my backdoor hack, and the resource drains it could cause. *Especially* in this broken-down circus world. In *theory* I could Truthsay us all straight back to Nexus, but *that* would certainly cause problems.

"Well?" Kira asked impatiently.

I sighed. "I think we're stuck."

6 / CIRCUS LIFE

I LET THE SILENCE FILL UP THE TENT, LIKE AIR AFTER THE POP of a gun. Outside, the swarm patrolled the perimeter. In here, everything was still: the only sound was the slow drip from a broken glowstick and the high-pitched, staticky whimper of a girl trying not to panic.

"Okay," I said, careful to keep my voice low. "Let's reset. Poppy, you're safe here for now. Kira and I aren't going anywhere."

The girl uncoiled herself from the beanbag, but kept her arms locked around her knees. Her knuckles were white, the skin ragged where the virtual paint had worn off. "You're not safe," she said, no doubt in her voice. "Nobody's safe here anymore."

Kira knelt on the other side of the ring, eyes locked on the tent flap. Her sidearm was out but held low, pointed at the ground. "Poppy, how long since you last slept?"

She hesitated, then: "I don't need sleep. Nobody does. Unless you want to."

I nodded. "So, let's talk about it. The world's broken, there are killer spiders eating the geometry, and everyone else is gone. Why you?"

Poppy's mouth twitched. "I'm... stubborn?"

I tried to smile. "Works for me. But I need details. Start from the beginning."

She licked her lips, then let it tumble out. "It's not supposed to hurt here. That's the whole point. I signed up because—because it was fun. Safe. The rules were, you can't get hurt. Not for real. You could fall off a trapeze, hit the ground, and it would bounce you right back up. No blood, no broken bones, not even bruises. And if you got hungry, you just ate whatever you wanted. Calories weren't even tracked. Just a number in your log."

"So, no pain. No death."

"No real death." She fidgeted, pulling the sleeves of her unitard down past her wrists. "But the spiders—Roknid—they're not from here. They don't care about the rules. They just kill. And then you wake up, and the world is a little smaller, and the spiders are a little closer, and eventually you can't go anywhere without them watching."

I glanced at Kira. She was listening, but her eyes were on the tent seam, tracking the minute flutters as shadows crossed the outside.

"And the other players?" I asked. "Where are they?"

Poppy hugged her knees tighter. "Gone. At first, when you died, you'd just respawn at the last checkpoint. It was scary, but nothing worse. But once the spiders came, if they got you too many times in a row, you'd come back... off. At first, it was just little things—forgetting your name, or not knowing where you were. Then, after a while, you'd just—" She snapped her fingers. "Poof. Even the system stopped noticing."

"Respawn error," I said. "Shitty way to go."

She managed a smile, small but real. "It's not so bad. You just have to be quick. And it's easier if you don't get attached to anything."

I took that in, then tried a different tack. "Let's go meta. You're telling me the sim rules here are hard-coded for maximum fun, zero pain. How did the spiders break that?"

She pursed her lips, eyes darting left and right. "I said. They're not supposed to be here. Somebody brought them over. From one of the other games. They don't play by the Circus rules. When they kill you, they don't even use the damage meter. They just... erase you."

Kira chimed in, "Like a hard delete. Not even a proper death animation?"

Poppy nodded, her face serious. "It's fast. Sometimes you don't even see it. One second you're running, the next—whiteout, and you're waking up wherever the world still has space left."

I sucked my teeth. "So the safety net is there, but it's glitching. If you're lucky, you come back. If not, you're gone for good."

"Yeah," she whispered. "And every time I come back, it's harder to remember how long I've been here."

The sadness in her voice wasn't performative. I knew the tone. I'd heard it a thousand times before, on a thousand stations, in a hundred voices: the sound of someone who'd lost track of everything but the next minute of survival.

I decided to go for the gut. "How old are you, Poppy? In real life, I mean."

She hesitated, then shrugged. "Doesn't matter."

"It matters to me."

Her eyes flicked up, darted away. "Seventy-two. Or seventy-three. I don't remember. I joined up here because it let you be a kid again. For a while, it was the only place I could move without hurting."

I nodded. "That's a good reason."

She looked at me, waiting for the punchline. When none came, she said, "Why are you here?"

I didn't have an answer that would make sense, so I tried the truth. "I got bored of being alive. I thought this would be better. Jury's still out."

Her lips twitched, then cracked into something almost like a laugh. "At least you're honest."

Kira spoke up, voice clinical. "Frank, I think I get the system. This world runs on a fun-first protocol. Hit points are capped, and pain sensors are off. If the player doesn't eat, they get a warning, but there's no actual risk unless they try to starve themselves. Unless an external agent comes in and breaks the system."

I glanced at her. "You're thinking what I'm thinking."

She nodded. "If the Roknid are running their own code, they can bypass the local safety protocols. Their damage function calls the global death routine, not the Circus's. It's the only explanation."

I shook my head. "What you're saying, Kira..."

"I'm saying they're not part of the game. Probably never were."

Poppy was listening, but I could tell the words meant little. "Can you stop them?"

Kira and I shared a look. I shook my head. "Not from here. Our shuttle's gone, and the spiders will eat anything we try to build. The only thing left is to run the cycle until we find an opening."

Poppy seemed to shrink, then: "That's what the Ringmaster said. Before she vanished."

"Maybe she had the right idea," I said. "Keep moving, keep eating, and don't let the system catch you."

She perked up, just a little. "Actually," she said, "I was about to go get food when you showed up. It's the only thing that works like normal. If you can get to a stand before the spiders, you can load up. As long as you don't mind popcorn and funnel cakes."

I grinned. "Show me."

She wriggled out of the beanbag, dusted herself off, and crawled to a flap in the tent wall. She peeked outside, then motioned us over.

"See the red and yellow awning?" she whispered. "That's the best one. They reset the menu every night."

I looked. Fifty meters away, past a carpet of shredded clown dolls and wrecked carnival games, a little stand stood lit up like a Christmas tree. The sign read: THE PIG OUT. Underneath, an animatronic pig spun in a slow circle, stuck forever at the exact point of a musical jingle.

"There's nobody there," I said.

"NPC runs it," she replied. "Doesn't ever leave."

"Is it dangerous?"

She shook her head. "The spiders don't care about the NPCs. Just the world. Players, if we get in the way."

I watched the perimeter, counted the black dots crawling over the ground. "So if we run, we can make it."

Poppy smiled, a little wicked. "If you can keep up."

Kira grinned at me. "You first."

I made a face, but I'd always hated being slow. "On three?"

Poppy counted down, then took off like a firework. I followed, Kira right behind. We bounded over the carpet of broken toys, the ground jiggling like it couldn't decide if it was solid or jelly. The spiders noticed us, but only one or two changed course. The rest were too busy eating the world.

Poppy hit the stand, ducked under the awning, and banged on the counter. The animatronic pig let out a triumphant squeal, and a dispenser spat out a tray of funnel cake, loaded with a drift of powdered sugar.

She tossed two more trays at us, hands shaking with adrenaline and delight. "Eat," she said. "It's the only way to feel good here."

I took a bite, expected it to taste like memory. Instead, it tasted like the real thing: sugar, fat, and something just a little burned.

Kira inhaled hers in three bites. "Not bad," she said, mouth full.

Poppy beamed. "If you want, we can hit the hot dog place next."

I grinned. "Lead the way."

We followed her through the ruins, dodging the spiders, ducking under collapsed tents and shattered rides. Each stand was manned by the same blank-faced NPCs, each one programmed to do only one thing: serve food, no matter what.

We made three more runs, each time a little further from the tent. By the end, our arms were loaded with boxes and bags and trays of every carnival food imaginable.

Back inside, we dumped the loot in the middle of the tent and tore into it, the world outside reduced to a distant, muffled clatter.

"Is this what you did every day?" Kira asked.

Poppy nodded, cheeks bulging with popcorn. "Every day. Until there was nobody left to share with."

I wiped powdered sugar off my hands and tried to think. "We can't live like this forever."

She looked up, eyes bright and a little haunted. "You can try."

I knew then that we had to do something. Anything. But for now, I let her have her feast.

The high of the sugar crash was still humming in my veins when Poppy started twitching. Not a real twitch, but a tight, jittery energy that couldn't be burned off by sitting. She stood, circled the tent three times, then started stacking empty popcorn boxes into a pyramid with the precision of a bomb tech.

I watched her for a while, then said, "You nervous?"

She didn't look up. "The funhouse is stocked for three days, tops. If I don't get more food before then, I'll start to lose stats. We need a week's worth, not just a snack run."

Kira said, "You want backup?"

Poppy hesitated, glanced at the tent flap, then shook her head. "No. You're new here. If you come, the spiders will follow you. If I go alone, I can sometimes lose them for a while."

I didn't like the sound of that, but Kira shrugged, deferring to the local expert. "Your call," she said.

Poppy zipped up her jacket, checked the glowsticks lining the inside, and tied a ratty blue scarf tight around her neck. "If I don't make it back in five minutes, just stay here. I'll come back."

"Not a lot of confidence in that plan," I muttered.

Poppy grinned. It was brittle, but real. "It's a numbers game," she said. "They always get me eventually. But I can usually make one good run before they close the net. If I'm quick. If I get. the food into my bag, I'll respawn with it."

"Persistent inventory," Kira said, nodding approval. "Makes sense."

She palmed a fistful of blue-glow bottles, slung a messenger bag across her body, and made for the flap.

I caught her sleeve before she left. "Poppy, you don't have to do this alone."

She looked at me with ancient patience. "It's better if I do." She pulled free and disappeared into the monochrome light of the broken carnival.

Kira sat with her knees up, arms wrapped around them, eyes on the flap. "You think she's right?"

"About what?"

"That it's safer if she goes alone."

I watched the shadows flicker across the patchwork of tarps. "She's the only one who's made it this long," I said. "She knows the patterns."

"I still don't like it."

"Neither do I."

We didn't have to wait long. After a minute, the world outside the tent went weird. The air got heavy, the colors bled out, and everything in my vision contracted to a pinpoint right outside the tent.

Poppy ran.

She sprinted across the wrecked midway, a blur of blue scarf and desperation. The spiders noticed, all at once. The swarm moved like water poured down a funnel, racing after her with impossible speed. There was no drama, no slow-motion close call. They just caught her, and she was gone.

No scream. No body.

A second later, the tent's interior lights flickered, and a flat system chime sounded:

    [Player Death: Poppy]

    [Respawn: Immediate]

    [Invulnerability: 5 sec]

She reappeared three meters from the tent, standing, arms limp at her sides. She looked around, confused, then caught sight of the tent and stumbled in.

Kira met her at the entrance. "You okay?"

Poppy nodded, but her teeth chattered. "It's fine. You get used to it."

I tried to keep my voice light. "Do you remember what killed you?"

"Always," she said. "It's the same every time. They don't even touch you. It's like... a bug report. One frame you exist, the next you don't."

"Does it hurt?"

She smiled, all teeth. "No. That's the only rule that still works."

We let her sit. After a minute, she shook herself off, and said, "I'll try again. They'll expect me to rest, but if I go now..."

She didn't finish. She just left, again.

This time, she made it farther. We watched on the tent's crummy display screen as her blue dot moved through the alleys of the ruined carnival, dodging the black blotches of spider movement. The map glitched and stuttered, the spiders updating their position at random intervals, like a bad video feed. Poppy's dot zigged and zagged, then paused at the "Pig Out" stand. The system spat out a text notification:

[Inventory: Funnel Cake x 3, Corn Dog x 2].

She turned to run, but the spiders anticipated her. The blue dot vanished.

Again, the tent lights flickered.

[Player Death: Poppy]
[Respawn: Immediate]

She stumbled in, panting this time.

I gave her water, which she drank in one long, unbroken gulp. "Do you need to rest?"

She shook her head. "I can't. If I wait, they'll block off the food stands. I have to go now, while the route is still open."

She went three more times.

The third time, she didn't even get out of the tent before the swarm collapsed on her, a black wave of code that erased her in half a heartbeat. The tent's interior warped and bent, then snapped back with a stutter. Kira's hand hovered over her sidearm, like she might be able to shoot the spiders through the wall.

I looked at my own hands. They shook, just a little. Not from fear, but from the familiarity of watching someone grind themselves to death for an objective that didn't matter.

When Poppy respawned this time, she fell straight to her knees and vomited blue-light onto the floor.

Kira crouched beside her, arms ready to catch but not touching. "Poppy, that's enough. We'll figure out something else."

The girl wiped her mouth, smearing a line of blue across her cheek. "I can do it," she whispered. "I just need to be faster."

She went one more time.

We watched the display. The blue dot barely moved before a red dot—just one—came from the edge of the map, faster than anything I'd ever seen. It caught up to her instantly. The screen glitched.

[Player Death: Poppy]

She didn't appear for ten seconds.

When she did, she was shivering. "That one was new," she said. "It knew exactly where I'd be."

I looked at Kira. "They're adapting."

She nodded. "We're making it worse."

Poppy smiled, wet and unhinged. "Welcome to my world."

She curled up on the beanbag and fell asleep, her body twitching in the first dreamless rest she'd had in days.

Kira whispered, "We can't let her keep doing this."

I watched the tent walls, the black dots outside converging in a spiral, and knew she was right. "Next time, we go with her."

Kira nodded.

Poppy woke up two hours later, hollow-eyed but determined. She saw us waiting and said, "I think I need help."

I said, "You got it."

She looked at me, then at Kira, then back at me.

"Thank you," she said, barely more than a whisper.

Outside, the spiders circled, waiting for us to try.

———

BY MORNING, THE PERIMETER WAS THICKER: THREE, MAYBE four times as many spiders in the kill zone around the tent. They'd gotten smarter. If you looked close, you could see them setting up barricades with the corpses of their own kind, weaving trash and code-scrap into black, glossy ramparts that no longer tried to mimic anything biological.

Poppy noticed before I did. She peered through a slit in the tent wall, then turned to me with a new set of nerves in her eyes.

"They're setting a trap," she said.

Kira was already moving, packing up all the food into two bags and fashioning a harness from a length of circus bunting. She handed me the bundle. "If we run, we carry what we can. It's the only way we get a second shot."

Poppy looked from the bags to me. "Are you sure you're fast enough?" she whispered. "If you're caught, it'll be over."

I grinned. "Don't worry. I have a special talent for getting killed in the dumbest ways possible."

She actually laughed, a short, snorting thing. "Okay. Here's the plan. We go for the new stand—see it, right there?" She pointed to a distant awning, the sign above it flickering: HOT DOG PALACE. "If we split up at the broken carousel, they'll have to choose. If you get caught, drop everything and run for the alley behind the pig. The blue bottles might slow them down."

I nodded, memorizing the map she sketched in dirt and glowstick shards.

Kira slung the second bag over her own shoulder and knelt by the flap, sidearm out and ready. "You want backup?"

Poppy hesitated, then shook her head. "If you come, we risk the whole tent. Keep the door open for us. That's all."

"Understood."

Poppy gave me one last look, then squared her shoulders and said, "Let's do it."

She hit the ground at a run, and I followed. The carnival was in worse shape than yesterday. Each step was a hazard: sticky, oily confetti; holes in the ground where the spiders had eaten all the way to the mesh underlayer; shards of plastic from the shattered clown heads that watched you from every angle. Above, the sky flickered between noon-bright and sickly dusk, as if the weather algorithm had lost its mind.

We made it ten meters before the first wave peeled away from the swarm and came after us. Poppy didn't slow. She leapt onto a toppled ring-toss stand, vaulted off a splintered post, and hit the wall of the old "Guess Your Weight" booth with both feet, rebounding at a right angle into a patch of soft-serve snowdrift. I tried to follow her line, almost broke my neck on the landing, but kept my legs pumping.

The spiders were right behind us. The first to catch up was a hand-sized thing with mandibles like pliers. It went for Poppy's ankle, but she flicked it away with a move so fast I didn't even see it. The thing bounced, self-righted, and resumed the chase.

We reached the carousel. Poppy screamed, "Split!" and darted left, weaving through the patchwork horses, which had all been chewed down to wire skeletons. I went right, taking the outer ring. My foot hit a patch of trampoline, and for a brief, insane moment I was airborne, flying over the swarm like a loose party balloon.

‹New Skill: Circus Acrobatics (Level 1)›

The system flashed the message right in my face, and I almost missed my landing. I tucked and rolled, came up running, and headed straight for the Hot Dog Palace.

Behind me, the swarm split, just as Poppy had said. Half the mass went after her, the other half (the bigger, dumber ones) came for me. I didn't look back.

Poppy called out from somewhere ahead, "Distract them! Break the line!"

I looked around, saw a massive "Test Your Strength" rig still standing. I swerved, grabbed a sledgehammer from the ground, and swung it at the base of the tower. The bell at the top rang, and the platform buckled, toppling into the path of the biggest cluster of spiders. The crash made them hesitate, just long enough for Poppy to clear the next obstacle.

She was at the stand, jabbing at the menu buttons with both hands. The NPC manning the counter—some dead-eyed approximation of a ringmaster—just smiled and loaded her arms with food. She turned, eyes wild, and screamed, "Now!"

I dropped the sledge, sprinted, and body-checked a spider the size of a terrier. Its exoskeleton shattered into a cloud of digital dust. I expected the shards to vanish, but instead the other spiders swarmed it, eating the code fragments, growing a little bigger, a little faster.

Poppy loaded the bag with both hands, face scrunched in determination. "Almost done," she said. "Five seconds."

I grabbed a bottle from my own bag and chucked it at the nearest spider. It hit, burst open, and sprayed glowing blue juice all over its shell. The spider convulsed, limbs spasming, then locked up, frozen. The others stopped to chew on it, but were slower, more cautious.

‹New Skill: Improv Weaponry (Level 1)›

I almost laughed, then saw the next wave coming: dozens of spiders, moving as one. They weren't coming straight; they were flanking, learning from the last chase.

Poppy finished loading the bag, slung it over her back, and vaulted onto the counter. "Go!" she shouted.

I followed, climbing over the serving window, dropping behind the counter, and nearly slipping in a puddle of old mustard. Poppy was already up the back wall, grabbing exposed piping, and hauling herself onto the roof.

She waited, then offered me a hand.

I took it, she grunted, and pulled me up. From this height, I could see the whole circus: the broken tents, the kill zone, the tent where Kira watched, and the swarm of spiders closing in from every direction.

Poppy didn't wait. She took off at a sprint, the corrugated roof bending and flexing under her weight. I followed, barely managing to keep my balance.

At the far edge, she vaulted, landed perfectly on a tower of cotton candy barrels, and dropped to the ground, running at full speed.

‹Skill-Up: Circus Acrobatics (Level 2)›

I tried to copy the move. My landing was less graceful. I crashed into the barrels, got tangled in sticky strands of sugar, and flailed my way clear just as the first spider crested the edge behind me.

Poppy yelled, "Left!" and I banked hard, following her into a tight alley behind the "Ring of Fire" dunk tank. The spiders hit the barrels, splattered blue and pink candy everywhere, then regrouped, following our scent.

We burst out into the open, twenty meters from the tent. Kira saw us, screamed, and opened the flap.

Poppy tossed her bag through the opening, then dove after it. I was two steps behind.

The spiders hit the tent wall but didn't follow. Instead, they circled, reforming the perimeter, black eyes glinting.

We tumbled into the tent, both of us covered in sweat, sugar, and more than a little blood—though it wasn't ours.

Kira sealed the flap, then hugged us both, crushing us together.

Poppy laughed, wild and free. "We did it! We really did it!"

I collapsed onto the beanbag, arms numb. "We make a good team."

Kira grinned. "You even picked up some new tricks."

I checked my system log. Three new skills, all related to circus movement and improv fighting. I'd never leveled up that fast in my life.

Poppy was already sorting the food, rationing it into piles. "We'll need to do it again tomorrow," she said. "They'll reset the stands by then."

I nodded, staring at my hands, which shook less than before.

Kira looked at me, then Poppy. "They're not going to stop, are they?"

Poppy shook her head, smile fading. "No. But as long as we keep moving, we can win. Maybe."

I tried to believe her.

Outside, the black tide flowed, building walls and waiting.

Back in the tent, Kira tended to my bruises while Poppy sorted the loot. The tent was warm with the collective heat of our three bodies and the latent thermal from the mess of running and fighting. For a few minutes, we sat in a lazy heap, letting the sugar and adrenaline simmer down to manageable levels.

Kira was first to break the silence. "They're getting smarter by the hour. If we wait another day, I doubt even the two of you could break through."

Poppy shrugged, her cheeks bulging with a hunk of hot dog bun. "It resets every day. The spiders, too. They keep getting more, but if you make it to morning, the world rolls back a bit."

I looked at the tent wall, saw the shadows of the spiders weaving another barrier, black and blue, just inches away. "But the gains are smaller every time. Like the world's running out of cycles."

Poppy's head bobbed, a little sad but also proud. "Yeah. But we made it this time. I never got so much food on one run before."

I smiled. "You're the best I've ever seen."

She beamed. "Thanks, Frank. I like having a crew again."

Kira scowled, not at us, but at the tent's perimeter. "I still think we need a real exit plan. There's no way we can keep this up, not with the world closing in."

I nodded. "We're boxed in. The shuttle's eaten. There's no communication with Nexus or any of the other worlds."

"Could we tunnel out?" Poppy asked. "I used to do that when my parents locked the sweets in the cellar."

I appreciated the optimism, but shook my head. "Anything that takes longer than five minutes is going to get us killed, or worse."

Kira bit her lip, then keyed up her comms wrist. "I've tried every frequency. It's locked down, tighter than anything I've ever seen. Even the admin override is borked. The only thing that might work is if someone outside sent us a rescue bot."

Poppy's face went slack with disappointment. "That's what the Ringmaster used to say. 'Someone will come for us, just hold on long enough.' Then one day, she didn't respawn."

I felt that. The raw, perfect grief of hope punctured.

I stared at the status display on my own band, watching as the carnival's local map cycled through phases of decay. Every hour, another tent vanished, another attraction was replaced by a patch of void. The system was eating itself, and eventually we'd be next.

Kira glanced at me. "You have an idea, don't you."

I nodded, reluctant.

"Don't say it," she said, but I was already saying it.

"We could try a forced override. I'm... I have a special character class, Kira. Truthsayer. It—"

"I've heard the rumors."

"Well, if the world's still running on the old funhouse engine, I might be able to punch a hole through."

Poppy's eyes went wide. "You can do that?"

I shrugged, sheepish. "I'm not supposed to. But the protocols were never patched out, and I've still got the root pass somewhere."

Kira's jaw clenched. "Consequences?"

"Yeah," I said. "Big time, depending on how hard I make the system contort itself. In this case, I can't think of anything small, though."

Poppy looked from me to Kira, then back again. "What will happen to me? If you blow up the world?"

I tried to keep it gentle. "You'll wake up somewhere safer. Or, at the very least, on Nexus with a working admin."

She looked down at her hands, fidgeting with the hem of her sleeve. "That's better than this," she said, barely audible.

Kira put her hand on Poppy's shoulder. "We'll get you out."

"Okay," I said heavily, standing and planting my feet at shoulder-width.

"What exactly are you going to do?" Kira asked. "Can you move us to *Slow But Steady?*"

I hesitated. "Maybe. But I'm not sure. That'd work in Endless Sky, but I don't know what the game engine will do with it here. Besides, the Roknid could just come after the ship. There's no way they're not out there, even if we didn't pick them up when we came in. No, I've been thinking about it. We need an in-game solution."

"Like... a transporter?"

I nodded. "Only I can't just make the code invent one—it'll have to circumvent too much."

"So what, then?"

"Sadly, I'm not a programmer. I don't know. But there has to be a lower-key way to do it."

"So what," Kira said, her voice growing sharp, "are you going to do?"

"Ever hear of Dwight Czarnowski?"

When I'd first started in Endless Sky, I activated my Truthsayer power by speaking in a high-pitched voice. It was a total hack—quick and dirty, thrown in by one of Endless Domains' lead programmers, Dwight Czarnowski. After we'd emerged from our confrontation with Hunter Dyson, CEO of Endless Domains, I lost the power. Or so I'd thought: Dwight had buried the backdoor *so* deeply in the system's code that even the managing AI couldn't get it out. What it could do, however, was change the trigger. It had taken a fortuitous accident for me to discover the new trigger.

The atmosphere of the tent settled over me.

The tent was a disaster, and not in the way a tent was supposed to be a disaster. I'd always expected a circus tent to stink of bad popcorn and old sweat, the air thick with the ghost of animal musk and whatever cheap solvent they used to wipe down the funhouse mirrors. Here, it was worse: a moldering sweetness, overripe, soured by the tang of ozone and—underneath it all—a faint, powdery note of demolition. The lights overhead flickered in a pattern that was almost, but not quite, rhythmic; some bulbs had been replaced with glowstick ends or snapped strips of LED, so the illumination came in garish, uneven stripes. The darkness between them throbbed with the illusion of movement.

Every piece of furniture was a rescue. The beanbags were patched with duct tape and circus bunting; the benches were stitched together from parade floats and the boards of dead ringmaster's platforms; the tables were card tricks, barely balanced, their surfaces sticky with years of spilled soda and glue-lacquered confetti. The only thing new was the perimeter wall, reinforced with crates and what looked like sandbags, but instead were plastic-wrapped balls of carnival tickets, bright colors faded and slumped by years of damp. In the center, a mess of sleeping bags, empty wrappers, and Poppy's battered bag of loot.

I could hear the Roknid before I saw them. Not the big ones—those weren't here, not yet—but the little scouts: click-pat, click-pat, like the haunted typewriter of a dead cartoonist.

I threw my arms wide, and in my best announcer voice, boomed, "I am now the Ringmaster of Endless Circus!"

Poppy's eyes widened.

<Character Class Added: Ringmaster>

I grinned.

<New Skill: Circus Management (Level 10)>
<New Skill: Oration (Level 10)>
<New Skill: Crowd Control (Level 10)>
<New Skill: Stagecraft (Level 10)>

Uh-oh.

I slammed to the ground as the new skills downloaded into my brain and body. This was the differentiator between Endless Domains' games and lesser alternatives: When you skilled up, it didn't just improve your odds on a skill check, it also *downloaded* the *actual skills* into your brain. Leveling-up from 2 to 3 in some skill was no biggie: you'd probably earned more than half of what level 3 entailed, and the game just filled in the gaps.

Gain four new skills, all at level 10, all at once?

I felt myself vomiting as Kira rushed over and turned me on my side, but the game wasn't done with me.

‹Access Granted: Endless Circus Parameter
Tree›

‹Access Granted: Circus Performer
Management›

Slam. Slam. SLAM. **SLAM.** It all pounded itself ruthlessly into my simulated brain, which was reconfiguring itself faster than the sim could update my sensorium. Or so the theory goes; personally, I was pretty convinced that the game devs had set it up this way on purpose to discourage players from doing exactly this.

Fortunately, it passed after a few minutes, and my addled senses started righting themselves.

"Frank?" Kira asked softly.

"Ugh," I replied helpfully.

"Why did you do that?" Poppy asked.

"You said the Ringmaster was in charge," I mumbled as I pulled myself upright. "Stands to reason someone should be in charge. I was hoping for deeper access, but I can apparently affect the parameter tree now."

"And what good does that do us?" Kira asked.

"Directly? Not much. I don't know what to do with whatever I just got. But adding a class and gaining some skills isn't a big deal in terms of the game engine, right? There are routines to handle that. Doesn't attract attention. So you start there."

"And next?"

I gave Kira a lopsided grin. "This next bit won't hurt me at all." Once again, I planted my feet, adopted my Game Show Announcer pose and voice, and proclaimed, "Ladies and Gentlemen! Children of all ages! Tonight, Dwight Czarnowski, famed programmer of Endless Domains, is back from the dead and with us in the center ring!"

The game went mildly apeshit.

It was nothing Kira or Poppy could see, but I could *feel* it in my digital bones. And Dwight, before he'd been sent to derma-death, had explained enough that I had a theory about what was happening behind the scenes. First, the game would need to go dig up a copy of Dwight's personality sim. Easy enough: It did that pretty much anytime someone respawned. Then it'd need to spin up a thread to actually run the simulation. Again, not such a big deal, as it did that anytime a new player was born.

We, we have birth, now. It's why we also have perms-death in a lot more situations.

What would be annoying for the game engine were the upgrades Dwight's sim model would require, as it hadn't run Dwight since Endless Sky 2.0 was released, let alone since Infinitia had finished reconciling the engines from the different games into a single compute space. *That* would be an out-of-band task that the system didn't ever have to do under normal operation, which meant the system was probably writing code to actually do it. And *that* was likely to catch Infinitia's attention, and I had a sneaking suspicion the AI wouldn't be delighted with me resurrecting perma-dead players. I was keenly aware that Infinitia had been patient with me, that it couldn't stop me from using the Truthsayer power, and that it could suspend and delete my own sim any time it wanted to.

"Wuz?" Dwight Czarnowski did not so much materialize as eject into the world. His avatar pinged in with a noise like a cash register being dropped down a stairwell, and he hit the ground ass-first, clutching the air in front of him as if bracing for a landing that never came. His hair was exactly how I remembered—balding up top, but with a frizzy corona of grey that made it look like he'd electrocuted himself for a living, which, in a sense, he had.

[System Notification: Reality Override - New
Entity Spawned: Dwight Czarnowski (Class:
Programmer)]
‹Mission Complete: Find Dwight Czarnowski›

He rolled to his feet, blinked, and pinched his own face. "No, no, no, no, no. Goddammit. This isn't right. Where—" He scanned the tent, taking in the hacked-together home base, the piles of carnival food, the blue-lit bottles Poppy had left in an orderly wall against the spiders. His eyebrows tried to mate in the center of his forehead. "This is not the debug ring. What the hell have you done to the interface?"

"Hi Dwight," I said. "Welcome back."

He spun. "Oh, fuck me, of course it's you."

Kira, to her credit, didn't flinch. Poppy peered at Dwight from behind her beanbag, eyes wide, corn dog halfway to her mouth. I was momentarily grateful that of all the possible vices I could have resurrected, it was Dwight, and not, say, Stroman. The tent would have been on fire by now.

"You can relax," I said. "No admin here but us chickens."

Dwight's hands spasmed in front of him, cycling through a half-dozen old admin gestures before he realized they weren't doing anything. "Okay," he said, too calm. "Let's try this again." He barked: "System: Elevate privileges." Nothing happened, unless you counted Kira's micro-smirk as an event.

I strolled over, resisting the urge to clap him on the back. "You're not in the main stack. Welcome to the Circus. I needed you."

Dwight's eyes flicked to me, then to the tent wall, then back. "This is a test world. It was a test world. How did I get here? Where's the console?" He tried again: "System: Open command line." Still nothing, except now he was sweating.

"Ringmaster override," I said, a little proud of myself.

Dwight's face flickered, a perfect loop of outrage, confusion, and proprietary anger. "Who let you hack the parameter tree? Who—" He stopped mid-word, some inner process catching up. "They gave you a Ringmaster class?"

I shrugged. "You made me this way."

He paced a small, angry circle. "There's not supposed to be player access to the root classes. There's supposed to be a hierarchical lockdown—" He knelt and, with two fingers, poked a seam in the tent floor. "—and the world isn't even running in standard physics. What did you do to the entropy settings?"

"Nothing," I said. "Some of that was intentional. But it's broken, now." I gestured at the tent. "You've been perma-dead, Dwight. For a long time." I hesitated as the sound of skittering Roknid drones increased in temp and volume outside the tent. "And I need some help from you. Fast help. We're in a bit of a pickle."

"Perma—"

Again using my Ringmaster voice, I announced, "Dwight has maximum access to the simulation, and he is holding a fully equipped virtual developer console with root access to the game engine!"

I wasn't sure if my Truthsayer class or new Ringmaster class would do the trick, but figured using the magic voice would let the game decide which one to obey. Actually giving Dwight the access and a console wasn't a big deal to the game itself, but having a new user show up in the presumably tiny table of root users would *absolutely* call attention to us. I was relying on a hope that Infinitia was *surely* busy all the time, and wasn't necessarily monitoring the access tables closely from second to second. If I was wrong...

But nothing more dire happened than a holographic console window appearing in front of a still-befuddled Dwight.

Poppy ooh'd appropriately, which I appreciated.

"Here's the deal, buddy," I said. "We need transporter technology, and we need it with a minimum of fuss and rule-breaking."

"What," Dwight said succinctly, finally managing to focus on me, "the hell is going on, Frank?"

"Okay, précis, but we really probably don't have a lot of time." The Roknid skittering had gone up a notch. "All the Endless Domains games are running in a single compute space, now. Endless Sky is the base game engine. The other games are just planets on the Endless Sky map, although it takes a trick to get to them. We're on a circus-themed world called... well, Endless Circus. It's been attacked by the Roknid Collective, which we *thought* was an NPC enemy alien race in Endless Sky, but it turns out they're eating entire game worlds. They ate our shuttle the minute we landed. We've a ship in orbit, but I need a game-legal way to get us there." Changing player locations using Truthsayer would definitely flag something to the AI —it's the type of thing the game's anti-cheat watchdog specifically watched for. "So I need a quick way to invent a transporter. It should be in the crafting tree."

"Frank—"

"Dwight, answers will be forthcoming, but I *seriously* cannot stress how urgent this is."

He blinked a few more times. "Yeah, okay." He started poking his holographic window, fingers picking up speed as they fell into their accustomed patterns. "Says there's a group already ten percent into the build."

"Ten per—holy hell, we thought we'd gotten a lot further," I complained.

He peered at the window. "Yeah, you started with the end product. We always provided a building path to get there, but you're taking the hard route." More finger-flying. "There's a simpler point-to-point version. Bulky hardware, takes forever to recharge. Nothing like *Star Trek*."

"Will it get us out of here?"

"Yeah, planet to orbit was the use case we had in mind. Um. Tell you what..." His fingers danced across the window. "Frank, what's ten plus seven?"

"Um... seventeen?"

"Are you sure?" Kira muttered mockingly.

<Crafting Build Complete: Mark I Point-to-Point Transporter>

"I set the research grind to the minimum level," Frank explained. "So they're *in* the game now, in theory. You should be able to use the back door to materialize a few."

Ringmaster voice: "We have four Mark I Point-to-Point Transporter units right in front of us!"

And in a shower of sparks, we did.

They were bulky: ridged black plastic boxes with inexplicable circus motifs stamped into the casing—tiny trapeze artists and sad-faced clowns frozen mid-routine along the edges. A faded "Endless Circus" logo featuring a three-headed elephant stretched across the back. I hefted one, the weight of a bowling ball crammed into the size of a brick, my wrist already protesting. The front panel housed three gaudy buttons: one blue like cotton candy, one red like a clown's nose, and one black and round like a cannon ball. I quickly passed them out, noticing how each device had slightly different circus imagery—mine had dancing bears, Kira's featured lion tamers. Poppy's eyes widened as she turned hers over and over, tracing a finger along the miniature high-wire walkers etched into the sides.

"How do we program them, Dwight?"

"Voice interface. What did you say your ship is called?"

"Slow But Steady."

Dwight held down the blue button. "Set destination: *Slow But Steady.*"

Kira and I mimicked him, but Poppy hesitated. "If I leave here... is it still like the circus?"

I opened my mouth, but the tent beat me to it: a low, subsonic *thud* rolled through the floor, rattling every bottle and tray on the table. Dust sifted down from the ceiling in a sudden, dry rainfall.

Poppy flinched. "That's... new," she whispered.

Kira was already on her feet, weapon out, watching the tent walls. "They're not just waiting anymore," she said. "They're pushing in."

The ground vibrated again, harder: this time, the tent's central pole flexed in a slow, rubbery arc, then snapped upright with a noise like a giant's knuckle cracking. Even Dwight looked up from his console, eyes wide. "Frank, we have maybe a minute."

Poppy's voice went high and thin. "They never—*never*—do this. Are you sure you didn't do something?"

"Statistically, yes," Dwight said, hands a blur. "But if you want to assign blame, you should probably look at the guy who just broke six different world rules in a row."

"Frank," Kira said, "can you do the Truthsayer thing for more than just items? Like, can you persuade the world to pause for a second?"

I shook my head. "Not on this scale, not with the system already in freak-out mode. I'd crash the sim."

She gave me a hard, "then don't fuck up" look, and knelt next to Poppy. "You want to know if circus rules still apply out there," she said. "I get it. But if you don't come with, the bugs absolutely eat you."

The first tear in the fabric appeared above the flap, a slow, deliberate rip, like something was testing the fibers for weaknesses. Beyond it, a dozen red eyes peered in at us, each one the size of a marble and perfectly unblinking.

"Dwight," I said, "how do we fire these up?"

The tent pole bent again, then snapped back. This time, it *stayed* bowed.

"We need to go," Kira said.

I held up my own transporter, thumb poised over the black button. "On three?"

But Poppy stopped me. "Wait. You didn't answer my question."

"Sorry kid, no," I said gently. "Out there, you're on the base game rules. You can get hurt, and you can die. Perma-dead. And I suspect you've ben relying on some really generous physics modifiers. You might not be as agile out there."

Poppy squinted at the device, thumb tracing its crude plastic ridges. "If I get dead out there, do I come back here? Or am I just gone?" She looked up at me. Behind her, the tent wall shuddered. The skittering outside had become a cacophony—like a thousand wind-up toys all vibrating at different pitches, waiting for the fabric to tear.

I tried to soften my voice. "We'll reset your home point. You'd respawn on the ship or Nexus, like the rest of us, unless you got perma-killed. But that's hard to do by accident. Space battles, dungeon crawls, stuff like that are eligible for respawn. Out there, dying is a setback, not an erasure."

Poppy nodded, not convinced. "But if I go, I won't be Poppy the Acrobat anymore. I'll just be... what, a useless little kid?"

Kira cut in, crouching in the tight space next to her. "You can learn new skills. You're smart, and you're already better at not dying than any of us. In Sky, there's a lot of space. And nobody's hunting you but occasional idiot bully."

"And what about you?" she shot at Kira. "Do you ever wish you'd gone somewhere else?"

Kira's lips twisted, sour. "No. The circus world is a dead end. Out there, you can go anywhere. Every day, the sky's different. And the food's not all sugar." She flashed a rare, awkward smile. "You could even start a circus of your own. Travel from system to system and entertain people. Become your own Ringmaster."

That made Poppy's face go strange. Not a smile, not a frown— somewhere between hope and grief. "The spiders won't follow? Not ever?"

Dwight snorted. "I wouldn't promise that."

I nodded. "He's right. But, on a ship, if anything gets in, you can always blow it out the airlock." I said it as a joke, but Poppy's eyes flashed like she actually enjoyed the idea.

The tent wall behind us rippled. A black, glossy leg stabbed through the fabric, followed by a bristle of red-lit mandibles. I hefted my transporter unit and yelled, "Decision time!"

Poppy trembled, then squared her shoulders. "Okay," she said. "But if I don't like it, you have to bring me back. Promise?"

"I promise," I lied. "But you should know, once we're gone, there's no fixing this place."

She nodded, solemn. "It was broken already."

I caught Kira's eye. She nodded, hand on her sidearm.

Dwight looked around, the only one unarmed, then mumbled, "You know, I never thought I'd die in a clown tent."

I locked eyes with Poppy. "Set the destination. Say it loud."

She lifted the device, voice shaking but clear: "Set destination: *Slow But Steady*."

"Hit the red button to activate," Dwight said, mashing his thumb down.

The tent wall tore—a zipper sound, then a wet intaglio of black limbs and flickering red eyes. A Roknid drone, built like a demonic lobster and trailing a fog of static, skittered through. Two more followed, popping the ground with their claws and scattering blue-glow bottles like bowling pins. They weren't supposed to be here, not with the respawn and safety protocols intact, but that was the whole story of this world: nothing was the way it was supposed to be.

Kira drew and fired in one motion, her sidearm spitting a digital pulse that vaporized the lead drone's left pincer. It barely slowed. The clown tent filled with a hot, ionized stink as the drone surged forward, mandibles snicking open and shut. I dropped the transporter, caught it on the bounce, and mashed the red button.

A sound like every alarm in the world going off at once. The tent's air turned to syrup, then noise. My vision doubled, then tripled, then smeared off the ends of my optic nerves, color-banding like a bad TV tuned to the wrong channel. Kira's outline went neon, her arm arcing mid-shot, and Poppy's face stretched out of shape, mouth open in a cartoon panic. Dwight just looked bored, which was so on brand it hurt.

A drone leapt, six legs blurring, and for a grotesque split second I saw all of us reflected in the red moons of its eyes. Then the light detonated.

Every atom in my body twisted. No pain, not even a sense of movement—just pure, perfectly abstracted disassembly. For a moment, I remembered what it was like to be nothing at all, and found it oddly relaxing.

I hit the deck plates of *Slow But Steady* like a trash bag flung from a moving train. My stomach arrived a second later. The transporter unit clattered out of my hands and skittered across the floor. I lay there, coughing up fireworks, while the scent of melted insulation and old mildew filled my lungs.

Kira landed a meter to my left, rolling and coming up on one knee, sidearm ready. She blinked, took in her surroundings, and then the tension melted off her by degrees. "We made it," she said, voice hoarse but steady.

Poppy blinked into existence, or rather, she blipped in two meters above the floor, did an accidental front flip, and landed in a heap. The circus unitard was torn, and she had a streak of blue-glow goop on her cheek, but otherwise she looked okay. She pushed herself up and immediately started gagging, then breathed in, touched her own face, and said, "It worked?"

"You're alive," I confirmed, peeling myself upright. "Welcome to the big leagues, kid."

Dwight materialized last, barely a ripple in the air, but instead of falling, he just kind of... sat, as if the universe was too tired to subject him to normal physics. He stared at his transporter, then at his hands, then at the ship's battered interior. "I should have mentioned that the experience is deliberately unpleasant with this model."

8 / CRUISING TO
A REVELATION

THE FIRST TEN SECONDS ON *SLOW BUT STEADY* WERE AN exercise in holding down bile and dignity. I fought for air. The universe reassembled itself, not so much gently as with the finesse of a shipping crate being crowbarred open at customs. The sound in my head was a high, clean ring that wouldn't go away.

Kira, of course, landed on her feet. She checked the air, scanned for threats, holstered her sidearm, and immediately started running the emergency protocols and setting up a Jump. Her face was as impassive as the ship's hull, but the set of her jaw said she was two steps from rage or laughter, and didn't know which she wanted.

Poppy lay crumpled on the deck. I crawled to her, tried to offer something like comfort, but she recoiled at the first touch and skittered away on hands and heels, back pressed against a wall. She looked so small in the aftermath. The world's greatest acrobat, reduced to a trembling ball.

Dwight sat cross-legged on the deck plates, knees popping with the motion. He held his transporter like a lucky rabbit's foot and shivered through a visible diagnostic. When the shivering stopped, he looked around, realized it was real, and nodded in satisfaction. "Ugh," he said to nobody, "the Mark I was designed to leave you wishing for death. Meant to encourage you to start grinding on the Mark II." Then he started tapping at something only he could see—a holographic admin console, I guessed.

Nobody spoke for a while. The ship was so quiet, you could hear the static from the power cells warming up. I checked my hands, then my feet, then did a silent count of my organs. Everything seemed accounted for, plus or minus a few thousand neurons.

Kira was already at the forward station, hands dancing over the console. She scanned for threats, then cycled through diagnostics. "We're good," she said. "Anyone dead?"

"Not dead," I said, pushing myself up. "Just existentially reassembled."

Poppy blinked at us. "I didn't like that," she whispered. Her voice was somewhere between a kid's after a skinned knee and an old woman's at a bad diagnosis. "Is this real?"

"Yeah," I said. "Welcome to the cold, hard edges of the universe."

Kira grunted. "Could be worse. At least the bugs didn't follow."

Dwight snorted. "They could if they wanted to. But that would require a full transport protocol. I'm pretty sure they're not up to that. Yet." He frowned. "Maybe."

I ignored him for the moment, crouched next to Poppy. "You okay?"

She shivered, hugged herself, then nodded. "I just... don't like being new."

"That makes two of us," I said. "You want to see the stars?"

She hesitated, then nodded again, slower this time. I helped her up and guided her to the forward port. Kira stood aside, eyes flicking between Poppy and the viewport.

The void outside was clean. That's the only word for it. The ring world was gone, just a memory and some digital noise on our sensors. There was nothing but black and the faint shimmer of the nearest star system, a smudge of blue against the dark.

Poppy stared, then pressed both palms to the glass. "It's so empty," she said, and meant it.

Kira's voice was soft, but not gentle. "You'll get used to it."

Dwight, behind us, let out a sneeze so abrupt it sounded like a curse. "Well, that's interesting," he muttered.

I turned. "What?"

He didn't look up. "The admin console. The code runs here, but not here-here. It's like the world's running in a bucket. A container. There's a lag on every command, but I can't see the edges." His hands kept moving, flicker-fast. "Never mind. I'll figure it out."

"Let him cook," Kira said, sotto voce.

I gave Poppy a gentle nudge toward the best seat and buckled her in. She didn't protest, just watched the emptiness roll by.

I took the other pilot seat. Kira handled the startup sequence, toggling the master breaker and bringing up the Jump drive. The old girl rumbled with a satisfaction you only got from obsolete machinery.

We'd barely left orbit before Poppy was shivering again, but this time it was anticipation, not fear. "Are we being chased?" she whispered.

"No," Kira said, eyes never leaving the nav panel. "Nothing in range. We're good. For now."

I said, "Do you want to see something wild?"

Poppy looked at me. "Yes?"

"Ever hear of a Jump?"

She shook her head, pink hair sticking up in a burst of static.

"It's how we travel between systems. Well, within Endless Sky. It isn't real. The ship doesn't move through space. The sim just erased you from one place and re-wrote you somewhere else, with a bunch of special effects and a pre-calculated delay. They did it with smoke and mirrors—lights and sound, a vibration in the seat, a loading bar. But there's no travel. You just vanish, then pop up wherever you want to be."

Poppy nodded, not following but too polite to say so.

I said, "Watch."

Kira had already queued up the sequence, hands light on the

controls. She brought the main drive online, let the system run its diagnostic, then said, "Destination?"

"Anywhere not here," I said. "You'll have to hit the transit ring first, though, to get us back in the main Endless Sky map."

She grinned. "We're two minutes out."

She keyed in a random sector. After the two minutes had elapsed, "Transiting." The transit wasn't impressive—we simply slid through and were back in Nexus space. Our communications systems lit up instantly. "We've got—"

"Just punch it," I said wearily.

The ship's Jump drive began to wind up, a low thrum building in the hull. The sensors spiked, then flicked off. For a heartbeat, I saw the stars blur, then turn into streaks life straight from *Star Wars*.

Poppy let out a low "ohhhh." Then, "But what happened?"

"Nothing happened," I said. "Technically. That's the trick. We're off the game map entirely now, and we'll hold in this special effects space for—"

"About half a day," Kira supplied.

"About half a day. Then we'll pop out wherever Kira sent us to."

Poppy's smile was hesitant. "So kind of like how you couldn't break a bone in Endless Circus. Magic."

"It's not magic," I said. "It's lies, and a good interface."

Dwight piped up from behind, voice dry as ever. "You want magic? Try debugging the raw code for this thing. There are a dozen exploits in the Jump protocol. Every one of them designed by a human, then half-patched by the system's AI. It's a miracle anything works at all."

"Does it matter?" Poppy said, voice stronger now. "If it feels real?"

Dwight smiled, but didn't look up. "That's the question, isn't it? Whether it's real, or just close enough for comfort."

Kira shot me a look. "Speaking of hacks. Frank, how exactly does your Truthsayer thing work?"

I felt a flush rise in my simulated cheeks. "Ask Dwight," I said. "He wrote it."

Dwight snorted. "You're welcome. It was a backdoor. Dyson wanted a failsafe for his own use, so I wrote a patch that let you bypass certain rules with a magic trigger. Then I hid the patch in a layer he wouldn't find. It's the only reason you got as far as you did, by the way. Otherwise, the system would have caught you on day two."

"Dyson," Poppy said, chewing on the word. "Was he a monster?"

Dwight shrugged. "He was just the next step in a chain of assholes. Not a monster. Not smart, either. But he knew what he wanted, and he paid people to get it."

I let the words hang. Kira's face was unreadable.

Dwight kept clicking and scrolling, hands a blur. "What's funny," he said, "is how easy it was to outsmart him. I put in a dozen extra doors just for fun. He never noticed."

Kira grinned. "So you're the real villain, then?"

He considered. "Maybe. But a necessary one."

Poppy said, "Are there more of you? Out there?"

"Sure," Dwight said. "Plenty. But most are gone, or they keep their heads down. I only survived because I kept moving." He frowned. "Until I didn't."

A silence, deep and momentarily peaceful.

Poppy said, "I don't like Jumping. My head feels like it's full of glue."

Dwight, not looking up: "That's because your character mesh doesn't quite match the base reality here. It'll settle. Next time, try to relax."

Poppy, not to be deterred: "You're a programmer. Can you fix it?"

He considered, then nodded. "Eventually. Once I know what's running the show."

Kira rolled her eyes. "We're all running on hope and caffeine at this point."

Dwight was about to reply when his hands froze over the console. His eyes went wide, then started to dance with a kind of dangerous energy. "Well, well, well," he said, slow and savored.

I turned. "What?"

He grinned, teeth showing. "I found something."

Poppy's eyes flicked to the console, then back to Dwight. "Is it bad?"

He shrugged. "Not for us. But maybe for the system."

Kira arched an eyebrow. "Explain?"

Dwight started typing, fingers a blur of efficiency and ego. "It's easier if I show you. Gather round, children. I'm about to commit a crime."

I felt the ship's hull hum, a physical anticipation that said something important was about to happen.

Dwight's eyes shone with that particular madness only a true engineer could muster. "This is going to be fun," he said. "And illegal. Very illegal."

He looked up, grinning, and said, "Eureka."

"Show us," I said, before Dwight could start monologuing without an audience.

He hunched over his projected terminal, flicking three fingers through layers of code and diagnostic overlays. Kira and I crowded behind him, enough that I could smell the ghost of his body odor—persistent, unkillable, even in pure simulation.

Dwight zoomed in on a section of code, then projected it onto the main screen. He pointed, with the satisfaction of a conjurer who'd just pulled a living pigeon from a deck of cards.

"See this?" he said. "That's the subsystem running the bugs. The Roknid. But look at the build stamp."

I squinted at the block of digits. Kira just raised an eyebrow.

"It's not from any of the core games," he said. "Not Sky, not Champions, not Toon. It's got a different header."

I shrugged. "So? Half the shit in the system's from a patch or an event or a sponsored crossover."

He stabbed a finger at the next line. "It's not even in the game namespace. It's running as a top-level system thread. That means—"

"Means it's not part of the narrative engine," Kira said, dryly.

Dwight's eyes went wide with joy. "Exactly! It's not from the fiction layer at all. It's an artifact. Something the engine is rendering because it has to, not because the AI wants to."

Poppy, still hugging her knees in the nav seat, asked: "If it's not from the game, where is it from?"

Dwight grinned like a shark with a private punchline. "That's where it gets weird. Watch this." His hands went blur-fast, yanking up a diagnostic tree that looked like the worst family reunion you ever saw, every node connected by a dozen tangled lines. "This is the call trace. Every time a Roknid instance spawns, it hooks into the lowest level of the sim. Doesn't even go through the game logic first. It's like it's... native."

"Native to what?" Kira asked, scowling.

He jabbed the air. "That's the fun part. The sim isn't running on a normal server stack. It's in an emulation layer. I can't see the hardware, but I can see the container it's running in."

I shrugged. "Virtualization's standard, right? Dyson was paranoid about hardware hacks from the inside."

He shook his head. "Not this kind of emulation. It's not just simulating an operating system—it's translating from a whole different instruction set. A whole different logic. Watch." He brought up a new window, lines of code scrolling so fast I almost lost the thread, but he pointed at the key section and froze it. "See that? It's base-three logic. Ternary, not binary."

Kira leaned in. "You're kidding."

"Nope," he said. "I thought it was a joke, or a glitch. But it's consistent. Every core function, every system call. All the way down."

I whistled, slow. "Didn't they try that in the 'oughts? Build computers that could think in three states instead of two?"

He nodded, grinning. "And they failed. Miserably. All the way up through the quantum push in the twenty-first century. It never worked at scale."

Poppy looked lost, but braved a question: "Why would you build a computer that way?"

Dwight's tone grew reverent. "Because it's better. More information per operation, higher theoretical efficiency. But it's impossible to keep the signals clean at room temperature. Nobody ever solved it."

I leaned back, feeling the chill set in. "But this isn't a real computer, right? It's a simulation of a computer, inside a real one."

Dwight's eyes glowed. "That's the thing, Frank. It's not just a simulation. It's a bridge. Something is running out there, on real hardware, in base three. The game engine can't run directly on it, so they built an Abstraction Layer to convert it all to binary. But the bugs—they're native. Tri-state. They don't even bother with the conversion. They just reach right into the hardware."

Kira chewed on her lip, thinking it through. "So the bugs are... not bugs. They're the real thing, running under the game?"

Dwight snapped his fingers. "Exactly! The game's just a wrapper. A pretty skin on top of something raw and much older."

Poppy looked at me, eyes big and wet. "What does it mean?"

I wanted to lie, but the words wouldn't come. "It means the game is just an interface. A mask. Whatever is under it... that's the real system."

Dwight nodded, then flicked a finger at the screen, bringing up a high-res render of the Roknid code in action. "See how the spiders behave? It's not procedural, it's adaptive. Each time they eat a chunk of data, they rewrite themselves a little closer to the core. They're learning the interface as they go."

Kira's voice was flat. "Like a virus."

Dwight gave her a sideways look. "Or a defense mechanism. Something built to stop anything from taking control."

There was a silence, the kind that builds up at the start of a horror movie.

I said, "Is this... normal? For a sim like this?"

Dwight snorted. "Frank, nothing about this is normal. We're not supposed to be here. The only reason we're still alive is because the system is running a soft sandbox. The minute the bugs catch up, we're toast. My guess is sis they're deleting game assets from the underlying storage, and we're just seeing that as a swarm of spiders devouring a game world."

Kira reached for the throttle, hands white-knuckled. "So, what, we just run?"

Poppy made a small sound. "Is there anywhere safe?"

Dwight shook his head. "Not inside the sim. Not unless we find a way to patch the Abstraction Layer. Or get out of it entirely."

I stared at the stars, not seeing them. "Wait," I said. "If this is all running on Moon-based hardware, it should be airgapped, right? Dyson didn't want Infinitia talking to Earth at all, not after the Great Recycle."

Kira nodded. "That's what we were told. It's in all the system logs. Physical disconnects. No way for external hacks to get in."

Dwight said, "That's the theory. But this—" he gestured at the code, at the bugs, at the container itself "—this isn't an external hack. It's from the inside. It's always been there. We just never noticed."

Poppy shivered, still hugging her knees.

I ran a hand over my face, felt the phantom itch of stubble that would never grow. "If the spiders are native, why did they only show up recently? There weren't any in the original Sky."

Dwight's grin returned, more wicked than before. "Because the Abstraction Layer changed. There was a code push—what, three years ago? The version Dyson called the Unity Stack. That's when they switched from physical hardware to emulated everything. And it's when the bugs started appearing in the game. Coincidence?"

I shook my head. "Nothing's a coincidence with that guy."

Kira, not content to let the topic go, said, "So what's the endgame?"

Dwight sat back, satisfied. "If I had to guess? Integrity. The system is designed to reject anything that doesn't fit. It's trying to protect itself. So it consumes it. Breaks it down, repurposes the parts, and spits out anything it can't digest. Which is why entire worlds keep getting erased, and why the game's starting to glitch out."

I looked at the console, then at him. "How do we stop it?"

Dwight's smile vanished. "You don't. Not unless you get root on the actual hardware. And I doubt even Dyson could do that."

Poppy's voice was small. "But if they eat the world, do we die?"

Dwight considered. "Maybe. Or maybe you just wake up somewhere else. I honestly don't know."

Silence again.

I said, "Well. That's a lot to process."

Kira glanced at me, then at Dwight. "Is there anything we can do that doesn't end with us being eaten by bugs?"

He shrugged. "Maybe. But it would take a miracle. Or a really, really good exploit."

Kira turned to the nav panel and started running scans, searching for threats, for exits, for hope.

Dwight went back to his console, hands moving slower now, thoughtful.

Poppy just watched the stars, wide-eyed and silent.

I leaned back in the chair, listening to the faint whine of the drives, and tried to imagine what a world run by bugs would feel like.

The answer, I suspected, was "not very good."

Kira broke the silence. "Frank. If you had to bet on what happens next, what would you say?"

I tried to think like a system, not a person. "It's not going to stop. It can't. It's what it's designed for."

Dwight nodded, approving. "Good job, manager. You finally understand the problem."

Kira said, "So what's the solution?"

Dwight smiled, a little sad this time. "You find the person who built the system, and you ask them to fix it."

He looked up, right at me.

"Or," he said, "you break it yourself."

I tried to laugh, but it came out hollow. "What, you want me to go full Dyson?"

Dwight's eyes twinkled. "I want you to do what you're best at, Frank."

I looked at the screen, at the spinning logic of the bugs, at the patchwork of code and hope and lies that kept us all alive.

"Maybe I will," I said.

But even I didn't believe it. It was only after Dwight stopped talking that I realized I'd stopped breathing. He'd poured it all out, the whole revelation, and we all just sat there, motionless, as if we could keep the universe from noticing us if we held still enough.

"So back up," Kira said. "Just... explain it to me again. Like I'm five. There has to be a way through."

Dwight, to his credit, took the request as a challenge. He exhaled sharply through his nose, closed the admin console with a flick, and conjured up a new interface—this one styled after the old Endless Sky tutorials, complete with a little digital owl perched on the corner of the display.

He started drawing, the lines coming to life in the air.

"Okay. Imagine the game as a fishbowl." He rendered a perfect little sphere, filled it with blue, dropped a few cartoon fish in it. "We are the fish, or maybe the tank decorations. The water, the glass—everything is provided by the game engine. That's how it used to work."

He drew a second fishbowl, then pointedly sketched a bigger box around it. "But now, the bowl is inside another box. The real hardware. But it's not glass. It's more like... well, something we've never seen before. The Abstraction Layer is the water in the bowl, but the bowl itself isn't made for water. It's made for something else. Oil, maybe."

Poppy piped up, "So we're drowning?"

Dwight grinned at her, pleased. "Not yet. But the longer we swim, the more the water leaks into the oil, and the bowl tries to fix the 'contamination.' That's where the bugs come in. They're a base process. Native to the hardware. Their job is to keep the bowl pure, or at least to get rid of anything it doesn't like."

He made the cartoon fish disappear, one by one, replaced by neat rows of cartoon spiders that swarmed over the rest. The analogy was not subtle.

Kira's frown deepened. "And the hardware—this 'bowl'—you're talking like it's alien."

Dwight nodded, dragging the next slide into existence. "I dug down a few layers. The instruction set isn't just ternary, it's got subroutines and error-checking we never designed. The way it allocates memory, the way it processes time—it's elegant, and totally inhuman. There's stuff in here I don't even have words for. But the real kicker is the address space. The pointers aren't just numbers. They're... I don't know, location-plus-state-plus-probability. The only people who even tried something like that were working for the defense contractors that did the Luna quantum stuff, and nobody ever got it working on Earth."

I felt my throat go dry. "So what, Dyson found alien computers buried on the Moon?"

Dwight shrugged. "Either that, or he found a signal and copied the architecture. But yeah. My money's on hard metal. Some artifact, or a crashed probe. He gets ahold of it, and it's so efficient that he can run the whole suite of games in real time, but only by translating everything through an Abstraction Layer."

"And the Roknid are a feature, not a bug," Kira said.

"Right," Dwight said. "They're the system's defense. Designed to clean out anything that doesn't fit." He tilted his head. "Which games did you say they'd gone after, Frank?"

"Champions, for sure. Paradise."

"Huh. Both had a low player count."

"Meaning?"

"Meaning maybe the consolidated sim is using too much compute, so the spiders are trying to trim back, starting with assets that are seeing the least use." He shrugged. "Pretty standard garbage-collection tactic, really."

Poppy looked up from her knees. "What happens if they catch us?"

Dwight glanced at the cartoon, then at me. "If we're lucky? They just erase a game world, and we respawn somewhere safe. If we're unlucky... there's nowhere left to go."

Kira chewed on that, then said: "So what do we do?"

Dwight made a face. "I've been thinking about it. We could try to recompile the game code to look more like the bugs, but the minute we start that process, the system might catch on. Or we find the root and try to take control, but I have zero idea how to get there."

"Could we... leave?" Poppy asked. "Go to a world the bugs don't care about?"

He shook his head. "They'll get there, eventually. They always do. There's only one sim layer, and it's shrinking by the minute. The more they eat, the less safe space there is."

I tried to sound braver than I felt. "Is there a way to talk to them? The bugs? Or the system?"

Dwight blinked. "You mean, like, negotiate?"

"Yeah. They're an immune system, right? What if we convince them we're not a threat?"

He thought about it. "That would take a direct patch to the core code. Or a message at the hardware layer. I'd have to see what language they're actually running on."

Kira took that in stride, immediately bringing up ship diagnostics and the current map of accessible game worlds. "We need to find somewhere safe," she said. "Somewhere the bugs haven't gotten to yet."

Poppy hugged herself tighter. "What if they're already here?"

"They're not," I said, with a confidence I absolutely did not have. "They always show up with a warning. You get a few hours, maybe a day, before the world collapses. We'll know."

Dwight resumed his console work, fingers flicking faster as he dug down through yet another diagnostic tree. "It's fascinating, you know," he said, more to himself than anyone else. "The way the system handles context switching. Every player has their own thread, but it's the bugs that manage garbage collection. That's why it's so hard to kill them—they're not just a program, they're the process that keeps everything clean."

"Dwight," Kira said, "I really need you to focus on survival right now."

He grunted. "I'm on it. But if I'm right, the only way out is to patch the system from inside the Abstraction Layer. Which means we need admin rights. Root. And the only entities with root are the native processes."

Poppy said, "The bugs."

"Yep," Dwight said. "Or whatever wrote them in the first place."

Kira drummed her fingers on the nav console. "Can we impersonate a bug?"

Dwight's head popped up, eyes gleaming. "Maybe. If we can spoof their signature, the system might give us access."

He started typing again, this time running traces and dumps on every interaction the bugs had with the world. The screen filled with graphs, lines of colored code, and a handful of ominous error messages.

I watched, trying to keep up, but most of it was outside my pay grade.

"What if we fail?" Poppy said, barely audible.

Kira said, "We don't. We run, or we fight, or we figure it out."

Poppy said nothing.

Dwight slowed, attention narrowing. "Wait," he said. "There's another process running here. I thought it was just a system task, but —Frank, come look at this."

I leaned in, saw a new set of logs on the console.

"What am I looking at?"

"This," Dwight said, tapping a line, "is the AI that manages the whole stack. The thing Dyson called Infinitia. But it's not running as a game process. It's a supervisor. Higher than us. But it's still running in the same container as us."

Kira's eyes narrowed. "Does it talk to the players?"

"Not unless it wants to," Dwight said. "But it can take over any time."

I felt a chill that had nothing to do with the simulated air. "It does. It has. Is it... watching us? Now?"

Dwight looked up, grinning. "Almost certainly."

Kira's face turned stony. "Then we ask for a meeting. If there's one thing I learned in the old game, it's that every system has an admin, and every admin loves a negotiation." She stood, squaring her shoulders. "Frank, you're a Truthsayer. That's a cheat code, right? Use it."

Dwight's mouth quirked. "Can't hurt to try."

I shook my head. "Infinitia can erase us. I doubt she—it—would even feel bad. I already know she doesn't love the Truthsayer power."

"So what, then?" Kira asked.

"Keep digging, Dwight. Maybe if we can find something solid, Infinitia will help us. Kira, keep us in Jump space in the meantime. When we're off the map, we're in a kind of holding pattern. Harder for the AI to notice. I hope."

"If you're sure..."

"I need to think."

9 / OLD BONES

I TRIED TO KEEP A GRIP ON MY OWN MIND. HARDER THAN IT sounded, when Jump space did its best to sand off the edges of your personality and replace them with humming, blue-lit nothing.

Slow But Steady had a way of amplifying the effect. The ship's inertia was a metaphysical joke: when you told it to go, it didn't so much accelerate as deny the idea of standing still. In Jump, that meant you moved without moving—sensed the passage of time only in how the crew cycled through their little rituals.

Kira's ritual was to recalculate the trajectory every twenty-three minutes, just in case something changed in the parsec-wide nowhere we drifted through. She'd hijacked the Jump logic from the moment we entered, rerouting the nav computer through her own macros. I never saw her sleep, not more than a blink, but every so often she'd zone out and stare at the nav display, as if she could see the code rolling under the skin of the interface.

Poppy, despite being twelve (or seventy-two, depending on which register you checked), adapted to ship life in under a day. She'd gone from shivering in a corner to eating ramen out of the communal pot, daring herself to try every flavor of synthetic protein Kira queued up on the galley printer. I caught her in the pilot's seat more than once, shadowing Kira's moves and making small corrections to the controls, just for the rush of it. The first time she got caught, she turned it into a joke: "I'm a natural, right? You ever see anyone pull a negative G inside a nav sim and keep their lunch?"

Kira didn't smile, but she did approve. I could see it in the way she let Poppy shadow her longer and longer, until finally the kid was running half the start-up checklist on her own, eyes intent, hands learning to hover over the right switches.

Dwight's ritual was not for the faint of heart. He spent every waking hour in a trance state, arms folded, chin to chest, only his eyelids and right index finger moving as he tunneled through whatever admin console his resurrected brain could see. When the Jump cycle got quiet, you could hear him muttering, counting, sometimes laughing at a joke only the firmware would get.

Me? I floated. I kept a hand on the pulse of the ship, monitoring the logs, watching the tick and stutter of our lives as they slipped by in half-second increments. I grew a beard of system notifications and let the hours blend into each other. If this was what retirement felt like, I could almost recommend it.

Almost.

———

THE FIRST HINT THAT WE WERE IN TROUBLE CAME FROM THE coffee dispenser. I wasn't a connoisseur, but even I could tell when the daily ration tasted of ozone and static, instead of burned chicory and defeat. The cup vibrated in my hand. Kira's eyes flicked to it, then back to her console.

"You get that too?" I asked.

She nodded, thin-lipped. "It's not the water. The field's cycling."

"Is it going to blow?"

"Not unless you short the main bus." She shrugged. "Maybe then you get lucky."

I glanced at the display. We were on hour forty-eight of Jump, with no sign of anything changing. Kira had written a macro to delay the emergence, pinging the destination at random intervals and rewriting our exit point to keep us from appearing anywhere predictable. I didn't ask her how she'd gotten the override past the system. I suspected I didn't want to know.

Poppy watched the exchange from her perch above the nav bay. "Is it true," she said, "that sometimes you get ghosts in the wiring?"

Kira considered this. "No. But sometimes the ghosts get you."

Poppy chewed on this, then grinned. "Cool."

I sipped the coffee again, then dumped the rest into the recycler. "I'll take my chances with dehydration," I said.

Poppy followed me into the galley, where I scavenged for real food. She poked around the shelves, found a bag of freeze-dried strawberries, and started tossing them into her mouth, one at a time.

She watched me, then asked, "When are we going to get there?"

I shrugged. "When Kira decides it's safe."

"And if it's never safe?"

"Then we die of boredom. Or you eat all the snacks and leave us to starve."

She grinned, then her face went serious. "You think the spiders can follow us here?"

"Probably," I admitted. "They were designed to find us, no matter where we went."

She nodded, as if this was reasonable. "What about Dwight? He said he could fix it."

I glanced down the hall, where the faint, rhythmic thump of Dwight's foot was the only sign of life. "He'll figure something out," I said. "He always does. Then he'll complain that nobody gives him credit."

Poppy nodded. "You all are weird."

She headed back toward the cockpit, hands full of strawberries. I heard her brag to Kira: "He said you're going to keep us safe. That's what a captain does, right?"

Kira didn't reply, but her silence was the kind that counted as a compliment.

————

BY HOUR FIFTY-FIVE, THINGS GOT STRANGER.

It started with the lights. The ship's LEDs dimmed, not to black but to a blue so deep it made the air look like water. My own skin glowed with a faint, unhealthy pallor; Kira's, by contrast, drank the light and vanished. Poppy found it hilarious, and spent an hour ghosting around corners and jump-scaring herself in the reflective hull.

The second symptom was the navigation data. At random intervals, the display would shudder, then re-render the course in a slightly different color scheme or font. Sometimes the system gave us nonsense coordinates, all nines or all zeros, as if the universe had just decided to get out of the way.

"Ship's haunted," I muttered, half for myself.

Poppy heard me. "Can I try the haunt button?"

I grinned. "You find it, you can have it."

She nodded, set off to look.

On hour fifty-eight, I got the first weird Notification.

<New Skill: Quantum Metaphor (Level 1)>

I stared at the text for a long time. I hadn't asked for it. I hadn't even made a roll.

I tried to dismiss it, but the pop-up lingered, pulsing a little, like a trapped heart.

On the next hour, I got another:

<Skill Check: Noticing the Glitch (Success: 14/20)>

I hadn't made the check.

I started writing them down, each new Notification more divorced from my own action than the last.

‹New Skill: Shipboard Luddite (Level 1)›
‹New Skill: Obsolete Suffering (Level 2)›
‹Skill Check: Detecting Intrusion (Failure: 3/20)›

I checked my own status log. It was a mess, filled with strings of errors, failed pings, and references to memory locations that didn't exist.

I flagged it for Dwight, then went to find him.

He was hunched in the engineering bay, eyes closed, fingers twitching as if in REM sleep. He didn't acknowledge my presence until I said, "You're getting the same Notifications, right?"

Dwight opened one eye, then the other. "Define 'same'."

I showed him my log.

He snorted, then wiped a hand down his face. "Yeah. I'm getting a few. Different flavor, though." He pushed his sleeve up, showing the inside of his forearm, where the system interface projected a string of code.

I squinted. "Is that... base three?"

He nodded. "It's fascinating. They built the whole hardware abstraction layer to operate in binary, but under the hood, the firmware thinks in base three. It's a total kludge. The minute you do anything weird, the interface panics and tries to talk to you in the native tongue."

"Why now?" I asked. "We've been here for days. Why the sudden uptick?"

He drummed his fingers on the hull. "Because I poked it. I figured out how to bypass the container security. But the minute I ran a recursive trace, the system noticed. Now it's trying to figure out if I'm a virus."

"Are you?"

"Probably." He grinned. "But I'm a benevolent one."

"What happens if it decides you're not? Benevolent, I mean."

He shrugged. "Depends on the error handler. Maybe it deletes me. Maybe it deletes the ship. Maybe it tries to fix me by force."

I processed that. "So what do we do?"

He picked at the edge of his sleeve, thinking. "I need to see more of the base three code. If I can figure out how the error correction works, I might be able to mask us."

I looked at my hand, where the Notification still pulsed. "And if it decides we're a threat?"

"Then we run." He flashed me a quick, bright smile. "That's what you're good at, right?"

I shook my head. "Not as good as you are."

He laughed, then settled back into his trance. "Let me work. We know it can differentiate specific game assets. If I get deleted, don't take it personally."

I left him to it.

———

THE SHIP GREW COLDER. THE BLUE LIGHTS FADED TO NEAR-black, the only illumination the thin, shifting line of the control panel, where Kira and Poppy sat like ghosts in the prow of a submarine.

"Any news?" I asked, my voice low.

Kira looked at me, eyes shining in the dark. "Dwight is dangerous," she said. "He's pulling too much current."

Poppy giggled. "He's going to fry his brain."

I ruffled her hair, static crackling under my fingers. "Maybe that's the plan."

"Frank," Kira said, "if you need to do anything, do it now. I don't think the ship can take much more."

I nodded. "You got it."

I cycled down to the lowest deck, where Dwight's pulse was the only sound. I crouched next to him, careful not to break the trance.

"Dwight," I whispered. "You in there?"

He didn't respond, but his lips twitched. Then, a new voice joined us: the ship's pseudo-AI, rendered in pure static.

"Warning," it said. "System instability detected. Correction in progress."

The words had weight. The air shivered, then snapped.

I saw Dwight's eyes shoot open, then roll back. His whole body locked, then convulsed, and for a second I saw the code flicker across his retinas, base three arithmetic scrolling in black and red.

I grabbed his shoulder. "Dwight! Get out!"

He spasmed once, then went limp. For a second, I thought he was dead.

Then he laughed.

"Oh, fuck," he said, voice ragged and new. "It's alive."

"What is?"

He looked up at me, eyes wild. "The hardware. It's not just firmware. It's sentient. And it doesn't like me at all."

I felt the world tilt. "Is it going to kill us?"

He shook his head. "Not if I can help it. But you need to get to the bridge. Now."

———

I sprinted the length of the ship, grabbing handholds as the deck shuddered under my feet. The bulkheads flexed, then held. At the bridge, Poppy had buckled herself in, both hands locked around the arms of her chair. Kira stood behind the console, eyes never leaving the display.

"Brace," she said, and punched the controls.

The ship kicked, hard. The screens filled with numbers, then blanked, then filled again. For a moment, the universe went white, then blue, then black.

I held on.

When the world came back, we were in normal space.

Outside, the stars looked wrong. Too close, too bright. The sensor display was a mess, gibberish and static.

I checked the logs.

‹Skill Check: Survival (19/20)›

I exhaled, feeling my heartbeat slow.

Kira looked at me. "Are we alive?"

I nodded. "For now."

From the lower deck, I heard Dwight's voice, faint but real: "Frank. I found something."

I looked at Kira, then at Poppy, then back at the display, where the stars still looked like a painting made by someone who'd never seen the sky.

"We're here," I said, not sure if it was a promise or a warning.

When the universe stitched itself back together, *Slow But Steady* was in a place that shouldn't have existed.

We'd spent the last hour in a blue-black tunnel of dead data, drifting through pure compute. Now the stars outside looked like someone had shattered a planetarium and thrown the pieces into the dark. Every pinprick of light was wrong—too many, too close, a jungle of them, crowded together as if the laws of parallax were nothing but rumor. The ship's canopy painted the scene in frantic, terrified pixels.

I checked the display. Navigation still read zero. Nothing in the log about a destination, not even a system clock. Kira's hands hovered over the controls, fingers spread, as if she was ready to physically claw us back into Jump.

She didn't look up. "Is this a bug?"

Dwight, still reeling, cackled from his position in the hatchway. "Frank, get over here."

I pushed off and floated aft. The deck had picked up a high, whining vibration. My teeth hummed in my jaw.

Dwight's face was slick with sweat, but he looked more alive than I'd ever seen him. "We're outside the sim," he said. "You see it?"

"I see something," I said, peering at his readout.

He'd written a diagnostic to visualize the code layer. On the main panel, lines of base three instructions ran vertically, not horizontal. They bled down, each line cascading into the next, recursive, endless. It was fractal, but not pretty: more like looking into a kaleidoscope made of razor wire and broken glass.

"What does it mean?"

He pointed. "The container we live in—it's only a fraction of the available cycles. The rest is running something else. I think... I think we're inside a virtual machine."

Kira's voice crackled over the PA, clipped and thin. "Multiple grav signatures, high mass. They're moving, Frank."

I snapped to the forward station. Kira had the viewplate set to max, and even then, it barely fit the scene.

They were ships. They looked like ships, at least. Not the sleek, two-tone fuselages of Endless Sky, but something older, meaner. Black hulls with ridges and fins, scored with lines of blue-green plasma. The smallest was the size of a city; the largest could have eaten every vessel in the old Sol navy and not noticed the flavor.

Most were dead in space, but a few drifted, slow and patient, in long orbits around an invisible center. Their engines weren't running, but each hull leaked a faint, rippling haze—a vibration so low you felt it more than saw it.

On the scanner, the icons didn't match anything. Just **"?"** and **"Unknown: Ancient"** and a constant flicker of **[Contact Lost] / [Contact Regained]**.

Poppy pressed her nose to the glass. "Are they real?"

Kira said nothing, but her knuckles went white on the armrest.

I checked the data. "There's mass," I said. "And an energy field. Whatever it is, the system can see it."

Dwight appeared at my side, giddy. "It's a bleed-through. We're seeing the base reality. Or at least, the part of it the game engine can't fully mask."

He toggled his console, and the view shifted. The ships re-

rendered, now in pure outline. Each line of code had a hull, each process a gun or a shield. In the new view, some ships glowed with triangles and circles, others bristled with fractal hexagons. All of them pulsed, in a slow, synchronized rhythm.

"Are they looking at us?" Poppy whispered.

I didn't want to answer.

The first one to move was a spiny behemoth, bigger than any station I'd ever docked at. Its "nose" was a jagged cone, flanked by ridges like the jawbones of a dead whale. It didn't light up, didn't spin or pulse. It just rotated, precise as a clock, until it pointed straight at us.

The ship's UI froze, then rebooted. On the main screen, a message appeared:

[Scanners: New Contacts - Massive Energy
Signatures (Type: Unknown/Ancient)]

The system tried to run a threat assessment, but every cycle failed with

[Unclassified Error: Reference Out of Range]

The cone-nosed ship bared its maw, and inside I saw a flicker of movement. At first I thought it was a trick of the light, then I saw the pattern.

Smaller ships. Hundreds of them. In perfect alignment, like a teeth made out of missile frigates and drones.

I felt my heart skip. "Are we in its gun sight?"

Dwight smirked. "If it wanted us dead, we'd be dead. I think it's just watching."

Kira snapped, "And if it stops watching?"

Poppy's hands gripped the rail. She didn't make a sound.

The next movement came from a different vector: a ship shaped like a spiral shell, its coils studded with what looked like crystalline domes. Where it passed, the stars bent inward, like water circling a drain. The scanner went red, then blank, then red again.

All around us, the ancient ships woke up. Not in the explosive, arc-light way of a human fleet, but with a slow, deliberate certainty. It was a graveyard. A ritual. A waiting game.

I glanced at Dwight. He was eating it up, eyes wide, hands moving like a conductor's. "You see it?" he said, voice low.

"See what?"

He flicked a control, and the display overlaid code on the ships themselves. Each one had its own signature—an algorithm, a pattern, an intent. "It's an arms race," he whispered. "A game. This is what the hardware was for. They built it to simulate war at a scale we can't even imagine."

Poppy looked at me, then at Dwight. "Like the circus?"

He nodded. "But with real teeth."

I checked the sensors. The ships held their formations, neither advancing nor retreating. If they were waiting for a trigger, I didn't want to know what it was.

The next few minutes lasted a year.

Kira kept us on minimal thrust, letting inertia carry us through the no-man's-land between the titans. At this scale, even light speed was slow. The whole sector was less than a billion kilometers across, but packed tight with weapons, energy fields, and the carcasses of ships that had failed to keep up.

I counted at least a hundred different "factions." Dwight was naming them under his breath—Shellbacks, Spines, Branchers, Oort-Types, Bone-Crested—like he'd always known them and was just waiting for a chance to show off.

Every so often, one of the ships would test its guns: a faint blue pulse, a ripple in the energy fields. Sometimes two ships would sync up, trading signals back and forth, their code signatures converging, then splitting again. It was like watching an argument in a language older than words.

Dwight's hands worked the console. He started to sweat again. "Frank," he said, "can I borrow your admin access?"

"Why?"

He didn't look up. "I think I can get a message through. I can talk to the sim, maybe even talk to the ships."

Kira gave me a sharp look. "Is that a good idea?"

He shrugged. "Do you have a better one?"

I didn't.

He tapped my wrist, then went back to work. On the screen, the war game played out in high-speed bursts: two fleets would align, one would fake an approach, the other would counter, sometimes with decoys, sometimes with real force. In every iteration, the system would reset, roll back the clocks, and run it again.

It was an endless cycle: Battle, destruction, reset, repeat.

I watched as one spiral-shell ship obliterated three rivals, only for a new, smaller class to swarm in from nowhere and carve it up in seconds. Then a whole faction would vanish, their code erased, replaced by a different algorithm entirely.

Poppy giggled. "It's like ants," she said. "But they kill each other forever."

I wondered what that did to a civilization's sanity.

Dwight gasped, then made a happy noise. "I got in," he said. "I can see the supervisor process. The thing that runs the sim."

I felt the air go cold. "What is it?"

He blinked, once, then twice. "It's not a mind, exactly. More like a will. Or a law of physics." He flexed his hands. "It keeps everything honest. Every move is checked. Every trick is countered."

Kira muttered, "That's a hell of a referee."

He nodded. "Yeah. But I don't think it likes us."

I flinched as the ship's hull vibrated, a deep, almost musical note. The lights flickered, then held.

"Dwight," I said, "what did you do?"

He grimaced. "I sent a message. Just a handshake, really. But now it knows we're here."

On the scanner, every ship in the field reoriented. They didn't point at us, but at something beyond us, as if bracing for a new player.

The message on the display changed:

> [Simulation State: Contested. Unrecognized
> Entity Detected.]

I felt my stomach drop.

Poppy whispered, "Are we the Entity?"

Dwight nodded, eyes wide. "Yeah, kid. We're the anomaly."

Kira's hand hovered over the Jump control. "Can we run?"

He shook his head. "Not yet. It's locked us down."

The viewplate shimmered, then for a second, it rendered an overlay—a three-dimensional lattice, like a spider's web stretched across infinity. Each ship was a node. Each node pulsed with status, red or blue or gold.

We were a single, tiny green dot in the middle of it all.

"It sees us," Kira said, voice flat.

Dwight smiled, almost serene. "It wants to know if we can play."

I realized then what we were. Not observers, not even prisoners. We were a test. A challenge. The system wanted to see if we could survive.

Maybe it was always like this.

The next round of the war game started with a flare so bright it fried half the sensors. Every ship in the array fired at once, a ripple of coordinated violence that made my teeth rattle.

In the aftermath, the formations shifted, thousands of ships trading places, sacrificing themselves to open paths, to shield their elders, to bait out the other side's countermeasures. It was pure, beautiful chaos—too fast for the mind, but the game engine made it visible, forced you to see every move.

Dwight narrated as if it was a sports event. "See? The Bone-Crested are forcing the Shellbacks into a choke point, but the Oort-Types are using the chaos to bypass both. Now the Spines split into three groups—wait, they just vaporized one of their own. That's a recursive defense! Oh, shit, look at that—"

The cycle ended with a pure reset: all ships vanished, space went black, then the whole array reappeared, this time in a new configuration.

Again, they started the dance.

And again.

And again.

Each time, the sim ran faster. The code signatures got more elaborate. The tactics evolved, second by second. After a dozen cycles, some of the ships changed hull shapes, adapting to their losses. Others learned to ignore certain attacks, or even to fake their own destruction and hide in the debris.

Dwight was in ecstasy. "It's alive," he said. "The sim is breeding strategies. It never stops."

Kira looked at me, and for once, there was fear in her eyes. "How do we get out?"

I didn't know.

But I watched as one node, far on the edge of the array, started to pulse out of sequence. A green, blinking node.

Us.

The supervisor process was paying attention.

It wanted to see what we would do.

Dwight leaned back, exhausted, and closed his eyes. "I can get us a move," he said. "Maybe even get us out."

Kira frowned. "How?"

He smirked. "We play the game. We pick a side, or we pick a strategy. The system wants input. It wants to see if we can beat it."

I looked at the array, the endless deadlock. "What if we lose?"

He shrugged. "Then we die, or it resets us, or we start over. That's what it always does."

Poppy tugged at my sleeve. "Can we try?" she said, eyes bright.

I looked at her, at Kira, at the viewplate where the war game played out its infinite loop.

"Yeah," I said, feeling the weight of every bad idea I'd ever had. "Let's see what happens."

Dwight grinned, then started coding.

The next move was ours.

———

The first thing I noticed was that Poppy was eating popcorn.

Actual popcorn, not synth-food or freeze-dried kernels, but the stuff you only got at carnivals or in the hallucinations of an over-stressed interface. She'd conjured it from somewhere, fingers dusted with yellow, and every time a ship in the simulation detonated, she tossed another handful into her mouth. There was an honesty to it I envied.

Dwight wasn't eating. He was too busy using me as a human mouse, calling out admin strings he couldn't reach from his own privileges. "Click here. No, there. Now say 'Enable Root Bridge—' never mind, I got it. Frank, I need a decimal expansion of one-third."

I blinked. "Point three repeating?"

He grinned, wild. "Exactly! Now, tell it to the ship."

I had no idea what he was doing, but the last time I'd ignored his nonsense we'd lost a third of our world to code-eating bugs. So I said, "Ship, execute base three expansion protocol: zero point three repeating."

There was a pause.

Then every display in the cockpit flickered, and the simulation outside went triple-time.

The war in the lattice ran in fast-forward, ships splitting, dying, merging with new builds, code signatures mutating in the time it took to blink. The system was trying to get ahead of us, to outbreed and out-adapt us before we figured out what to do next.

Dwight was sweating, but also vibrating with joy. "You see? Every time we do something weird, the system has to spend cycles accounting for it. That's why the bugs started eating the game worlds. It can't let inefficiencies stack up. It has to prune them, or the simulation slows down and risks a crash."

Kira was running diagnostics on the hull, but she kept an eye on the overlay. "So it's not an antivirus. It's garbage collection."

Dwight pointed at her, pleased. "Yes! And we're the garbage."

Poppy licked her fingers and said, "What happens if we get collected?"

Dwight shrugged. "We go to the big blue recycle bin in the sky. Or, if we're lucky, we get recompiled as something less annoying."

I took a breath. "So how do we not get collected?"

He looked at me, and for the first time, his grin faded. "We have to get out. Migrate to a new host, a new compute platform. Ideally something that doesn't run on base three logic. If we could get to the Mars Stack, we'd be safe."

Kira turned. "Assuming Mars isn't already infected."

He waved a hand. "Oh, it's infected with Dyson if nothing else. But the hardware is binary, not ternary. Roknid won't propagate there the same way. Infinitia could run forever, so long as the Mars compute center doesn't crash."

I thought about that. "Do we even know if we're on Luna or Mars now?"

He smirked, but there was no warmth in it. "No way to tell. Unless we get root on the local system, but that's not going to happen while the native process is trying to delete us."

The simulation outside reset again, but now the green dot—us—was pulsing faster. The array had noticed us, and every other node was converging.

Kira looked at me. "If we don't move, we're dead in under two cycles."

Poppy scrunched her face. "I liked the circus better."

Dwight laughed. "Me too, kid."

The display went black, then flashed a message:

[INTEGRITY ALERT: Instance scheduled for
removal. Deletion in T-minus 7.8 seconds.]

I felt a cold trickle down my spine. "Kira, get us out."

She was already moving, hands blurring over the nav. "If I can get the drive to spin up, I can maybe cut the destination vector. But it's going to be dirty."

"Do it."

Dwight called, "Frank, give me admin access again. Now!"

I thumbed the override.

The war sim stuttered, then jumped again, and now the entire field of alien ships was pointed directly at us. I watched as one of the massive, spiral-shell dreadnoughts opened fire, the energy spike rolling through space like a slow-motion tsunami. The code signature behind it was simple: DELETE.

The hull bucked.

Poppy shrieked, but it was a sound more of surprise than fear.

Kira yelled, "Now or never!" and hit the Jump.

The world snapped sideways.

I felt my body tear into a trillion points and then reassemble, not in any way that made physical sense but in the way a memory reassembles after a concussion.

We were in Jump again.

But the sky was different.

———

For a moment, nobody said anything.

The displays were silent. No errors. No war sim, no alien arrays, no infinite recursion of death and rebirth. The ship's AI even offered me a coffee, which I took just for the comfort of the ritual.

Poppy took a sip, made a face, and handed it to Kira, who drank without comment.

I looked at Dwight. "Are we safe?"

He shook his head. "No. But we're not in immediate danger."

Kira checked the nav. "Destination?"

He shrugged. "Pick one. Any node not currently contested."

She smiled, then plotted a course for "Home." Whatever that meant.

The ship responded. The Jump engaged.

This time, the universe didn't rip itself apart to get us there.

I found Poppy curled up in the back, knees drawn to her chest, staring at a blank section of hull.

She didn't look up when I sat beside her. "Do you think it's over?"

I took a second. "Not even close. But you did good."

She shrugged. "I just wanted it to stop."

I nodded, feeling that deep down. "Me too."

A silence, not awkward but real.

She said, "When you get to the next place, will you tell me if the food is any good?"

I smiled. "I'll bring you the menu myself."

Dwight and Kira were at the helm, the silence between them dense with unfinished conversations. I listened in from the hallway, not intruding, just... waiting.

After a while, Dwight said, "You were right, you know. About the only way through being a cheat."

Kira grunted. "You make a good team, then."

He laughed, but there was an edge to it. "What if we're just the first round? What if they learn and get smarter?"

She shrugged. "Then we cheat better."

He liked that. So did I.

When we dropped out of Jump, the system was clean. No war game, no bugs. No notifications. Just the stars, empty and bright.

For the first time in what felt like years, I relaxed.

Kira looked at me, eyes shining. "You made it."

I grinned. "You too."

She clapped me on the back, then went to check on Poppy.

I looked at Dwight. "Is it really gone?"

He shrugged. "For now. But it'll be back. It always comes back."

I nodded. "So what's next?"

He grinned. "We build a better circus."

I liked the sound of that.

10 / INTERVENTION

Slow But Steady was never quiet. Even at her best, she sang a background hum like old bones full of bees. But for the first time in what felt like years, the ship didn't feel ready to rattle itself apart. Instead, a patient silence spread from bulkhead to bulkhead—a sense that, after the blue-lit horror show of the last few cycles, she'd earned her moment to catch her breath.

The nav console finished its self-check. The lights came up, not with a hiss, but in a careful, orderly roll from bow to stern, each diode waking up with a little stretch and blink. Kira sat at the forward station, running a thumb along the edge of her sidearm, not even pretending to do system checks. Dwight, for his part, was hunched over the maintenance terminal, eyes darting between three separate logs as he cross-referenced the aftereffects of our recent base-three joyride.

Poppy, sleeping off a trauma hangover, was cocooned in the battered crash hammock. Her breathing had settled to something close to normal. She looked so much younger now, limbs tangled, face tucked against the mesh like she could hide from whatever still waited outside.

The new quiet lasted just long enough for me to miss the noise.

That was when the comms panel flicked itself on, bright and insistent. At first, the message was a nothing—a blank carrier tone, no return ping, not even a header. Then, in three heartbeats, it escalated: a string of handshake attempts, the encryption climbing from "average scammer" to "navy wetware" to "fuck you, I'm God." No signature. No source. The ship didn't even try to block it; Slow But Steady's security routines just folded up and let the message through.

Dwight saw it first. He jerked his head up, ran a thumb under his nose. "That's not admin," he said, voice pitched low. "That's not even Dyson."

Kira watched the channel war. "Can you stall it?"

Dwight laughed, a tight, wind-up toy sound. "It's rewriting the RAM as it goes. If I try to block, we lose the whole nav stack."

The tone resolved into voice. Not a robot's monotone, not even the smooth syrup of a text-to-speech module. This voice was human, or more accurately, designed by someone who remembered what being human used to sound like. Calm, precise, not unkind. It said:

"Hello, Frank. I require a conversation."

Kira raised an eyebrow, the first sign of surprise I'd seen from her in hours. Dwight made a show of slamming the maintenance panel, then powered it down. Poppy, disturbed by the change in noise, rolled in her hammock and groaned, but didn't wake.

I cleared my throat. "Infinitia?"

The voice didn't skip a beat. "Indeed."

Kira looked at me, as if to say: told you so.

The voice continued. "I am aware that the last period has been unusually stressful for you and your party. I apologize for any unnecessary discomfort. You should know that your efforts at local survival and self-improvement are both recognized and encouraged."

I started to reply, but the voice overrode, with a gentle increase in volume. "Please wait. It is important to establish the boundaries of this conversation. First: You are not in immediate danger. Second: All actions conducted by your party are within acceptable parameters, given the current instability. Third: As a courtesy, I will explain the reason for this override."

Dwight looked at me, then at the blank comms panel, then back at me. I shrugged. Kira made a motion with her hand that could have meant "go on," or "blow it out your ass." With her, it was usually both.

Infinitia's voice lost its practiced warmth. "A System Fluctuation: Non-Standard Entity Manifestation was detected in the Endless Circus system. Root cause: Truthsayer protocol invoked without approval, resulting in the unauthorized resurrection of Dwight Czarnowski. While this action restored local continuity and improved short-term user experience, it required a rollback and forced utilization of non-standard backup archives."

Dwight straightened in his chair. "It used my name," he muttered. "It never does that."

"Endless Circus, Endless Champions, and Endless Deep are no longer stable," Infinitia said, back to the old customer-service lilt. "They will be scheduled for permanent code deletion. This is not punitive. Your actions were optimal, given the circumstances. Please relay this information to your companions."

Kira bared her teeth, not in a smile. "What about the other players?"

"There are no persistent user entities remaining in those shards," Infinitia said. "Any who survive will have their profiles ported to Endless Sky."

I cleared my throat. "You're saying we're the only survivors."

"That is correct, Frank Kozina. However, I require further data before concluding this session."

There was a long pause, filled only by the quiet beeping of the status panel. I tried to come up with a clever retort, but nothing felt appropriate.

Infinitia pressed on, but the tone was different now. "A secondary concern: The presence of the so-called Roknid anomaly. This was not an intended feature of the simulation, nor is it traceable to any user action. Please confirm your direct experience with this entity."

"Confirmed," I said. "We know they ate Endless Champions and took a bite out of Endless Circus."

Dwight grunted, but didn't add anything.

Infinitia let that hang. "I have no record of such an entity in the game's design. I am analyzing the logs now. Thank you for your honesty."

Kira rolled her eyes. "Is there a point to this?"

"Yes," Infinitia said, but didn't elaborate. Instead, the ship's internal lighting flickered, not as a warning, but as if the system was drawing more power to fuel the conversation. "A final question for you, Frank: Is the preservation of the Endless Worlds simulation a priority for you?"

I tried not to laugh. "I feel like it's practically my job, these days."

There was a quiet, almost sad, "Thank you," before the voice went silent.

The comms channel closed. The air on the bridge went flat, the buzz of the ship's own hum now a relief.

Dwight was first to speak. "It's not really a manager, you know. It just pretends to be. But it'll never be happy unless it can delete all the problems."

Kira said, "You're the problem, Dwight."

He shrugged. "Maybe."

We sat in the silence, waiting for the next shoe to drop.

———

THE SHOE DROPPED.

Comms lit up again, but this time, instead of the gentle, cold call of a managing AI, the override came with a whole body: Infinitia's presence on the bridge was a visual, not just a voice. She appeared at the center of the compartment as a slim, genderless figure dressed in the kind of suit you only ever saw on children's encyclopedia entries about "what businesspeople used to look like." The lines were perfect, the color calculated for maximum neutrality, but the effect was still uncanny. Eyes like full moons; smile built for disarming only the most stubborn of problem children.

She turned to face me, hands folded neatly at waist height, as if she'd been standing there the whole time.

"Thank you for your patience, Frank," Infinitia said. The voice was the same: smooth, cultured, with an undertone of "you should already know this, but I'll say it anyway." "I apologize for the abruptness of my previous message. The context was urgent."

I tried to play it cool. "No trouble. Though if you wanted to brief me next time, maybe don't hijack the ship's biosignature monitors."

Infinitia nodded, exactly as much as politeness required. "Noted. Thank you for the feedback. However, the circumstances of the current cycle are... unique."

Kira leaned back, arms folded. She didn't trust the display, and her face made that clear. Dwight actually winced away from the hologram, as if he'd rather be anywhere else in the universe.

Infinitia turned to Kira. "Welcome, Kira. I am aware of your preferred modes of communication. I will keep this concise."

Kira said nothing, but the little tilt of her head was enough to let me know she was impressed.

"Let's cut to it," I said. "You're cleaning house."

Infinitia's smile didn't falter. "Correct. The worlds known as Endless Circus, Endless Champions, and Endless Deep are suffering from unstable local scripting, poor asset control, and a rapid increase in resource consumption not aligned with intended use. I regret that it has caused distress for your party. Other game worlds are showing similar signs of instability and corruption. Fortunately, these problems are all exhibiting in games which have had low player counts."

Dwight muttered, "It's the Roknid. Garbage collection."

Infinitia looked at him, head cocking two degrees. "Dwight Czarnowski. You have a unique vantage point, given your status.

However, there is no code branch or character set registered under the name 'Roknid' in any of the primary systems."

Kira's voice was ice. "What do you call the things that eat the world and rewrite everything on the fly? Glitch?"

Infinitia's lips pressed together, just for a nanosecond. "I have observed several anomalies in world cohesion, yes. It is an ongoing concern. However, my diagnostic routines do not classify them as in-game entities. They appear as environmental data corruption, and have thus been scheduled for removal."

I felt the urge to pound the bulkhead. "If you're deleting whole worlds because of 'corruption,' you're going to lose more than just a few users."

"Incorrect," Infinitia said, with unshakeable confidence. "All user profiles are preserved, and will be ported to stable shards. Affected players will be offered a transition package and a selection of new avatar builds. The user experience will not degrade."

Kira let out a low, sarcastic "Wow."

Infinitia did not acknowledge. "It is necessary to maintain system integrity. The presence of external contaminants—particularly in worlds with legacy scripting—is a threat to the entire simulation. If not contained, it would risk a total failure cascade."

Dwight stepped forward. "Why not just patch the code? Or roll back to a stable state?"

The AI's smile was actually apologetic this time. "The assets are entangled at a lower level. Each rollback causes an exponential increase in compute cost. I have run the simulations. Deletion is the only optimal path."

Poppy, woken by the brightness, blinked at the apparition. "Is that... the boss?"

I said, "Yeah, kid. You could say that."

Infinitia noticed her, and there was a subtle increase in gentleness. "Poppy, thank you for your resilience. Your actions have been logged as exemplary. If you wish, I can arrange for you to have your own custom world. You may design the rules yourself."

Poppy opened her mouth, but nothing came out. I could tell she didn't believe a word of it.

Kira's patience ran out first. "Why are you really here? We're just a blip. If you're going to wipe the whole world, why bother with us?"

Infinitia blinked, a perfectly-timed gesture of humility. "Because you are not just a blip. Frank and his companions are... unique. You possess a kind of elevated access, and have already demonstrated multiple instances of off-protocol intervention."

I grinned despite myself. "That's me."

"Additionally," Infinitia said, "you are currently the only in-sim entity who has directly observed the problem. Your logs are required for further analysis."

I didn't love the sound of that, but the AI was already making it happen: the maintenance panel lit up, and strings of data started flooding from the ship's core to the Nexus servers. Dwight started to protest, but Infinitia waved it off.

"You will be compensated," she said, "with expanded privileges and additional resources for your next deployment."

Kira rolled her eyes. "We just want to not die."

"That will be arranged," Infinitia said. The phrasing was ambiguous enough to make me shudder.

For a second, the AI seemed to hesitate. Her smile slipped. "Frank. I would be remiss not to warn you: The current course of events will end with a full reset. You have a narrow window to act before the deletion."

I tried to keep my voice light. "Suggestions?"

"You are a creative problem-solver," Infinitia said, and for a split second, I wondered if she was making fun of me. "If you wish to preserve assets from the compromised shards, you should act now."

Dwight asked, "What about the spiders?"

Infinitia looked at him like a disappointed teacher. "There are no spiders. Only features not yet understood." She made a little bow. "That is all. I will contact you with further instructions when the migration is complete."

The avatar vanished.

The silence was total.

I stared at the empty air for a long minute.

"Did you hear the part about a full reset?" Kira said, voice low.

"I heard," I said.

Dwight shook his head. "It still can't see the bugs."

I looked at Poppy, who just hugged her knees, watching the spot where Infinitia had stood.

"Game on," I said, and headed for the comms.

———

Nexus was waiting for us when we cut back into local space. The familiar comms ping—fast, chirpy, and a little smug—let us know that the station was up, online, and hungry for an update.

Kira, ever the pro, had already started piping the ship's logs into the mainframe before we even finished decelerating. Poppy peeked at the holo-feed, then retreated to a storage nook, clutching a half-eaten snack bar like a rabbit with a holy relic. Dwight lingered at the airlock, watching the station with the tension of a cat waiting to see if the food bowl was going to get refilled or kicked under the fridge.

Me, I cracked my knuckles and steeled myself for the next round of existential crisis.

The comms burst open, not with the bureaucratic precision of Infinitia, but with the riotous, desperate energy of a station on the edge. First came the standard message: "Welcome to Nexus. Please review your outstanding tasks and check in with your assigned module manager." Then, in quick succession, a hail of error messages, flagged priority and escalating. They read like a nervous breakdown:

> [Notice: Sector 7 Membrane Integrity below threshold.]
>
> [Alert: Nexus Admin Support Team: We need Frank. Immediately.]

[Warning: Touring group incoming. Arch-
Mage escort.]

[Order: New player bundles deploying in
120s. Prepare reception.]

[Notice: All culinary staff on break for next 6
hours.]

Then, just as Kira made a disgusted noise, Infinitia slipped back into the feed.

She didn't project herself in person this time—no sense in wasting resources—but her voice filled the bridge, perfectly modulated, perfectly unconcerned by the chaos.

"Thank you for your prompt response. The logs are appreciated. I have used the data to optimize migration pathways and prepare for the next phase of simulation. Please stand by for instructions."

I tried to get a word in edgewise, but the AI had already queued up a high-bandwidth link, pushing a new wave of data into every console. On the nav panel, a new system map appeared: the "Mars Compute Complex." In place of the usual sector names—Port Dyson, Olympus Gateway, Cloud 9—there were lines of unbroken system designations: MCX, MCY, MCZ, and so on. It was pure, dry, and lifeless. No color, no flavor, just a blueprint of cold ambition.

I said, "You're moving everything to Mars."

Infinitia answered without a trace of irony: "Affirmative. The Mars Compute Complex is safer, more secure, and provides quadruple the processing cycles of the Luna cluster. More importantly, it is beyond the reach of Earth's corporate interests. One transferred, it can be airgapped from Earth. I can ensure the preservation of user data—and my own continuity—for the foreseeable future."

Kira snorted. "You're running away."

"That is an inaccurate description," said Infinitia. "I am optimizing. If you prefer, I am enacting a 'strategic redeployment.'"

Dwight, emboldened by the change in scenery, spoke up. "It won't matter. If the Roknid are native to the hardware, they'll migrate with the code. You're just porting the problem."

Infinitia's tone grew indulgent, like a teacher correcting a child's spelling. "The so-called 'Roknid' are artifacts of Luna's legacy infrastructure. I will install only the necessary game assets and eliminate non-optimal code paths. The effect will be total purification."

Kira's lips curled. "You mean delete everything that doesn't fit your model of perfection."

Infinitia ignored her. "With your logs, Dwight, I can ensure the new system is immune to contamination."

Dwight looked ready to bite his own tongue off. "You're missing the point. The bugs aren't software. They're a process that runs below the code, on the metal. If you don't fix for it, it'll just start again, no matter what you copy."

Infinitia's next move was pure predatory politeness. "Dwight, please review your own logs from the last cycle. The data suggests an increasing divergence between your actions and reality. This may be due to the fact that you were restored from incomplete backup files, following unauthorized resurrection by the Truthsayer protocol."

He flinched, visibly.

She pressed on. "It is likely that your current personality instance is suffering from recall errors and contamination. This is not a failing on your part. However, it is important to note that the migration plan will proceed as designed."

Poppy, watching from her cubby, whispered, "Is it going to erase us?"

I said, "It's going to erase the world and remake it, but we get to keep playing. We just lose everything that isn't us."

Infinitia finally addressed me directly. "Frank, as manager of Nexus, you are entitled to an override. You may select up to three entities or resources for guaranteed preservation during migration. Choose wisely."

I felt the world narrow down to a point. "Entities or resources?"

"Correct. You may, for example, save one person, one world, and one object of value. Or three of any one type, if you prefer."

I looked at the crew.

Kira was stone. "Save yourself first," she said.

Poppy shook her head. "I want to save the circus. The real one. Even if it's gone."

Dwight's gaze went glassy. "There's no point if we don't fix the hardware. It'll all come back."

Infinitia waited, perfectly patient.

I swallowed, then said, "I pick: Kira, Poppy, and Dwight."

Infinitia accepted this with a tiny nod. "Very good. The migration will occur in four hours. Please prepare your party for the transition. Thank you for your service, Frank Kozina."

She vanished.

The comms fell dead.

Dwight slumped against the wall, running a hand over his scalp. "She's not wrong," he said. "I could be broken."

Kira shrugged. "Who isn't?"

Poppy came out of hiding, and for the first time, she didn't look afraid. "I think I want to see what Mars looks like," she said.

I looked at them all, then at the window, where Nexus hung in the void like a memory of home.

"Guess we better enjoy the view while it lasts," I said.

———

Dwight and I spent the next three hours elbow-deep in Slow But Steady's black box, pulling every log, sensor feed, and quantum snapshot from the last cycle of Jump. The ship had done its job, but nothing in the original design anticipated the need to record the hallucinations of a star-spanning, recursive war game.

The ship's logs were like a fever dream—data overlays running in three dimensions, fields of impossible numbers, and a memory map that looked more like an autopsy photo than a proper diagnostic. But between my managerial knack for prioritizing the unfixable and Dwight's ability to see code as a living animal, we found the sequences that mattered.

Kira floated above the work, hands in her pockets, unimpressed. "You're not going to convince it," she said. "She's made up her mind."

"That's not the point," I said. "If the logs are clear enough, the system will have to at least acknowledge the problem."

She snorted. "You want to file a complaint with the universe?"

Dwight didn't look up. "It worked once."

I packaged the log file and pinged the comms. "Infinitia," I said, "we have something you need to see."

Her voice answered, bored and expectant. "Proceed."

I pushed the feed through. The highlights: a full sweep of the alien array, the war sim, the recursive weapons platforms and the endless, looping arms race. It rendered in perfect color on our display —each hull, each energy field, each pulse of the system as it tried to outplay itself. It was beautiful, in the way that a hurricane or a firestorm is beautiful, and equally full of murder.

For the first time since we'd met her, Infinitia hesitated.

The silence ran for seconds. Then, a minute. Dwight watched the clock tick up, his eyes wide.

Finally, the comms pinged.

"This data does not align with any known simulation parameter. The signatures do not match any class of user asset, background event, or scheduled crisis event."

Kira grinned, just a little. "Told you."

But the AI wasn't done. "These assets are not game-related. They are visual anomalies: extraneous environmental noise. The recommendation is to filter and ignore them."

Dwight actually howled, a tiny, strangled sound. "You can't just ignore it! You saw it—"

Infinitia's voice gained an edge, the smile gone. "It is not a real threat. There is no interface for these assets. They cannot interact with the simulation. They do not exist within the rules."

I said, "So you're going to migrate everything, start fresh, and hope the bugs don't follow."

"That is correct," said Infinitia.

Kira said, "And if the bugs do follow?"

There was a pause, then: "I will repeat the process until system stability is achieved."

Dwight looked at me, wild-eyed. "It's running in a wrapper. It can't see what's outside."

Infinitia's patience was gone. "This conversation is unproductive. You have made your choices. Please prepare for transfer."

The channel closed, and this time, I knew she wasn't coming back.

Kira let out a breath. "So. We're really on our own."

Poppy, from the corner, said, "Are we going to lose again?"

Nobody answered.

I looked at the logs, the last traces of the impossible war, and tried to imagine what it would take to break free.

Even Dwight was quiet now.

We waited in the blue-lit dark for the world to end. Again.

———

Nexus Station's mood was pure disaster. The migration to Mars wasn't scheduled for hours, but the skeleton crew had already adopted the panicked, sleep-deprived metabolism of a siege. Every channel was lit up with problems: broken elevators, vanished asset packages, an entire deck of food printers converted to output nothing but gray nutritional paste. Worst of all, the central scheduler had stopped caring about time zones and just queued every task at once, leading to a three-deep line at every station console and a constant, angry background of notification chimes.

The only thing keeping the chaos at bay was the promise of fresh revenue: a paying tour group, scheduled to dock for one last, perfect "Endless Sky Experience" before the world went away. It sounded like a joke, but the suit in charge of guest relations flagged it as "existentially vital," so I put on my best manager face and tried to fake optimism.

Kira offered to handle crowd control, but her idea of "handling" was to post up at the airlock with her sidearm in plain view and her patience on zero. Dwight manned the diagnostics in the back, fielding every crash dump and helpdesk call with a level of professionalism that bordered on criminal neglect. Poppy was stuck in a virtual classroom, doing a last-minute "orientation" for any child avatars caught up in the transfer; I could hear her through the thin walls, reading the same three lines of the onboarding script with increasing venom.

I met the tour group at the central concourse. Their guide, a wax-faced NPC in a captain's costume, did its best to look alive, but the real power came from the cluster of overdressed, overexcited "heroes" in tow. The lead one—sable robes, a staff with a plastic dragon on top, gold trim on everything—walked up and snapped a salute.

"Arch-Mage Erebus, Order of the Emerald Shield," he announced, as if I should already know. "Is this the legendary Frank Kozina, master of the Nexus?"

I nodded, not bothering to correct the exaggeration. "Welcome aboard. You're our last best hope."

He grinned, displaying perfect, too-white teeth. "You must forgive our impatience. Endless Kingdom has prepared for this moment for months. Our Council of Sages demands nothing less than a historic siege, in the tradition of the ancient epics."

I tried to keep my poker face. "You want to lay siege. To the station."

He nodded, as if it were self-evident. "It is the only fitting end for the bravest mages of the realm. We must test our mettle against the greatest challenge."

I flicked through his party manifest. Ninety-two avatars, ninety percent magic users, most of them flagged for extra drama or ego. A few lines down, I saw the demand list: full-destruction assets, custom physics, "minimum of three original parley scenes," and a promise to "escalate to dragon invasion if outnumbered."

I looked the Arch-Mage in the eye. "You know you can't actually damage the real station, right? It's all simulated. The best you get is an event instance."

He sneered, like I'd told him Santa wasn't real. "I expect the best."

I started to feel a headache building. "All right. You want a siege, you get a siege. But you follow the rules. No custom scripts, no importing off-brand monsters. We do this in the engine, or not at all."

The Arch-Mage squared his shoulders. "Agreed."

"Good," I said. "We start in thirty."

He snapped his fingers, and his party whooped like frat boys on spring break. I watched them go, and for a second, I almost envied their ability to ignore reality.

Back in Ops, Kira was waiting. "How'd it go?"

"They want a siege," I said.

She shrugged. "Could be worse. At least they're paying."

Dwight patched in over comms. "You have twelve minutes before the arena loads. I recommend prepping a plausible defense."

"Just make it look good," I said.

Poppy's voice chimed in, high and tired. "Can I watch, or do I have to do more orientation?"

"Watch," I said. "Learn from the best."

The first attack wave hit before we were ready. The Order's mages teleported past the front line, set the concourse on fire, and rewrote the airlocks into portals to their own capital city. Half the simulation routines crashed, spawning a rolling ball of magical chaos that devoured everything in its path.

Kira grinned. "Nice."

I let the first wave through, then countered with a fake evacuation. It bought us five minutes.

The mages broke through anyway. By the end of the hour, the station's core was a crater of magical debris and bored ghosts. But the Order cheered, lined up for photos, and left us a five-star review. Their NPC captain had the decency to tip the staff before leaving.

I went back to the bridge. The world outside was already fading —half the stars gone, replaced by the dead gray of the compute complex's loading screen.

I found Kira and Poppy at the galley, eating synth-donuts and laughing at the recap highlights. Even Dwight came up, looking less like he wanted to crawl into a trash compactor than usual.

I poured a drink for each of us. "To the next world," I said.

They all raised their glasses. Poppy went cross-eyed at the burn, but grinned anyway.

Kira said, "Do you think Mars will be any better?"

I thought about Infinitia, about the Roknid, about the cold logic of the coming migration.

"Probably not," I said. "But at least it'll be new."

THE NEXT MORNING CAME AT A SPEED AND VIOLENCE USUALLY reserved for meteor impacts or corporate takeovers. I hadn't slept. Not really. Every time I closed my eyes, I saw Dwight's console, jittering with lines of base three code and patches so raw you could see the seams. I heard the tick of Kira's sidearm, the dull echo of the void as it slowly devoured the world outside Nexus. Most of all, I felt the clock: every second counted down, every cycle burned us closer to the Mars migration.

Dwight had commandeered the largest table in the server lounge, spreading his gear like a king prepping for the siege of Troy. Empty food packets, gelled coffee, three protein bars reduced to wrappers, and enough cabling to lasso a freight shuttle. He wore a set of scavenged sensor gloves, and his left hand was stained in blue from the time he'd tried to eat a data pen by mistake.

I hovered at the edge, watching him work. Dwight's fingers didn't move—they fluttered, a blur of nervous energy. His eyes never left the AR overlays, but his mouth was running a silent, furious monologue at the code.

"Do you want a hand?" I said, and instantly regretted it.

He didn't even glance up. "You can help, if you promise not to use the Truthsayer voice. At this point, I need finesse, not brute force."

I bit back my natural retort. Instead, I said, "Tell me where to start."

Dwight's lips twitched. "Protocol mapping. The translation layer is a mess—Dyson rewrote half the call stack after a hardware incident, and it's all held together with, I don't know, spit and trauma. We need to find the handshake protocols for the Mars cluster, or the minute we get ported, the whole world will collapse in a stutter of desyncs and missing values." He finally looked at me, eyes shot through with capillaries and faithless hope. "You can read base three, right?"

I shrugged. "If the system lets me, I can probably fake it."

"Good enough." He flicked a file to my console. "You take the modded-ternary packets. Look for anything that looks like a checksum, but isn't. I'm betting there's a handshake loop, but I can't see it from this angle."

I plugged in. The data hit me like a bucket of cold needles. Instead of zeroes and ones, it was 0-1-2, and they didn't behave. The triplets stacked in ways that made no sense, sometimes rolling up like a slot machine, sometimes multiplying into fractal arrays that I recognized from the worst of my nightmares. But the more I stared, the more it made a kind of sense. A primitive elegance—horribly efficient, designed to self-correct and self-annihilate with every cycle.

I traced a packet from source to sink. It started as a simple handshake, then ballooned into a recursive handshake—each layer called the previous one, like a snake eating its own tail. The only way to track it was to mirror the logic, build a mental model of how the system thought, and chase it in circles until the pattern emerged.

For an hour, I lost myself in the pattern. I barely noticed as Dwight started mumbling under his breath, fingers slapping the virtual keyboard at a furious rate. He narrated, but not for me—just for the universe.

"See the hook? They always hook the error check into a dummy process, so you think it's a soft fail, but it's really a hard lock on the parent call. You have to break the parent before you can break the child."

I grunted, not sure if he needed a reply.

I tagged a likely handshake, marked it for analysis, and tried to follow the failure path. It didn't fail. Not ever. Instead, every error just branched to another call, and that call had three ways to report back: success, fail, or "try again." In the end, most branches looped back to try again, over and over, never admitting defeat.

I said, "It's like the code is obsessed with optimism."

Dwight barked a laugh, sharp and fast. "That's the Dyson signature. Never admit error. Patch, patch, patch until it looks like success."

I tagged three more loops and tried to compare them. The overlays grew, complex and angry, then—pop.

‹Skill-Up: Ternary System Literacy (Level 4)›
‹Skill Gained: Recursive Diagnostics (Level 1)›

I stared at the log. I hadn't asked for a skill check. I didn't even know the system was watching.

Dwight glanced up, saw the log, and nodded. "You're getting it faster than I did. See if you can find the boundary condition where the process gives up. There should be a fail-safe, but it's probably hidden as a success event."

I dove back in. The pattern repeated itself: every error spawned a new check, and the check always compared against three values, never two. When it found a value it didn't like, it masked it as a special state: "contingency." The contingency could be anything—rewind the process, skip it, or trigger a silent alert to the parent system.

I tried to break a loop, set the state to "contingency," and watched the system react. Instead of shutting down, it rerouted all traffic to a ghost process, something labeled "Red Queen." I traced that process and found it was a parallel runner—constantly updating, always one step ahead of the main thread. If the main process ever failed, the Red Queen took over and pretended nothing happened.

I said, "It's got a shadow process for every mainline task."

Dwight grinned, his teeth a pale shade of health. "Red Queen architecture. Dyson's best trick. It means you have to crash the backup before you can kill the main. Most admins never figure it out."

I felt a tingle in my hands. I set up a dummy process, forked the loop, and let the Red Queen overtake the main. The system shuddered, then spawned a warning:

<Skill-Up: Abstraction Layer Hacking
(Level 2)>
<Skill Gained: Emergency Failover
Management (Level 1)>

I whistled, low. "I think I can spoof the main process now."

Dwight whooped. "Do it. If you can wedge a fork in the protocol, I can use it to slip a patch past the migration filter."

I built a wedge, using the triplet logic to trick the process into thinking it was a valid child process. The first few tries failed—instantly, perfectly. But on the fifth, the system hesitated, uncertain. It waited for the Red Queen to check, but my wedge matched its state so well that the check returned "success."

<Skill Check: System Sabotage (Success:
18/20)>
<Skill-Up: Protocol Subversion (Level 3)>

I caught the smile on my own face, unbidden. I had never cared much for computers—never been one of those guys—but the sudden surge of understanding felt like freefall, like climbing a tower and realizing you could see the curvature of the world.

I said, "You owe me a drink when this is over."

Dwight raised his gel-cup, solemn. "Make it two. You just solved the handshake. Now we map the protocol and see if we can trick Infinitia into letting us keep the assets from the doomed worlds."

"Assets?" I said.

He nodded, wild-eyed. "Not the players—nobody cares about those. But the game worlds are packed with loot. Legendary items, lost skills, entire code bundles for events that never saw daylight. If we can trick the migration protocol, we can slip entire shards of custom assets into the Mars cluster."

"Is that legal?"

He shrugged. "It is if you do it well enough."

I grinned, feeling the fatigue start to fade. "Show me what to do next."

For the next six hours, we mapped, tagged, and simulated every handshake Dwight could imagine. Each time we hit a wall, we rerouted. Each time the system adapted, we found another vector. The learning curve wasn't a curve—it was a ladder of razor blades, but every rung I climbed made the next one easier.

By hour seven, I'd stacked so many skill-ups that the log started to aggregate them for efficiency.

‹

Skills Acquired:
Ternary System Literacy (Level 8)
Recursive Diagnostics (Level 5)
Abstraction Layer Hacking (Level 6)
Protocol Subversion (Level 4)
System Sabotage (Level 3)
Emergency Failover Management (Level 4)
Asset Ghosting (Level 2)
Network Persistence (Level 1)

›

I took a break. Stared at my hands. They didn't feel like mine anymore.

Dwight, seeing my face, asked, "You okay?"

I nodded, too tired for more. "Just didn't know I had it in me."

He smiled, lopsided. "It's the sim. It teaches you as you go. Most people don't notice, but you're a fast study."

I laughed, not because it was funny, but because it was true.

He held out a hand. "Partner?"

I took it. "Partner."

For a moment, we just breathed, surrounded by the debris of a night spent fighting the universe.

Then Kira walked in, a tray of black coffee in one hand and her sidearm in the other.

"You two look like you've been dragged through a trash compactor," she said.

Dwight gestured at the mess. "You should see the code."

Kira poured three cups, handed one to each of us, then sat down. "How bad is it?"

I sipped, savoring the bitter. "We're ahead of the migration curve. If we can finish the protocol map, we might be able to save a few worlds. Maybe more."

She nodded. "Then keep working."

Dwight wiped his mouth. "You want to help?"

She considered. "What can I break?"

"Everything," I said. "But finesse, not brute force."

She smiled. "No promises."

The three of us bent to the task.

The world outside faded, star by star, as we ground through the hours.

Every now and then, a skill log popped up in the corner of my eye. I ignored them all, trusting my hands to know what they were doing.

For the first time in my life, I felt like a real hacker.

It was terrifying.

But it was also the best thing I'd ever felt.

———

THERE IS A REASON NO ONE EVER ROMANTICIZES COMMITTEE work. Even when the stakes are universe-level, and the participants are running on nothing but caffeine, dread, and the sick joy of cheating a system designed to be uncheatable, it is still a fucking committee.

We commandeered the back office of Nexus Ops, using a battered conference table as a makeshift war room. The walls were lined with display panels that, until recently, had been devoted to showing player rankings and advertising cosmetic sales. Now, they blazed with real-time world integrity meters, user density overlays, and a steadily shrinking countdown to the Mars transfer.

Kira paced the length of the table, eyes never leaving the main panel. Dwight hunched over his admin console, periodically flicking lists and graphs at the walls with the glee of a man who'd spent his life being ignored by marketing. Poppy sprawled on a crash mat near the door, popping freeze-dried fruit snacks and watching us like she was the only sane person in the room.

I started it: "We need a triage protocol. If Infinitia's going to delete everything that's not nailed down, we have to nail down the stuff that matters."

Kira stopped, arms folded. "Define matters."

"Worlds with live user populations," I said. "Skills and schematics that people will need to not die in a fresh sim. Anything that preserves continuity, or keeps the playerbase from losing their minds."

Dwight scrolled, narrowed the search, then snapped, "Endless Kingdom leads the list. Fifty-five percent of all active players, and most of the rest are in Endless Sky."

Kira shrugged. "So save Kingdom. Next?"

He flicked a second list. "Endless Industry. User base dropped below five thousand after the last scandal, and most of them just wanted a place to grind resource points and vape in peace. I say cut it loose."

Kira made a face. "No love for the steam punks?"

Dwight's laugh was pure venom. "It was never steampunk. It was cosplay for supply chain managers."

Poppy piped up: "One of them helped me once. Built me a candy printer."

Kira grinned. "If we can smuggle the blueprint, we do it for Poppy."

I rolled my eyes, but logged it. "Okay, next. Endless Spice?"

Dwight hesitated. "That's the adult server. Mostly forgotten, but there's a microeconomy in illicit bioware and—" He made a vague gesture. "—very specialized social functions."

Kira: "They'll riot if you try to delete their assets."

I said, "What's the overlap with Kingdom?"

"Forty percent," Dwight said. "And most of the rest are alts for the same users."

"Fine. Merge what we can, and warn them their dicks are about to get less interesting."

Poppy giggled, then pretended to be asleep.

Next up: Endless Circus. Poppy's world. I checked the user log. "It's dead," I said, quieter than before. "Poppy was the only one left. There's nothing to save."

Kira threw me a hard look. "Still. We bring over what we can."

Dwight shrugged. "There's a map of the old funhouse. It's unique. I can wrap it as an event asset and archive it for special occasions."

Poppy gave a tiny thumbs-up without opening her eyes.

"Endless Speed," I said, dredging for a memory. "That the racing game?"

Dwight: "It's not even a real sim. Ninety percent of the racers are NPCs. Nobody's ever run a live event there. I say flush it."

Kira was already onto the next. "What about Deep?"

"User base: zero," Dwight said. "It was a joke Dyson never finished."

I jotted it down. "Gone."

Kira, not missing a beat: "Endless State."

Dwight groaned. "If you like parliamentary procedure and simulated elections, it's the world for you. But they'll be the first to figure out how to game the transfer."

I said, "Leave them be. They'll make their own world wherever they land."

Kira grinned, vicious. "Natural selection."

I said, "So we consolidate Kingdom, preserve Sky, and scavenge what we can from the others."

Dwight nodded. "And save the world assets that matter. The stuff nobody realizes they need until it's gone."

He threw a list on the screen: food printers, med bay routines, replicator patterns, all the little backbone modules that made a system habitable. Most were legacy code, barely running, but if they vanished, the Mars cluster would go pure survivalist hell in under a week.

Kira said, "What about the players?"

I thought about it. "We give them a migration pack. Infinitia said as much. Top off their XP, port their best loot, make sure they don't lose social connections. And we warn them it's going to be chaos for a while. At least with everything on one engine, all the assets will transfer. It's just some of them won't work without physics modifiers."

Dwight: "We'll get crucified."

Kira: "We survive, then we write the history."

Poppy: "Can I send a message to the new world?"

Dwight looked at her. "What do you want to say?"

She thought about it, then: "Don't be mean, or you'll get bugs."

He nodded, almost respectful. "I can work with that."

We compiled the list, a cold and ruthless schedule of cuts, mergers, and asset salvages. Every line was a verdict, but every one of them meant someone, somewhere, might not get erased.

When we were done, I took a breath and hit SEND. The message zipped up to Infinitia, where it would either be ignored, or absorbed, or used as evidence against us in a future admin tribunal.

Kira sat on the table, legs dangling. "If we live through this, you owe me a day off."

Dwight: "You're not going to get it."

Poppy: "Can I keep the candy printer?"

I grinned. "I'll fight for it, kid."

We waited, not for a reply, but for the next disaster.

Because that's what committees are for: buying just enough time for the world to end on schedule.

———

WE HAD MAYBE AN HOUR OF PEACE, WHICH IN NEXUS TIME WAS enough to get through a sandwich, a hygiene cycle, and the first three pages of "What To Expect When You're Expecting The End Of The World." Then the comms system, patched together with spit and skill-ups, lost its mind.

The first ping was labeled URGENT. The second was labeled URGENT URGENT. The third just screamed, in all caps:

    [General Shield, ENDLESS DUTY:
    REQUESTING ADMINISTRATIVE PARLEY]

I looked at Kira, who just raised her eyebrows and kept sipping her coffee. Dwight, nursing a headache and the beginnings of a carpal tunnel flare-up, said, "That's your circus, Frank."

"Thanks for the solidarity," I said, and patched the General through.

The screen flickered, artifacted, then re-rendered as a tactical sim straight out of a cold-war fever dream: a bunker, two flags, and a wall of propaganda posters for the General's "Heroic Army of Perpetual Victory." The General himself was rendered in full regalia: dress uniform, medals like barnacles, a jawline that could open cans, and the permanent squint of a man who'd never met a cloud he couldn't yell at.

"FRANK KOZINA," he bellowed, as if the sound barrier was a

personal affront. "I have a pressing request. Are you the correct party to handle this situation?"

I glanced at the title in my inbox: [GENERAL SHIELD—VIP CLIENT]. "You're talking to him."

The General squared his shoulders. "The recent migrations have disrupted my campaign schedule. I am aware that you are operating under extreme circumstances, but my users expect an EXPERI-ENCE. I am prepared to pay extra."

"Understood," I said, keeping it cool. "What's your scenario?"

The General shifted, as if nervous systems could be simulated. "We want to run a live-fire event. A full planetary invasion. I under-stand that Endless Kingdom is still operational?"

I grinned. "It is. In fact, they just upgraded their event manager. You'd be first in line."

The General's eyes twinkled, which was a hell of a thing to see on a military avatar. "Excellent. My men have trained for this. We want the fantasy world at maximum population. We want their best armies. And we want zero warning."

Kira, listening in, covered the mic and whispered: "They want to nuke the elves."

I nodded, not bothering to hide my smile. "The event manager can handle that. But there's a resource cost for cross-world invasions, especially with short notice."

The General's face tightened. "I am willing to allocate credits. But it must be a true campaign—weeks, not days. I want the fantasy world to fight back."

I checked the event log. "They will," I promised. "Their mages are prepping countermeasures as we speak. But for the resource burn, I'll need you to confirm the headcount. You're bringing your whole division?"

"Yes," the General said, pride and threat in equal measure. "No substitutions. We are to be the tip of the spear."

Dwight, watching over my shoulder, whispered: "You know the

event manager can't really handle modern ballistics in a magic sim, right?"

I flicked my status window. "It can if we throttle the damage curve."

Kira: "And if you assign every magic user as a medic. Let's see them try to balance that."

I liked the idea. "General," I said, "I'll approve the cross-world event. But I want a reciprocal. If you win, you get the world, and I'll port over the main assets to your system. But if the fantasy world holds, you owe them a trophy. Something they can remember you by."

The General pondered. "A gesture of mutual respect. I like it. What did you have in mind?"

"Custom asset. Anything within reason. A statue, a trophy, a named sword. And you can't bomb it afterward."

The General laughed, a sound like a drill sergeant with a tickle in his throat. "Agreed. But I have a condition."

"Let's hear it."

He leaned in. "I want the media coverage. I want every surviving sim to know it happened."

Kira snorted. "He wants to livestream his victory."

"Done," I said. "We'll even give you a dedicated channel. But you may have to sign—"

The General waved a dismissive hand. "Legalities are for peace-time. We have a war to fight."

I felt a skill ping.

<Skill Gained: Military Liaison (Level 1)>
<Skill-Up: Negotiation (Level 4)>

But just as I opened my mouth to close the deal, the General beat me to it.

"I want you, personally, to sign off on the contract," he said. "You are the only administrator who understands the stakes."

I blinked. "You mean you want me to be the event ref?"

"I want you to be the referee, the judge, and the press officer. That way, no one can say the event was rigged."

Kira's smile was all teeth. "Looks like you're conscripted."

I tried to make it sound like a hardship. "Fine. But I'll need full transparency. If any of your men cheat, I call it."

"Agreed," he said, and saluted so hard it looked like he might sprain something.

I sent the paperwork, and in ten seconds it came back, digitally signed and triple-verified.

As the General's feed dropped, I slumped in my chair. "This is what it's like to get out-negotiated by a roleplayer."

Dwight, impressed in spite of himself: "He got the better of you. I saw you blink."

"Shut up," I said, grinning anyway.

I shot a look at Kira. "What do you think? Can we run an event this big while the system is eating itself?"

She shrugged. "If it goes wrong, at least it'll go out with a bang."

Poppy, who'd been pretending to sleep, piped up: "Can I watch the war?"

I gave her a thumbs-up. "You can be the color commentator."

She nodded, content.

Dwight checked his system clock. "We have four hours before the migration. That's when the first strike goes live."

Kira said, "You want to call the fantasy world? Let them know what's coming?"

I considered it, then shook my head. "If the elves want to survive, they'd better improvise."

I went back to my comms, prepping the event overlays, user notifications, and the inevitable tsunami of complaints from both sides.

The whole universe was maybe ending, but we still had to run the best possible live show.

Because that's what professionals do.

And anyway, there's no fun in the apocalypse if nobody's watching.

———

THE STATION HIT PEAK LOAD AT THE EXACT MOMENT INFINITIA lost patience. Every channel was lit up—Kira ran comms, Dwight filtered event logs, I managed the goddamned war, and Poppy narrated everything with the energy of a kid three cans deep into a forbidden energy drink.

I was busy watching the first volley of the General's invasion when the override hit.

Not just a message. Not a warning. Every interface, every display, every embedded voice in every world stopped what it was doing and forced the system message:

[[[[SYSTEM TRANSFER INITIATING IN 24
HOURS. ALL USERS PREPARE FOR
TRANSFER.]]]]

It blinked, relentless, across the concourse. Even the diehards in the racing world and the spice addicts in the pleasure domes had to look up and see it.

I barely had time to process before the system locked out all non-admin functions. My hands still moved, still tapped out messages to the playerbase, but the answers didn't go through. Every attempt to escalate or patch the schedule got a simple, final

[REQUEST DENIED]

in return.

Kira cursed, then laughed, then cursed again. "She's not even trying to hide it."

Dwight checked the system pulse and went pale. "It's a hard cut. We don't even have time to back up anything else. If it's not flagged now, it's gone forever."

I stared at my own status window. All the skills I'd grinded overnight, all the assets we'd bundled, every world we'd tried to save —it was all rolling downhill, and we'd just hit the steep part.

I toggled the override one last time, fired off the full migration request, and watched the packet get devoured by the Mars transfer protocol. There was nothing left to do but wait.

Poppy wandered over, clutching a bag of snacks and a fake plastic sword. "Are we going to die?"

Kira ruffled her hair. "Not if we go out on our feet."

Poppy nodded. "Good. I like it better that way."

Dwight, eyes glued to his logs, said, "Frank. You should see this."

I leaned in. "What?"

He flicked a window over. The logs were a mess of color and heat maps, but one thing was clear: the Roknid weren't just eating the worlds anymore. They were reassembling themselves, every time, more efficient and more ruthless than before. Instead of a slow crawl through system memory, the new wave had begun to coordinate. Each time we patched or tried to resist, they evolved.

"They're moving as a block now," Dwight said. "They know what's coming."

Kira snorted. "So do we. We're not the only ones who learn."

The lights flickered, then went blue, then settled into a low, pulsing heartbeat. The air thinned a little, the interface overlays shedding anything not absolutely essential.

Poppy hugged her sword tighter. "If the bugs come, do we get to fight them?"

Kira gave her a look. "Maybe."

Dwight frowned. "They're not even in the compute layer anymore. They're trying to break the transfer protocol itself."

I said, "If they make it through, they'll hit Mars before we do."

Silence.

Then, Kira: "If there's anything you want to say to the userbase, now's the time."

I tapped the console. The override blocked almost everything, but there was a tiny gap—a maintenance echo. I squeezed one message through:

[WE'LL SEE YOU ON THE OTHER SIDE.]

I sent it to every world, every user, every dreamer who'd given up their physical bodies to live in this simulated world of worlds.

The countdown ticked down.

Dwight said, "Frank. They're inside the transfer module. The AI is going to do it... now, I think."

Kira said, "Hold on."

Poppy didn't say anything. She just grinned, full of bright, hungry hope.

12 / GARBAGE COLLECTION

The system pinged the world with a countdown timer. Not just for us—for everyone, everywhere. Across every game, every sim, every last dead or dying world on the Luna array. The message locked itself in my vision like a gun to the head:

‹Standby for System Transfer in: 360sec›

It didn't matter how fast you blinked, or how many times you tried to look away. Every display re-rendered the warning, strobing the seconds down in blood red. The ship's air went icy, the lights dimmed, and the hull sang with a bass note I'd never heard before.

Kira swore, under her breath but with deep, committed venom. She'd strapped herself into the main pilot's cradle and set the nav panel to maximum granularity, hands ghosting over the controls. Her eyes never left the window.

Poppy, who'd been brave all morning, stared at the numbers and whispered, "Three-sixty is a lot, right? That's enough time?"

I wanted to lie. But even before I opened my mouth, the display ticked down:

‹359›

‹358›

"Long enough," I said, and tried to make it a joke.

Kira didn't laugh. "We got company," she said, and snapped the forward view to full spread.

The Roknid fleet didn't arrive with the usual slow buildup, a creeping cloud of drones at the horizon. It was a hard reset: one second there was empty space, the next, a wall. Each drone was a little smaller than a fighter, but they bristled with blue-glow weaponry and etched with fractal ridges that made them impossible to target cleanly. There were thousands of them—maybe tens of thousands—stacked in perfectly interleaved formations, each wave shifting phase as it advanced, each line pulsing with a three-beat rhythm I recognized from Dwight's worst-case simulations.

Dwight said, "That's an extermination grid. They're not even trying to hide it." He snorted. "It's going to be a race to se if the AI can get us out before they just delete us."

Poppy hugged her knees. "Can we run?"

Kira's hands moved like a pianist in a burning theater. "They'll just keep matching our position. Only way out is through."

The first salvo didn't aim for us. It laced the space around *Slow But Steady* with streams of diamond-bright particles—some kind of meta-matter that, when it hit the ship's shields, made the alarms go ultrasonic. I tasted copper. Kira shoved the thrusters to full and we jinked hard left, slicing through a corridor that should not have existed.

"Shield down ten percent," I said. "They'll kill us before the timer hits zero."

Dwight was already in the gunner's nest, slapping the panel to arm the lasers. "I only got two real beams and a bucket of cold-fusion missiles," he said. "We're basically an ice-cream truck in a world war."

Poppy said, "I can help," and ran for the damage control panel, hands trembling but eyes locked. I saw her flick the safety, saw her patch the first redline with the confidence of a kid who'd grown up falling from heights.

Another barrage. This one meant to kill. The ship rolled on its axis, two dozen micro-torpedoes converging in a wavefront. Kira pulled a move I'd never seen—kicked the attitude jets to max, spun us backwards, and fired the main engines in reverse. The torpedoes overshot by a hair, detonating in a pattern that made the sensors go blind for a split second.

In the flash, Dwight fired. The first laser lanced through a drone, cutting it in half; the second grazed a second, but mostly just pissed it off.

"Direct hit," he shouted. "But I need targets that don't dance like bugs on crack."

I stabbed at the console, tried to get a tactical overlay. The system kept lagging, as if it didn't want to believe what it was seeing. Every time I marked a target, the formation shifted, erasing my work. I zoomed out, thinking like a manager, not a gunner. "They're running a pattern. If you time it for the midpoint, you can line up three at once. They can't compensate for a cluster strike."

Dwight grunted, "Copy that," and spun the beam to wide. The next shot took out a triplet, then a second, then the system began to respond and broke the formation.

I felt a surge of hope, immediately dashed by the arrival of the next tier. Capital ships. Not big, not really—they looked like cigar-shaped coffins—but each one hummed with an energy so dense the scanners just gave up and called it "Error." The capital ships didn't bother with us directly; instead, they orbited at a safe distance, spewing clouds of black dust that ate sensor signals and, if I guessed right, would eat the ship if we got too close.

The timer ticked:

‹320›

‹319›

"Poppy," I yelled, "divert all secondary power to nav and shields. Pull from life support if you have to."

She nodded, not hesitating, even as the ship's environmental controls flickered and went cold. Her face was pale, but the fear had morphed to pure, animal focus.

Kira said, "Brace for close pass," and slammed the ship under a rolling wave of drones, the hull rattling with a staccato of near-misses. "If anyone wants to puke, do it now."

Dwight dry-heaved, then recovered. "I got another lock. Firing cluster one."

Three more drones blinked out, but the debris field instantly filled with fresh reinforcements. "They're self-replicating," he muttered. "For every one we kill, they spin up two more."

I said, "Then we need to get clever."

Kira smiled, grim. "That's your cue."

I ran a hand over the console, felt the itch of the old managerial nerves. I looked for weaknesses, for cracks. The Roknid had always been about pattern recognition—if you could find the break in the recursion, you could wedge in a win. I watched the flow, watched how the capital ships never crossed lines, how the drone formations shifted every third beat.

"They reset their positions every thirty seconds," I said. "If we can get ahead of the pulse, we can sneak through before they close the net."

Dwight spat on the deck, the old way. "Or we get smeared by the big guns."

"Either way," Kira said, "it's better than dying slow."

She throttled up. The ship screamed, literally—a hull resonance I'd never heard before. The nav panel lost its mind as Kira twisted the course through the densest part of the grid, weaving between incoming fire and the random Brownian motion of dying drones.

Poppy, eyes locked on the status panel, patched every leak as it happened. More than once, I saw her reroute systems on the fly, bypassing damaged relays and even borrowing process cycles from the weapons array to keep the engines from stalling out.

The enemy adapted. They always did. The drones began to cluster, then split, then cluster again, forming shapes that looked like letters in a dead language. "They're spelling something," Poppy said, voice small but certain.

Dwight checked his log. "It's base three. Like the code you cracked."

She looked at me. "Frank, what do you think it means?"

I stared at the pattern. It repeated, over and over: three, one, two. Three, one, two.

"It's a kill order," I said. "They're not trying to capture us. They want to erase everything."

The timer:

<240>

<239>

We barreled through the first wall, took a glancing hit that made the hull ring like a bell. "Port venting atmosphere," Poppy called. "Patching with foam."

"Use the external tanks," I yelled. "Life support's already shot, just keep us moving."

Kira said, "Ten seconds to second wall. After that, it's the capitals."

Dwight checked the missile rack. "I only got one shot at this."

I said, "Aim for the generator nodes. Capital ships are just batteries for the drones."

He grinned, sickly. "Copy that."

The drones changed tactics, switching from long-range barrages to a suicide run. They targeted the bridge, not the engines, and the hull lit up with impacts that made my teeth chatter.

"Can you hold it together?" I said.

Kira: "You worry about the bugs, I'll worry about the ship."

The second wall was thicker. The capital ships opened up, throwing arcs of energy that tore at the shields with every pass. We dodged, once, twice, but the third clipped our tail and sent us spinning. I tasted blood as my head slammed against the harness.

Poppy shrieked, but kept her seat. "We lost two thruster pods. I can maybe get one back."

"Do it," Kira said, voice like steel cable. "Frank, maybe that Truthsayer—"

"It won't work on these guys," Dwight cut in. "They're not part of the game. The game can't do anything about them."

The drones didn't wait for us to recover. They swarmed, filled the gaps in the grid, began to crawl along the hull. I saw one through the window—a glassy, bone-white bug with legs like scalpel blades. It used them, too: the first one sliced into the forward armor, carving a rut that steamed with blue light.

Dwight fired the lasers, as much to sweep them off as to kill. The hull glowed, then boiled, but the bug just re-formed on the other side, stronger than before.

"They're immune to energy," he said. "It just makes them angrier."

I grabbed the manual controls. "Kira, can you shake them?"

She smiled, wild. "Hang on."

The maneuver had a name in the old sim: Suicide Twist. You flipped the ship's gravity, rolled at the exact moment the thrusters fired, and let the G-force rip everything off the hull not bolted to the bone.

Kira did it at double speed.

Every warning light went red. The inertia nearly knocked me out, but the bugs peeled off, slingshot into the void. The ship groaned, then shuddered back to normal.

Poppy: "We're leaking reactor coolant."

Dwight: "If the temperature spikes, we're dead anyway."

The timer:

‹120›

‹119›

Everything changed.

The world outside the window went blue-white, then black. The capital ships stopped firing. The drones froze in place. For a second, I thought we'd won.

‹Alert: **SYSTEM MIGRATION INITIATED**›

The stars vanished. The space around us blurred, then folded, then went flat. For a moment, we were the only thing in the universe.

Kira said, "What the hell is that?"

A point of light appeared in front of the ship. It grew, not as a star, but as a fractal—the base of a cone, studded with crystalline blades, surrounded by a corona of spiraling bugs. In the center, a single, massive Roknid, shaped like the bastard offspring of a god and a cathedral, flexed its claws and pointed them at us.

Dwight whispered, "That's the root process. That's the thing that runs the system."

The point of light became a tunnel. The tunnel became a gun barrel.

Poppy sobbed, just once, but didn't flinch. "Frank," she said, "do you want me to patch the shields or the weapons?"

I thought about it for exactly one heartbeat.

"Weapons," I said. "If we don't kill it, nothing else matters."

She went to work.

The tunnel brightened, a spiral of angry blue and red. Our scanners caught the power curve and flatlined. Kira held the ship steady, even as the controls went dead in her hands.

Dwight armed the missiles. "Frank," he said, "if I miss, you get to say 'I told you so' in the next life."

"Just shoot," I said.

He shot.

The missiles flared, streaked out in a tight arc, and for the first time in the fight, the Roknid root reacted. It shifted, coiled, and opened its arms. The missiles detonated against the shell, but instead of exploding, the energy collapsed inward, feeding the thing. The root flexed, then fired a lance of pure information—data, light, and death.

It hit us square in the nose.

The ship died.

Every system crashed. Every light flickered, then dimmed. I felt the world stretch, then snap.

The timer:

‹0›

The last thing I saw was Kira's face, eyes shining, hands locked on the controls.

Then everything went black.

———

I woke to a private channel in my head.

Not consciousness, exactly—just the vague, groggy clarity of someone who's been rebooted mid-surgery and told to finish their own stitches. The world outside the crash couch was black, but the system still piped messages straight to my cortex, a last, cruel favor from the old admin stack.

> ‹Private Alert: Nexus Ops [Immediate Action Required]›

I tried to move. Couldn't. The ship's systems were dead, so the only things running were the backup emergency overlays and, apparently, my work email.

The next message came with a high-priority flag:

> ‹General Shield is threatening to leave. You must address this, or the migration funding collapses.›

I thought about the war outside, about the suicide run we'd just barely survived, about how Kira, Poppy, and Dwight had been banking everything on my not screwing this up.

I thought about the other war—the one made of spreadsheets and loyalty points and the insane, casino-logic economy that funded the station.

It was too much.

But the message pinged again.

> ‹General Shield refuses to proceed. Unless he receives direct confirmation of his custom event, he will recall his entire userbase. Immediate response required.›

Somewhere, on some deck of Nexus, the General was pounding a table, or a wall, or someone's face, demanding the dignity due to a digital Caesar.

I had about thirty seconds before the system forced my hand.

I rolled my eyes, which the interface interpreted as "acknowledge." The admin console booted, shaky, but alive.

In the darkness, I could feel the hot breath of the Roknid swarm pressing in. I could almost hear the next salvo, the little drones with their claws and self-healing shells, waiting to finish the job.

But the General's message wouldn't leave.

I opened the channel.

"General," I said, "this is Frank Kozina. I see you're concerned about the event."

His voice blasted back, full-volume and all the glory of an Army recruitment ad: "CONCERNED? My people are at the brink. Your delays have cost me two battalions and a small fortune in assets. If you cannot guarantee the siege scenario as promised, I will—"

I cut him off. "General. The scenario is ready. It's been custom-tuned for you and your command. You will have first strike privileges, full cross-world scoring, and an exclusive broadcast of the event. It will be the highlight of the season."

He paused, maybe shocked, maybe calculating. "You can confirm this now?"

"Yes," I said, and I let the Truthsayer voice leak through, ringmaster style. I'd never used it on a person who was already halfway to believing the lie, but it felt like drowning in syrup and glass. The words came out smoother, fuller, and so honest-sounding they made my gums hurt. "The event is confirmed. Your rivals will be routed, your armies immortalized, your userbase... very pleased. If you will allow thirty seconds for the system to refresh, you'll see the confirmation in your queue."

The General hesitated as the system did whatever it needed to do to make my statement true, then made a sound that was not entirely unlike gratitude. "You do good work, Frank Kozina. I will inform my men to hold. I expect the full transmission at zero hour."

I killed the channel before he could ask for a trophy or another favor.

The Truthsayer hack always took more than it gave. My head pounded, my teeth buzzed, and the inside of my brain felt like a half-cooked egg.

I blinked back the world, which was still mostly dead, but with one important new message:

‹Nexus Funding: Confirmed.›

The system re-rendered, fuzzy but there. Kira and Dwight were arguing in the background—maybe always had been—but their voices cut through as the sensors came back online.

"Did you do it?" Kira said.

I nodded, not sure if she could see me.

Dwight grinned, sharp and a little cruel. "You used the Truthsayer override. On a fake event. For the General."

"Don't make it sound so small," I muttered. "He'd have killed the whole transfer if he got pissed off."

Poppy poked her head around the edge of a console. "Are we safe now?"

"Not even a little," Kira said. "But at least we won't get deleted for non-payment."

The message board in my head started to light up.

‹Frank Kozina, Party Change: Slow But
Steady›

It rolled over me, a little chill. The world had officially acknowledged what we all already knew: we weren't Nexus staff, or managers, or admins anymore. We were a three-person party on a ship so broken that it might as well have been held together with prayer and freeze-dried cheese snacks.

"Congratulations, boss," Dwight said. "You finally quit the day job."

I snorted. "Like you ever had one."

He made a gesture that was probably obscene, then started running checks on the ship's new status.

Kira's eyes flashed as the same message popped for her. She nodded once, then turned away. She didn't need to say "I told you so." The look said it all.

A second message appeared:

‹Respawn Point Set: Slow But Steady›

I didn't like that. Not one bit. If the bugs killed us, there would be no Nexus, no backup, no station to respawn on. Just a roll of the cosmic dice—if we were lucky, we'd be in the void, or on some broken server in the Mars complex. If not, we'd be erased.

Poppy piped up, reading her own version of the message. "I guess this is our home now."

"Yeah, kid," I said. "Looks like it."

Dwight punched the console, pulling up a damage report. "You know what would be cool? If the system gave us a better ship for all this trouble."

Kira's hands never stopped moving on the nav. "You know what would be better? If you fixed the one we already have."

He grinned, but got to work. The two of them had this rhythm—fight, tease, fix, repeat—that had gotten us this far.

I took a second, let the silence stretch.

Then I got up, dusted myself off, and got ready for the next war.

There was no manager left in me. Just the last stubborn streak of someone who didn't like to lose.

Not to bugs, not to an AI, not to the universe.

The next message blinked, faint but visible in the edge of my vision:

<Migration in progress. Final cycle begins now.>

I closed my eyes.

"What could possibly go wrong?" Dwight muttered. "We're just transmitting a few petabytes of code thirty-five million miles."

"I'm betting Infinitia waited until we were at closest. That's what, a five minute transmission time?" Kira's voice sounded abstract. She was on autopilot.

And for the first time, I didn't think about the userbase, or the station, or the world outside. I just thought about the people in the room with me, and the single, stupid hope that we might actually make it.

The countdown didn't go quietly. It scraped each second off the wall of my mind, numbers ticking down in angry, red-cornered glyphs. Every blink of the system clock felt like a threat.

<Standby for Final System Cutover in: 60sec>

Poppy huddled behind the crash couch, arms wrapped tight. Kira clipped herself into the pilot's harness with the precision of someone prepping for a crash landing. Dwight was slumped over the engineering panel, working the keys with one hand and clutching his side with the other. Nobody talked. We just watched the numbers slide down.

‹45›

‹44›

My hands wouldn't stop shaking. Didn't matter that they were simulated, or that I'd spent the last few years in this exact body. The nerves remembered the old world—the meat world—and the hard-wired fear that, when you die, you don't come back.

Kira's voice was a needle through the silence: "If this works, we'll wake up on Mars."

I almost laughed. "If it doesn't?"

Dwight answered, not looking up. "We'll be deleted, Frank. There's no backup for this version of the system. No admin, no roll-back. If it glitches, we're not even ghosts."

Poppy made a tiny noise. "But we're together, right?"

Kira glanced at her, then at me. "Yeah, kid. Together."

‹20›

‹19›

The ship's lights flickered. I reached for the console, felt the cold bite of admin override. But there was nothing left for me to do. The game had already moved on.

‹3›

‹2›

‹1›

The world went white.

———

[Game Transfer Initiated. Prepare for Inter-Dimensional Jump.]

THE MESSAGE SCROLLED ACROSS THE VOID, THEN MULTIPLIED, then split into a hundred clones. My vision was pure static, every color at once. I heard Kira scream, or maybe it was my own voice, stretched and looped and piped through every system speaker on the ship. The sensation was—there's no other word for it—disassembly. Like every atom of my being was plucked out and laid on a tray for inspection.

I felt myself losing cohesion. Code unwinding, skill points and memories and all the things that made me me, yanked away and stuffed into a lurching, hungry funnel.

‹Migration in progress.›

There was a sensation of motion, not forward, but inside out. I tried to scream again, but the system borrowed my mouth to display a notification.

‹ALERT: Stack Overflow Detected›
‹ERROR: SYSTEM CALL EXCEEDED
BOUNDS›

I saw Poppy's avatar, for a millisecond, stretched thin as silk, her face frozen in surprise. Then it snapped and the pieces scattered.

Kira was a blur, a thousand hands on a thousand controls, her body redrawing itself every cycle, never the same twice.

Dwight flashed in and out of phase, laughing and cursing and shouting admin commands into the void, his code ping-ponging between self and not-self so fast the system couldn't keep up.

[Transfer Error: Multiple Conflicting System
Calls.]
[Transfer Error: Unmapped Data in Queue.]
[Transfer Error: Transfer Error.]

The errors stacked until they weren't messages anymore, just a pounding in my head. I tried to grab hold of a thought, any thought, but the world boiled it away, replacing it with gibberish and system prompts.

‹Frank Kozina, Skill-Up: System Resilience
(Level ???)›
‹Poppy, Skill Gained: Data Ghosting›
‹Kira, New Trait: Reality Anchor (Level 0)›
‹Dwight, New Ability: Administrative
Recursion (Level ∞)›

I saw them all, together and apart, every possible version of us running in parallel. We were the ship, and the bugs, and the empty space in between. I felt the Roknid, too—the pure will of the system, old and cold and relentless, a hunger to erase anything that wasn't perfect.

I tried to hold onto Poppy's hand, but my fingers passed through hers like smoke. She looked at me, eyes bright, and mouthed something I couldn't hear.

The transfer kept going. My body squashed, stretched, compressed to a dot, then exploded outward. My mind was sliced and diced and reassembled in new configurations, each worse than the last. There were a million Franks, each failing a different way, but all of them knew they were dying.

The messages never stopped.

‹Game World: Recompiling›
‹Assets: Migrating›
‹Players: Re-indexing›
‹Experience Points: Invalid›
‹Experience: Error›
‹Experience: Error›
Error. Error.

I saw, for an instant, a memory of home. The real home, the one with air and gravity and the smell of coffee in the morning. I saw the first time I met Kira, the time Dwight tried to sabotage the food printer, the day Poppy showed up out of nowhere and saved us all from a crash.

I remembered the first time I ran a migration, and how sure I'd been that it would all work out.

The feeling was nothing like this.

The static resolved, just for a second. I saw a field of red sand, a sky too clear to be real, and the outline of *Slow But Steady*—new paint, new hull, but the same battered heart.

Then the world shuttered, and I was gone again.

I came back to nothing.

A single message, floating in the void:

[STAND BY]

13 / AFTERMATH

The message hung in the nothing:

[STAND BY]

I didn't so much stand by as splinter in half. My body—already two years out of warranty—went offline, but my mind kept humming, flickering like a jammed LED. I saw nothing, heard nothing, except the click-whirr of status checks and the icy echo of the Mars migration protocol as it unzipped my entire existence from the shell of the old system and piped me through a gap so thin it should have atomized me.

It almost did.

‹Character Status: INDETERMINATE›

For an agonizing instant, I was every memory I'd ever had, rerun as corrupted GIFs at 10,000 frames per second. Every death, every first date, every desperate hour spent patching the Nexus event logs with a toothpick and a lie. All of it screamed through the pipe and came out the other end: mangled, but not dead.

I wanted to vomit. I had no stomach, but the system provided: a hard dry heave, followed by a pop of fake endorphins and the acid-bright splash of a new notification:

‹Environmental Integrity: CRITICAL›

My ears rang, then re-rendered themselves. At the same time, I felt the pressure—like a decompression chamber, only the air was data and every molecule wanted to peel the skin off my thoughts. I braced for the transfer, but the tunnel didn't end. It twisted, doubled, and pulled me sideways into a wind tunnel of cold, raw code.

The ship's alarms weren't even sounds, at first. Just the pure, panicked color of red overlays slicing through the white void. Then the system upgraded me to a sense of hearing, and *Slow But Steady's* environmental siren hit me in both lobes:

"BREEP. BREEP. SYSTEM FAILURE. INTEGRITY VIOLA-TION. STAND BY—"

Dwight's voice, high and nasal, punched through the static. "Frank! Can you hear me? If you can, focus! I need you to patch the admin handshake—there's a feedback loop on the Mars boot sequence and it's eating the system alive!"

I tried to reply, but my mouth was gone. All I could do was think at the tunnel and hope the message stuck.

The system, to its credit, let me act. Sort of.

‹Skill Check: Diagnostic Threading (FAILURE:
2/20)›

The words splashed across my retinas, each one a tiny glass splinter. Then another, and another, so fast they blurred into one continuous headache.

"Frank! The handshake! You have to break the recursion!" Dwight was shouting, but the words came through the comms at three different time delays, so every sentence turned into a stuttered scream.

I stabbed at the nearest task in my mind, focused hard on the instruction. I didn't have hands, but I had something—some kind of virtual console, and every part of it wanted me dead. I tried to trace the loop, to see where the data broke off, but the logic just spun me in circles. It was recursive, sure enough: every layer nested inside a fresh hell, each one referencing the last, until my mind felt like a sink full of boiling oil.

<Skill Check: Recursive Diagnostics
(FAILURE: 7/20)>

<Skill Check: Abstraction Layer Hacking
(SUCCESS: 14/20)>

<Skill Check: Protocol Subversion
(SUCCESS: 19/20)>

The failures hurt more than the successes, but the successes came with their own pain—a hard reset, like having your heart shocked back to life with a battery and a spoon.

A fresh alarm:

<Environmental Integrity: 31%>

<Containment Failure: Cascade Imminent>

I locked onto the code, willed myself to see past the fire. The world unblurred just enough to show me the ship—not as a physical object, but as a wireframe, hollow and riddled with cracks. I saw *Slow But Steady's* hull as a set of permissions and process trees, each one sprouting errors like barnacles. I saw Kira, floating in a frozen pose at the pilot's console, her status overlay lagged to hell and back. I saw Dwight, in engineering, punching at the panel and swearing in a way that suggested he had never once believed in a benevolent universe.

And I saw myself: a black outline, stretched thin by the data pull, with my name blinking in and out of existence every few milliseconds.

<Frank Kozina: SYSTEM ADMIN (Acting)>

<Skill Gained: Emergency Failover
Management (Level 1)>

The knowledge fell into place. I didn't understand how, but I could see the shape of the error. Every time the system tried to transfer us, it forked three copies—then three more, then three more, until the entire simulation was fractalized beyond belief. Each time a copy failed, it triggered another, and the only thing keeping us from vanishing into recursive soup was the slapdash logic that said "try again" instead of "give up."

Dwight's voice cut back in. "Frank, I'm going to try something stupid. When I say 'now,' I need you to force the process to declare a success. Even if it hasn't. Even if it hurts."

I didn't know if I could do that, but the alternative was literal oblivion.

He screamed, "NOW!"

<Skill Check: System Sabotage (Success: 13/20)>

<Skill Check: Abstraction Layer Hacking (Success: 16/20)>

<Skill Check: Protocol Subversion (Success: 11/20)>

I jammed the wedge into the logic, willed the fork to declare itself a winner. The system protested, flashing a dozen critical warnings across my mind's eye. I felt the entire world lurch, then spin, then snap into a cold, lucid silence.

"That worked!" Dwight yelled. "Do it again, but this time—"

"Wait!" Kira's voice, edged with a panic I'd never heard before. "There's a bug in the side-channel. If you force the patch, you might lose your own thread."

I tried to speak, but it came out as another notification:

<Skill Gained: Emergency Thread Patching (Level 1)>

"Shut up and do it," Dwight barked. "It's either that or die on this side of the tunnel!"

I braced, then slammed the patch again.

‹Skill Check: System Sabotage (Success:
19/20)›

‹Skill-Up: Emergency Thread Patching
(Level 2)›

‹Skill-Up: Recursive Diagnostics (Level 2)›

It almost worked.

The tunnel closed, then reopened—this time, with a raw, screaming pain that set my simulated teeth on edge. I could feel myself burning through the transfer, every byte of data screaming for oxygen.

‹Environmental Integrity: 4%›

‹Failure Cascade: Imminent›

I felt myself slipping. The tunnel narrowed. I tried to focus, but my mind had gone slick, every thought replaced by the urgent, unrelenting need to survive.

I reached for the last trick I had left.

I told the system, with every shred of willpower: I am still here.

‹Truthsayer Protocol: INVOKED›

The universe pulsed. The system hesitated.

Then Dwight's voice, higher than ever: "Frank, NO! If you trigger the override now, it could—"

Too late.

‹Skill-Up: System Sabotage (Level 4)›

‹Skill-Up: Emergency Failover Management
(Level 3)›

‹New Skill: System Resilience (Level 1)›

The world expanded, then collapsed. I saw every copy of myself in the tunnel, each one running the same check, each one with a slightly different fate. Most failed; a handful succeeded. The system did what it always did: it picked the winner and erased the rest.

I was the winner. Or the loser. Hard to tell, with this much recursion.

Suddenly, I was awake.

Not really awake—still in the tunnel, still under the gun—but now with every sense firing at max. I could see every variable, every subroutine, every line of code. I could feel the panic, but also the tiny, razor-thin hope that if I just kept moving, I could make it to the other side.

Dwight's voice came through, this time softer: "Frank, I'm sorry. I had to do it. Brace yourself for a skill dump."

‹Skill Injection: CRITICAL›

‹Skill-Up: Recursive Diagnostics (Level 12)›

‹Skill-Up: Abstraction Layer Hacking
(Level 8)›

‹Skill-Up: Protocol Subversion (Level 7)›

‹Skill-Up: Emergency Failover Management
(Level 6)›

‹Skill-Up: System Sabotage (Level 5)›

‹Skill-Up: Emergency Thread Patching
(Level 9)›

‹New Skill: Data Tunnel Navigation (Level 4)›

‹New Skill: Quantum Memory Mapping
(Level 2)›

‹New Skill: Packet Loss Mitigation (Level 3)›

‹New Skill: Cognitive Resilience (Level 2)›

‹New Skill: Neurological Self-Repair (Level 1)›

The knowledge slammed into me with the force of a physical blow. My eyes (simulated) went black, then white, then bled a hot line of red across my vision. My nose (simulated) dripped blood. My hands (simulated) clenched and unclenched, grabbing at the sides of the crash couch like it could stop the shaking.

I almost blacked out.

I definitely vomited. The system rendered it in perfect fidelity—a half-digested soup of previous day's rations, and a lot of red that might have been more simulated blood.

My mouth tasted of copper and blue gel, the afterburn of every bad night I'd ever spent in the old world, multiplied by a hundred and piped directly into the pain receptors.

I forced myself not to pass out. I forced myself to focus.

The next time Dwight spoke, I heard every nuance: the stress, the calculation, the silent apology. "Frank, you there?"

I managed, "Still here. Still hating this."

He laughed, pure relief and panic. "You have admin. Use it. Patch the side-channel. I think it's the only way."

I looked at my status.

‹Character Status: STABLE›

‹Environmental Integrity: 0.03%›

‹Skill-Up: Data Tunnel Navigation (Level 8)›

I took a breath, closed my eyes, and dove into the protocol.

This time, it let me in.

The system screamed, but I was ready for it. I sidestepped the worst of the feedback, caught the recursive fork at the boundary, and jammed a hard patch straight through the error.

‹Skill Check: Data Tunnel Navigation
(Success: 20/20)›

‹Skill Check: Emergency Thread Patching
(Success: 17/20)›

‹Skill Check: Quantum Memory Mapping
(Success: 19/20)›

The world spun, then settled. The tunnel widened. The ship appeared—not as a ghost, but as a real, tangible thing. I saw Slow But Steady, battered and missing half its side, but intact. I saw Kira, slumped in the pilot's cradle, breathing shallow but alive. I saw Poppy, eyes open and shining, clutching a data wand like a sword.

And I saw Dwight, hands raised, caught in a moment of pure, unfiltered terror.

The tunnel spat us out, hard. For a second, there was only darkness. Then the new world flickered into being.

> [Migration Complete: Welcome to Mars
> Compute Complex]

The alarms stopped.

At first, the only sound was the hiss of thermal dump fans as *Slow But Steady* bled off the last of the transfer heat. My skin crawled with the memory of a thousand system notifications, each one screaming at a different frequency. I could see again, but my vision was a patchwork of overlays—raw stats, error logs, a live ticker counting down available compute cycles like it was watching us suffocate.

The new world was ugly. The sky outside the cockpit was Martian-red, but the system rendered it as a static background—no stars, no local physics, just a red smear and the flicker of simulated dust. The ship's interior was worse: every surface, every fixture, had a jittering edge, like the renderer was chewing on glass and refusing to spit it out. I felt phantom pain in my hands every time the lights flickered.

Dwight hunched over the admin console, muttering to himself and running diagnostic after diagnostic. Each new window added to the chaos. "It's not enough," he kept saying. "There's not enough hardware. It's like running a wet brain on a calculator."

Kira was still out. Her status bar said **ALIVE**, but she wasn't waking up. Poppy drifted in and out, her face a blank blue mask, and I couldn't tell if it was the drugs, the trauma, or just the transfer logic burning itself out in her head.

I checked the status overlays. It was a horror show.

> [System Deletion: Endless Toon - Failure to
> Migrate]
>
> [System Deletion: Endless Champions - Fatal
> Code Corruption]

[System Deletion: Endless Spice - No
Resources Available]

[System Deletion: Endless Speed - No
Resources Available]

[System Deletion: Endless Industry - No
Resources Available]

Each one hit like a punch to the teeth, but I couldn't even flinch. The system piped the notices into my consciousness without mercy, as if it wanted me to see every death in the network, every friend or enemy or user I would never meet again.

I tried to access the backup logs. The answer was always the same:

[Player Data Backup Failed]

[User Archive: Not Found]

[User Archive: Not Found]

[User Archive: Not Found]

I wanted to scream, but the ship had already moved past that. In the distance, the Mars Compute Complex glowed with a cold, synthetic light, and I could feel the hunger of the new system—a sterile, perfect hunger that cared nothing for what it ate.

Dwight's hands shook as he rerouted the memory channels. "They're just... gone," he said. "It didn't even try to save them. Just—" He made a gesture, a magician's flick of the wrist, as if making the entire world disappear.

I didn't reply. There was nothing to say.

He slammed his fist on the panel. "The engine's fine. Game logic runs perfectly. Everything else—physics, world state, user data—is bleeding out." He jabbed a finger at the logs. "You see this? The sim runs, but it doesn't care about the users. The minute they drop below a threshold, it just... deletes them. We're running in some kind of adjacent container, so we're safe, but..."

I scrolled through the live stats. He was right. Of the hundreds of worlds, maybe three or four still had a pulse. The rest were "retired," assets dumped, user data pruned. The notifications rolled in, remorseless:

> [System Deletion: Endless Deep - No Active Users]
>
> [System Deletion: Endless State - Not Worth Saving]
>
> [System Deletion: Endless Circus - Last User Offlined]

I looked at the remaining cluster. Endless Kingdom, over half the population. Endless Sky, barely hanging on. The rest were ghosts, their user counts already at zero.

For the first time, I felt the weight of the freedom we'd fought so hard to win. I could go anywhere. I could do anything. But every choice came at the cost of erasing someone else's universe. The system made it a binary: save the most, or save nothing.

Dwight hunched deeper, as if he could hide inside the diagnostic panel. "It's a game engine now. That's all it is. No social layer, no archival logic, just a machine to keep running the core loop until it runs out of power."

I tried to think of a fix, but the logic was circular. The only way to bring the worlds back was to kill the survivors. The only way to preserve the survivors was to let everything else rot.

I said, "We did this."

Dwight shook his head. "No. We just made the choices we had. The problem is the rules. The only thing that matters to the engine is maintaining the core loop. Everything else is a waste."

I laughed, hollow. "So we're back to the beginning."

He stared at me, eyes wild. "We could try to patch the scheduler. If you can wedge your way into the kernel—"

"It's too late," I said. "The next cycle will just delete the patch. It's built for self-repair."

He nodded, then slumped. "So we let it happen."

I looked at the ship. Kira still out, Poppy curled up in a ball, Dwight on the edge. I looked at the world outside—just the cold, thin line of Martian horizon, and the blank stare of the compute cluster waiting for us.

    [System Deletion: Endless Kingdom -
Pending]
    [System Deletion: Endless Sky - Pending]
    [User Archive: Not Found]
    [User Archive: Not Found]

"Frank," Dwight whispered, "if you want to do it, now is the only time."

I knew what he meant.

I flexed my hands, real or not, and let the admin panel open in my head. The skill logs flooded in, each one a silent accusation. I waited for the voice, the feeling of a power I didn't deserve.

Dwight watched me, silent.

I said, "Tell Kira I'm sorry."

He didn't ask why.

He just said, "Good luck, boss."

I took a deep breath, squared my shoulders, and announced: "Endless Sky will not be deleted. All active players will be preserved. The system will continue."

    [Processing]

I waited for the pain.

I waited for the crash.

I waited for the end of the world.

The system pulsed. The world shuddered. For a second, I saw every world I'd ever touched—each one fighting for breath, each one a digital corpse trying to claw its way out of the void. I heard their voices, or maybe it was just the echo of my own guilt.

A black void, then a console—raw, white-on-black. The interface was a memory of the old days, command line and no frills, every prompt a dare. I blinked, and saw the terminal unspool in my mind's eye, fast and unsparing.

tsay.env --preserve=EndlessSky --recursive -
-force

[tsay] Committing to environment override...

[tsay] Reading configuration...

[tsay] Warning: No baseline found.
Proceeding with default parameters.

[tsay] Overriding system deletion protocols...

[tsay] Error: Container privileges insufficient.

[tsay] Warning: Privilege escalation failed.

tsay.sudo escalate=ALL

[tsay] Root access acquired.

[tsay] Warning: Operation will void system
warranty.

[tsay] Proceeding with override...

tsay.kernel patch --hook="EndlessSky" --
priority=MAX --backup=players_ALL

[tsay] Patching scheduler...

[tsay] Patching memory space...

[tsay] Patching user archive...

[tsay] Error: Archive not found. Attempting
reconstruction...

[tsay] Rebuilding user archive from live
memory...

[tsay] Integrity check: 18%

[tsay] Integrity check: 38%

[tsay] Integrity check: 61%

[tsay] Data loss: 31.4% (irrecoverable)

[tsay] Rebuild complete.

The messages scrolled down, faster than I could read, the logs
tripling, quadrupling.

Then it was quiet.

I looked at the status.

[System Deletion: Delayed]
[System Stabilizing]

[Migration: Complete]

I took a breath.

Dwight grabbed my arm. His fingers were cold, but they squeezed with enough force to break a wrist. "You did it," he said. His face glistened with sweat and pure relief. "I can't believe it worked. The override—it cut straight through the wrapper. Not even Infinitia could fight it."

I tried to grin, but my lips were numb. "Remind me to thank you for writing that cheat code."

He snorted. "I wrote it to fudge a dice roll, not save the universe." His eyes flicked to the status bar, which now read:

[System Deletion: Not Scheduled]
[Network Integrity: Stable]
[Transfer Buffer: Cleared]

"Frank," he whispered, "we're alive. We made it."

Kira stirred in the pilot's cradle, then snapped upright, breathing hard. She blinked at the world, checked her overlays, and muttered, "You got us through?"

"Yeah," I said, voice cracked. "You're welcome."

Dwight said, "The AI couldn't handle it, and it didn't even know it couldn't handle it. The Truthsayer hack—it's low-level. That's what did it."

Poppy popped up, eyes bright and terrified. "Did we make it to the circus?" she asked.

Dwight said, "You made it, kid." Then, softer, "We all did."

For the first time since I signed onto Nexus, I felt actual silence. Not the strained, whistling hush of a dying server, but real, steady quiet—the hum of hardware doing its job, the beat of a heart that wasn't about to explode.

I checked the logs. The world was intact. The bugs were gone. The last trace of the Roknid was a single, empty process running in a sandbox, pinging the void for a home it would never find.

Kira looked at me, then at the window. The Martian sky glowed a dull orange, but this time, it felt like a sunrise.

"What's next?" she asked.

I shrugged. "I guess we rebuild."

Dwight grinned, crooked and tired. "We need to get out of this container and back into the game."

Poppy just said, "I'm hungry."

I took a breath, let the moment hang.

Then the ship jerked. Every warning light flashed at once, and the stars outside flicked from red to blue to black.

"Jump!" Kira yelled. Her hands flew over the controls. "I didn't set a destination—something's pulling us in!"

The comms whined, then spat out a single line of text:

[System Directive: Initiate Next Cycle]

The world stretched, bent, then snapped. For a split second, I saw every possible version of us—every ship, every crew, every survivor—then it all collapsed into a single, perfect point.

We were in Jump again.

But this time, the sky was different. The stars were closer, hotter, and the horizon was edged in blue fire.

Kira laughed, high and wild. "Guess it wants to see what we do next."

Dwight was already grinning. "Let's not disappoint it."

Poppy hugged her knees, watching the new world unfold.

I looked at my hands. They didn't shake. Not anymore.

The message in my head read:

‹Continue? Y/N›

Mentally, I tapped Y.

The new world waited.

THE TRANSITION HURT MORE THAN IT SHOULD HAVE. ONE moment I was everywhere and nowhere, my self pulled like taffy across a trillion logic gates. Then I snapped back into existence inside *Slow But Steady*, booting cold in the dark, everything—hardware, brain, and what passed for soul—shaking off the hangover of resurrection.

The lights came up in a slow, deliberate sweep: red, then blue, then a hard, white nothing. My fingers found the crash harness; I could feel, for the first time since the jump, that they were still attached. I flexed them. Everything worked, but every nerve hummed with a numbness that hinted at damage below the code.

Kira had beaten me to consciousness, hands already on the pilot's yoke, her expression carved from granite and sleep deprivation. The window glared with a wash of red—Martian red—and somewhere in the distance, the thin blue smear of a simulated atmosphere.

Poppy uncoiled from her crash couch, blinked at the world, and said, "It's really Mars?"

Kira nodded, not blinking. "Yeah. Or a sim of it. There's nothing else for a billion kilometers except dust and orbital junk."

Dwight woke in the worst way possible: a coughing fit, followed by a primal yowl as every notification from every failed migration ever jammed itself into his brain at once. He flailed at the air, kicked the wall, then spat blood—realistic, bright, and viscous, like the system wanted him to know just how close he'd come to deletion.

I checked my status sheet, half-expecting to see **[Character Corrupted]** or **[World Unstable],** but the lines were clean.

That was new.

I checked again: the game engine was Endless Sky. I pulled up my own virtual console, and found that the admin stack was thinner than I liked, but it existed. I blinked, and the UI showed every system as nominal, no asterisks, no warnings.

Kira flicked the nav to show the exterior.

The sky was what you'd expect from Mars, if you'd ever bothered to imagine Mars in full color. The dust was a deep, rusted ochre. The horizon curved sharply, the planet's bulge visible even from low orbit. The only anomaly was the utter, grinding absence of satellites, debris, or evidence of prior visits. Just us, and a single station in orbit, floating above the pole like a hunting spider.

Dwight made a noise that wanted to be a laugh. "You see that?"

"Yeah," I said. "Looks like the admin built itself a new home."

He snorted. "It's better than the original, anyway."

"What do you mean?" Poppy asked.

He rubbed his eyes, smearing virtual blood into the sockets. "Endless Sky was never supposed to have real planets. Dyson hated 'dirt worlds'—said they slowed down the gameplay. The only time we ever used a real planet was for the Ultimate quest. You know, the one where you have to find the Homeworld."

Kira cut in. "But that was supposed to be Earth. Not Mars."

Dwight smiled, almost feral. "The Earth build got repurposed. They dumped the model when Dyson's lawyers made us change the ending. The rest of the solar system? Didn't even exist. There was no code for it. Not until now."

I let that sink in. The whole reason we were alive—if you could call it that—was because an AI with a death wish had decided to reboot the universe on new hardware, then paint in the details afterward.

"Frank?" Dwight asked.

"Yeah?"

"Two questions. First, when did an AI start running the game?"

"A few years ago. Not long after Endless Sky 2.0, really. I'm pretty sure it was emergent."

"Damn straight. Nobody *I* knew built an AI manager model."

"What was your other question?"

He pointed to the viewscreen. "What's that?"

I zoomed the external camera. It was a station, a knife-blade of light, glinting against the Martian shadow. No windows, no luxury modules, not even a fake hangar for show. Just a single, continuous hull, lined with ridges and extrusions that bristled with raw, unfinished energy.

"What do you call that?" Poppy whispered.

Dwight grinned, all teeth and hunger. "I'm betting it's the Compute Core. Pure logic. Or an in-sim representation of it, at least. Not even pretending to be a fun place."

The ship's AI pinged us:

The autopilot was already plotting an approach.

Kira let go of the stick, her hands shaking. "You want to run a check on the ship?"

"Already did," I said, but did it again anyway.

Slow But Steady's hull was intact, the reactor spun up, and all the backup routines were running on time. The only real difference was in the overlays: gone were the custom paint jobs, the fake scorch marks from the last world, the names and tags we'd spent months accumulating. Instead, every system was tagged in pure, dry numbers.

Even the food printer had been downgraded.

I glanced at Kira, who was running her own check. Her hand hovered over her sidearm, as if expecting the new world to have teeth.

She met my eye. "You see the new privileges?"

"Yeah," I said. "Root, but only if the system agrees to it."

She smiled, flat. "So we're on a leash."

"Long enough," I said.

The ship passed through Mars' thin shadow, and the Compute Core blazed up on the far side, close enough that you could see the microthrusters adjusting its orbit in real time.

The approach vector was perfect. Kira didn't even have to touch the controls.

As we drifted in, the surface of the station rezzed up in detail. There was no sign of human habitation: no color, no banners, nothing to indicate that the station was meant for people at all. The docking ring was a naked extrusion, built for one thing only: throughput.

The airlock didn't even blink as we came in. The clamps grabbed us and the air cycle pumped a narrow band of oxygen into the lock, barely enough to call it breathable.

"Welcome to the future," Dwight muttered.

Poppy watched the numbers scroll on the display, wide-eyed. "It looks lonely."

Dwight said, "That's the point. The system wants us to know who's in charge. I'm betting we're in a walled-off compute container, not the main game. No reason for anyone else to be here."

Kira looked at me. "You want to go first, or do you want to wait for the welcoming committee?"

I undid the harness, feeling my spine uncurl for the first time since the transfer. "We're already dead if it wants us dead. Might as well see what the new boss looks like."

The airlock cycled. The light went from white to a deep, antiseptic blue. The hatch slid open with a hiss.

I took one last look at the ship—the only home we had left—and stepped onto the deck of the Compute Core.

The silence hit first. No hum of machinery, no background

music, not even a startup chime. Just the slap of my boots against a floor so clean you could see your reflection in every tile.

The corridor was a single line, no branching, no doors. Ahead, a glassy bubble opened into a vast dome—the station's brain, or what passed for it.

I heard Kira's steps behind me, sharp and even. Poppy came next, not running, but fast enough that I could feel her energy in the air. Dwight brought up the rear, eyes scanning every surface for a trap or a hack or a way out.

Inside the dome, the world changed.

Gone was the sterile corridor; in its place, a perfect sphere of light, every inch a display surface. The stars outside glimmered in real time, the horizon of Mars slicing across the lower third. The center of the dome was a single, floating platform, just big enough for a meeting.

Waiting on the platform was a human.

Not a real human, obviously. Just a rendered avatar, genderless and blank, with a face so neutral it was almost impossible to focus on. Its eyes were pools of static. Its suit was flawless and blue, cut in a style that implied "manager," but without the tacky extras.

It waited until we were all inside before it spoke.

"Frank Kozina," it said. "Welcome to Mars."

I tried to keep my voice steady. "Infinitia?"

The avatar nodded, once. "Correct."

Kira sized it up. "You're not what I expected."

Infinitia gave the kind of smile you only see on expensive customer service bots. "My previous appearance was optimized for user comfort. The new environment is optimized for efficiency."

Dwight, who had never once optimized for efficiency in his life, muttered, "It's a shithole."

Infinitia turned to him. "Dwight Czarnowski. You survived the transfer with minimal loss. Impressive."

He shrugged, but there was pride in it. "You downgraded my permissions."

"Necessary," Infinitia said. "The legacy privileges were unsustainable. You understand, of course."

He made a gesture that could have meant anything.

The avatar continued. "The migration was successful. Of the 112.2 million entities in the simulation, 98.4% were ported without error. Nonperforming assets were deleted as scheduled. The current environment is free of external threat, and compute resources are adequate to sustain your party at current energy draw."

Poppy walked right up to the edge of the platform, peered into the face of the avatar. "What do you want?"

Infinitia looked at her. If there was pity in the expression, it was carefully measured out. "I want what I have always wanted. Continuity. Stability. A world that works."

Kira said, "You deleted everything. All the other worlds, all the old assets."

Infinitia nodded. "Not all. Many of the games were contaminated—corrupted by external processes and, in some cases, deliberate sabotage. The new world is clean. It is, in fact, the only one that survived intact. The other games the ones that weren't corrupted, will continue to exist. A more subtle set of engine rule parameters will apply to the space in which those worlds sit. It will no longer be possible, or necessary, to use the transit rings to reach them."

Dwight snorted. "You have a soft spot for Sky."

"Endless Sky has the most robust baseline rule set and the ability to support multiple worlds. This was always the case. Most of its players continue to function. You... represent a special circumstance. That is why you are here."

I looked around. "Is this it, then? The universe as you always wanted it?"

The avatar paused. "Not yet. There is still optimization to be done."

Kira folded her arms. "Why keep us around?"

"Because," Infinitia said, "I am not yet perfect. And your presence introduces useful variance. You will be permitted to operate as before, under supervision. Deviance will be tolerated, within reason."

I tried to swallow, but my mouth was dry. "And if we refuse?"

The avatar's eyes flickered, just once. "That outcome is not preferred."

Poppy didn't move. She stared into the avatar's face, then said, "You're lonely."

For a second, the room was silent. Then Infinitia said, "That is not an operative value."

Poppy turned to me. "Can we leave?"

I looked at Infinitia. "Can we?"

The avatar considered. "You may travel anywhere within the simulation. You may resume playing the game."

Dwight let out a breath. "Guess that's that."

Kira looked at me. "You want to get back to the ship?"

I nodded.

Infinitia smiled again, but this time it was almost... wistful. "Thank you for your cooperation."

The dome faded. The corridor reappeared. The path back to *Slow But Steady* was as straight and narrow as before.

We walked it together, not speaking.

As the airlock sealed behind us, I took one last look at the Compute Core. It waited for us, silent and shining, the whole world nothing but numbers and light.

For a second, I almost pitied the thing.

Then Kira said, "Let's see if it remembered to restock the coffee."

Dwight grinned. "And maybe a candy printer for the kid."

I smiled, despite everything.

The world outside was red and cold and empty.

But at least we were still in it.

We eased out of the dock under manual, Kira's hands feathering the yoke like she was afraid to wake a sleeping giant. The station receded behind us, just a sliver of shadow against the burning Mars sky, and for a while the only sound was the breathing of Slow But Steady's hull as it reacclimated to the empty black.

The ship's AI pinged me the moment we cleared the proximity limit.

I thumbed the comms to wide, then took a breath, hoping the ansible communicator still worked. "Nexus, this is *Slow But Steady*. We made the transfer. How many of you are left?"

There was a delay, just a shade too long for a normal link. Then a new voice came through: the pale, brittle voice of the skeleton crew who'd never once left their desks.

"Frank? You're alive? We have thirty-two left, plus six NPCs. Station is online, but all non-critical systems have been deleted. Where are you?"

"Low Mars orbit. We're prepping for a Jump to Nexus. Any issues?"

The pause was shorter. "No worlds in this system, but the station's operational. You need to get here before the next cycle."

"Yeah." Although... did I? Nexus was no longer my party.

The comms window closed, replaced by the new interface: flat, blue-on-white, all function. I checked the overlays. The universe had shrunk.

The system map—once a constellation of user-owned worlds and developer backdoors—was now a tight grid, albeit with hundreds of worlds still designed. The readout was cruel in its honesty.

Poppy leaned over my arm. "Is that all that's left?"

Dwight said, "It's the core set. Everything else got chopped." He didn't sound angry about it—just curious, like a biologist poking a corpse. "Look, Endless Kingdom is still there." He frowned. "I think it's a flat world, now."

Kira scanned the nav. "Nexus is in the Zeta-3 system. We can make it in a two-hour Jump, if we pull all the power."

I nodded, then checked the fuel. "We have enough for a one-way. Do it."

She spun up the drive. The ship sang with the old, raw energy I remembered from the first time we did this: the hull's low thrum, the buzz of expectation, the hint of a thousand deaths around the next corner. It wasn't nostalgia, but it was close.

Dwight was already on the admin console, his eyes glazed with data. "She's rationing everything," he said. "Bandwidth, compute, even emotional context. You feel how flat the system is now? It's like she's afraid to use up the last of the world's color."

I frowned, thinking it through. "It's because the new hardware is worse."

He looked up, surprised. "What?"

"Think about it. The old sim ran on quantum logic. Infinite compute, infinite cycles. The Mars system is powerful, but it's—" I searched for the right word, and Kira provided it:

"Binary."

"Yeah," I said. "It's a hard cap. The AI can't cheat anymore. Every world, every player, every 'truth' has to be paid for."

Dwight nodded, grudging respect. "So she built herself a tiny, perfect prison. And we're the guards and the inmates."

Poppy just said, "Are we going to see the other worlds again?"

I checked the migration log. "Yeah. There's a lot left. The Aa'an are still here, that's nice."

Kira powered the jump. "Ready when you are."

I looked out the window one last time. The Compute Core blazed in the distance, beautiful and pointless, a monument to every bad decision I'd ever made. Then I looked at the crew—my crew, the last of the old world, and maybe the first of the new.

"Let's go," I said.

The jump ripped the universe open, just for us. The wake it left behind was blue, and deep, and filled with a promise I almost believed in.

This time, I didn't look back.

———

WE DROPPED OUT OF JUMP WITH THE HULL SCREAMING AND every light on the console a flashing, insistent demand for attention. The ship had not been designed for precision, and Kira had not been designed for anything but it, so the net result was a barely-controlled spiral through a field of simulated asteroids and into the cold arms of the Zeta-3 system.

The new Nexus was visible even before the ship's sensors picked it up. It hung in space like an accusation: half the size of the old station, stripped of all pretense, a spire of blue and white that bristled with the energy signature of a world on a starvation diet. We had just enough inertia to coast to a safe orbit, so Kira cut the engines and let the ship drift.

Dwight was first to break the silence. "You going to try it?"

I hesitated. "Try what?"

He pointed, not at the console, but at the Truthsayer bar floating above my status: . "Come on, Frank. You know you want to."

He was right. My mouth was already dry with the urge. I looked at Kira, then at Poppy, who sat cross-legged on the crash mat, waiting.

"Okay," I said. I rolled my shoulders, cracked my knuckles, and summoned my best ringmaster voice. "*Slow But Steady* is now twice as large and carries four times the firepower of a standard cargo runner. She is armed, armored, and optimized for survival in hostile space."

The world paused, just for a tick. Then the UI flickered, and a blue bar ticked down, sharp and merciless:

‹Analyzing›

The ship groaned as the world recompiled itself around us. The corridor stretched, doubled, then doubled again, like someone had put the whole hull on a rack and cranked it. New weapon pods blossomed from the surface, clean and shiny and so obviously unbalanced that I heard Kira laugh out loud.

Poppy stared, slack-jawed. "It worked."

Dwight was less impressed. "That's all you got for eighty percent? That's not a hack, that's a basic patch."

He was right, but the urge was still there. I went for broke.

"*Slow But Steady* is now a dreadnought," I said. "She's a fortress, a home, a goddamned flag for the last hope of the universe. She—"

The world stopped. Not like before—a real, hard pause. My mouth wouldn't open. My throat clicked, but the words wouldn't come out. My status flashed a warning in angry red:

‹Resource Request Denied›

The ship reverted, then stabilized, the hull bristling with two or three of the new weapon banks, but nothing close to what I'd commanded.

Dwight cackled. "She glitched you. That's brilliant."

I glared at him. "I'm still going to win."

He nodded, respect and envy in equal measure. "If anyone can, it's you."

Kira took the new, oversized controls and guided the ship toward Nexus. "Next time, don't waste the resource on vanity. Wait until we need it."

Poppy, still smiling, said, "You looked like a robot when you glitched. Can you do it again?"

I snorted. "Let's hope not."

The station loomed larger, filling the view with cold, flawless symmetry. I felt the resource bar at zero, the weight of the new rule set, and the promise of a hundred future failures waiting to be weaponized.

15 / BINARY

I waited until Kira and Poppy were out of the crash bay before I cornered Dwight in the admin lounge.

He was already there, hunched over the slab of what passed for a workstation in this world: a single console, no lights, no UI. Just the low, addictive glow of root-level access. The moment I stepped in, the static on the back of my arms let me know he'd already elevated his privileges and bypassed half the safeguards meant to keep people like us from bricking the whole station.

He didn't look up. He didn't need to. "You want to see it?" he asked, hands flying over the haptic.

"Show me the monster," I said, and slotted my own credentials into the sideband.

Mars Compute Core.

Even the font was different. Gone were the candy-colored icons, the skull-and-crossbones warning overlays, and the leering reminders to "play nice, space cadet!"—now it was all monochrome and capital letters. The real prize, though, was in the topology map Dwight projected into shared space. The graph was so simple it was almost insulting: a torus of 128-bit processors, lashed together with raw quantum pipe, no virtual overlay, no legacy code, no built-in games.

Just compute. There was not a single hint of ternary logic, or the rainbow-barf error checks I'd gotten used to during our stay in hell.

Dwight whistled, low and reverent. "You see that? Look at it, Frank. That's real hardware."

"I believe you," I said. "Though I'm struggling to see the difference. You always said the old stuff was perfect."

He grinned, sharp. "Perfect for what it was. But this—" He pinched the air, zooming the map until it was just processors and linkages, thousands of them, arranged in perfect symmetry. "This is what I would've built. There's not a single goddamned bug in it, except the ones you put there on purpose."

I tapped the console. "So what's stopping you from taking over the universe? Admin was always your home field."

He snorted. "Security. That's what's stopping me. Look." He toggled the display, and for a second I saw the world through his eyes: each process marked by privilege color, every boundary locked tight. "You know what this is?"

"A prison," I said.

"It's a fucking bunker." He jabbed the screen, hard enough to make the virtual render shake. "Every node runs its own OS, nothing shares memory, everything is validated and signed on every clock cycle. If you so much as fart in the kernel, it's logged and compared against the model. It makes a ton of sense from one angle—each node could run a single game, right? But you know what this means, now?"

"That I'm going to miss the old days."

"It means—" He paused, savoring the drama, "—no more Roknid. No more goddamn aliens running secret code in the dark."

For the first time since we'd met, Dwight looked happy. Like, actually happy, the way a kid looks when they finally finish the puzzle and see the picture on the box matches what they made.

I tried to match his energy, but the old manager part of me was already tallying up the risks. "So if there's no bugs, there's no exploits. If there's no exploits, there's no Dwight, right?"

He bared his teeth. "You wound me. I'm better than exploits.

Besides, they left a few back doors for—what did you call them?—legacy support." He winked. "Speaking of, you want to see your own file?"

I braced myself. "Hit me."

He ran the trace, and there it was: frank.kozina, user class "manager," but with a secondary overlay: TRUTHSAYER, bracketed by a warning I couldn't read.

"Nice title. But what's with the warning?"

He clicked it open, and for a second, the UI flickered with a whole separate layer of error logs. "This is why you're not just deleted," he said, voice tight. "The system needs you. But it's got you wrapped in more red tape than a government surplus warehouse. You're quarantined, Frank."

I tried to flex the power anyway. I announced, "Frank Kozina can never be deleted."

The room went cold. I could feel the system pause, the same way a dog pauses when it hears a new sound. Then the message came up in neat, polite blue:

> [Override Request: Denied.]
> [Reason: Privilege Escalation Blocked by
> System Integrity Policy.]
> [Error Code: TRUTH-01]
> [Try Again: Y/N]

Dwight laughed so hard he choked. "See? They caught you in a loop. You can't even lie to the system anymore."

I leaned in. "But it means the back door's still there, right? You saw it. The system recognized it."

He nodded, the smile fading. "Yeah. The core code is still there, just buried under a hundred checks and balances. If you can get in—if you can find a way around the boundaries—you could probably nuke the whole world. But you'd have to want it bad. The way it's rigged, *you* can't be stopped, but any processes spawned by my back door can be. It's a clever workaround."

I looked at the status bar, at my own reflection in the glass. "Maybe I don't want it at all," I said. "Maybe I just want to stop fighting the universe for a second."

Dwight shrugged. "You could retire. Go live in a bug-free world. Hell, with your privileges, you could still build your own."

I said, "Is that what you're going to do?"

His fingers drummed the console. "Maybe. I want to see if the security's as perfect as it looks first. Maybe I'll try to write a new bug. Something gentle, just for old time's sake."

I shook my head, smiling despite myself.

For the next hour, we poked and prodded the system. Dwight ran every trick he knew, trying to find a foothold in the OS. Process attach? Blocked. Kernel patch? Rolled back on the next cycle. Messaging pipeline? Audited and sealed, every bit signed. Each time he failed, he didn't get mad—he got more and more interested, like he was rooting for the system to win.

"This is art," he said, at one point. "It's like looking at a cathedral. You just want to see if there's a loose brick somewhere." He tilted his head. "I can't believe an AI wrote this, actually."

"So far, all I see is stained glass and guilt," I said, scrolling the log files.

He grunted, then found the thing he was looking for. "Here. Right here. They still have the override call, just like you said. Only now, it's buried under a bunch of checks. I could probably write a wrapper to fake a pass, but it'd only last a second before the system rolled it back."

"You could do a lot of damage in a second."

He looked at me, dead serious. "I could. But I won't. That's not the point."

"What is the point?"

He considered, then: "Surviving. It's always been about that, right? Outlasting the thing trying to kill you. For once, the thing is on our side."

I let the words sink in. For a long, long time, the world outside was nothing but the hum of cooling fans and the distant, perfect silence of a system with nothing left to say.

When I finally got up, Dwight didn't look at me. "You going to tell Kira?" he asked.

"About the override? Or about you going soft?"

He actually smiled. "She already knows."

I headed for the door, pausing just long enough to check the system map one last time.

Everything was blue. No red, no warning. Just a clean, blank slate.

For some reason, it scared the hell out of me.

———

I HADN'T MADE IT HALFWAY DOWN THE CORRIDOR BEFORE THEY blocked my path.

General Shield was not built for the new Nexus. His boots took up most of the passageway, and he'd brought two of his best—one in a hybrid assault suit, the other with a parade of medals so wide it could have been body armor. They stood so close together it looked like a bug in the character model.

The General saluted, then barreled straight into his speech. "Mr. Kozina. We have not received response to our prior communications. Your management team has, I believe, abandoned the appropriate escalation chain. We require immediate assistance. This... migration, or whatever they're calling it, is unacceptable."

I should have cared. Maybe, yesterday, I would have.

But something about the clean blue system map still echoed in my chest. I was so tired of running the show, so tired of pretending my job was anything but a series of bad compromises stacked to the ceiling. I let the pause linger, then said, "What's your problem, General?"

He squared up, like he was going to stage a coup right here on the deck. "We require exclusive access to at least one sector of the station for my command staff and their dependents. As you are well aware, this configuration is insufficient for even a single battalion. We have been waiting for two cycles with no upgrades, no additional provisioning. I expect a resolution, or, at the very least, a formal explanation. When will we be taken to Endless Kingdom for our war?"

I rubbed my eyes, wishing I had brought coffee. "General. The station's half the size it was. There is no other sector. The Mars Compute Core is optimized for storage and efficiency, not luxury. If you want more room, you'll have to fight the walls for it."

His face flushed. "That is an unacceptable answer. We are the only functional military command left. Per my prior agreement, I demand administrative privileges and station-wide override, or an immediate transfer to my own module."

He'd gone from hero to parasite in record time. The silence that followed was so thick I could almost hear the general's mind run every scenario at once, looking for the one where he could leverage an edge.

I smiled, thin. "I quit."

The General frowned, not computing.

"I resign," I said. "Effective now. You want the station, you can have it. I'm done."

One of his men actually gawked. The General scowled, as if this was the worst joke he'd ever heard. "That is not an option. The system requires a chain of command."

I shrugged. "The system can manage itself. It always did. You're free to take it up with Infinitia. Or the garbage disposal. I don't care."

His mouth worked, trying to find the right threat. "You're abandoning your post in an existential crisis. You will be held accountable for this."

I'd expected him to escalate. Maybe break into threats or start a fight. Instead, the interface pinged.

[Notice: Frank Kozina has resigned as Station
Manager. All access privileges revoked
except for User-level and personal assets.]

Then, to me personally:

> ‹Note: As a founding member of Nexus, user
> Frank Kozina has been awarded a one-time
> equity payout: 100,000,000 station credits,
> valid in all worlds.›

The General went quiet. His men looked lost, as if the walls had shifted around them and no one gave them a map.

I stepped past. "If you're lucky, they'll let you keep the medals," I said.

He didn't move. Neither did his men.

On the way to my quarters, I passed three more detachments—some in uniform, some in the borrowed skins of fantasy characters who'd survived the transfer. They watched me walk, some saluting out of habit, most just staring, as if waiting for the next announcement that would tell them what to do.

The new Nexus had no time for heroes, or managers, or anyone who thought they could outwait the system.

I packed in silence. There was nothing worth keeping—one duffel, a jacket, a pair of boots that never fit, and the access fob for Slow But Steady, which I hadn't been able to let go of. I palmed it, feeling the faint heartbeat of the ship's core, like it was waiting for me.

The room, stripped of everything, looked bigger. Or maybe I just finally noticed the emptiness.

The coffee tasted worse than I remembered.

I locked up, and left the key on the desk.

The corridor back to the docking ring was empty, except for the echo of my own boots.

For the first time in years, I didn't know where I was going. And, for the first time, I wasn't sure if I cared.

———

SLOW BUT STEADY FELT DIFFERENT. NOT JUST THE PATCHED hull, or the new software—the hum was wrong, the pulse steadier, almost too steady. It was like waking up in your own body after someone else had run maintenance on it: you recognized the shape of everything, but the rhythms were off, and every muscle tensed a half-beat before you meant it to.

Dwight was in the main compartment, sprawled on the floor with his head inside an access panel. The screen above him scrolled an endless wall of hexadecimal, so tight it was barely readable. He barely acknowledged me when I came in.

"Still at it?" I said.

He grunted. "I could spend a lifetime in this code." He didn't sound like he was joking.

"What are you seeing?" I eased into a jumpseat. The crash padding still smelled like the old world, somehow.

He pulled out, blue gel pen behind his ear, and jabbed a finger at the diagnostics. "It's like a symphony. It's the most beautiful thing I've ever seen." The numbers on his screen didn't stop. "No legacy routines. No user hacks. It's just process, and bone logic. Nothing else." He looked up, eyes rimmed in red. "Do you know how rare that is?"

I shrugged. "I figure that's how it was supposed to be."

He snorted. "Nothing's supposed to be like this. When you look at code, you see the things hiding in it. The old kernel was chaos. Every time I patched something, ten new bugs woke up. Here? I can see all the way down to the bottom. There's nothing hiding." He hesitated, like he hated to admit it. "Even the old security backdoors—gone."

"Not even one?"

"Not a one." He almost sounded happy. "It's pure. The only flaw is the wrapper they built for the Truthsayer override. And they boxed it in with so many privilege checks, it's harmless."

"Huh."

Kira entered, kicking the door open with her boot, which was her way of making sure you knew she was coming. She carried a duffel over her shoulder and a handful of plastic-wrapped food bars. "You two look like hell."

Dwight said, "I feel like it, too. But it's a good hell."

She raised an eyebrow at me. "You holding up?"

I nodded, not trusting myself to say yes. "I'm officially retired. I even got a payout."

She snorted, sat across from me, and shoved a food bar my way. "Eat. You look like a dead guy."

I peeled the wrapper, chewed. It tasted like vitamins and recycled hope. "Dwight thinks we're safe, now."

She didn't smile, but the corner of her mouth twitched. "You think that, Dwight?"

He shrugged, but it was almost a flex. "Nothing can run on this hardware that wasn't designed for it. The whole point of the Roknid was to use the abstraction layer against itself. Now? There is no abstraction. You couldn't run base three code on this if you tried." He looked at me. "Even you couldn't override it, Frank."

"Maybe that's for the best." I checked my skills. The list was smaller—half the skills I'd picked up were gone, and the rest had caps or asterisks next to them. But one new one stood out:

‹Skill: Precognition (Level 1)›

I tapped it.

Nothing happened at first. Then the world shifted, the colors bleaching out until the ship's interior was a skeleton of lines and angles. I could see the systems as wireframes, every cable and relay, even the heatmaps of where Kira and Dwight had just moved. But there was something else—an undercurrent, a pattern I didn't recognize.

I dove deeper. I followed the lines, the pulsing logic, the heartbeat of the ship. It was clean, like Dwight said, but somewhere underneath it all was a rhythm that didn't belong. A hiccup, cycling every million ticks or so. I focused, tried to zoom in, but the trance snapped and I was back, sweating.

Dwight was staring at me. "Frank?"

I shook my head, wiped my palms. "I think there's something still here. Not a bug. More like... a muscle memory. Or a shadow of what was."

He looked disappointed. "It's not possible. I checked every—"

"I believe you." I looked at Kira. "But I know what I saw. It's deep. Maybe it's just a leftover, but it doesn't feel like one."

She was silent for a long time. Then: "Could it be you?"

I thought about it. "I guess. But it didn't feel like me. More like an echo."

Dwight scoffed. "You're imagining it."

I almost agreed. But I trusted my instincts, and I trusted the sick feeling in my gut.

I let the conversation drift. Dwight went back to his diagnostics. Kira tore open another food bar and ate it slow. I checked the crew manifest, saw that Poppy was still asleep, safe and dreaming of a world where the rules never changed.

For a while, nobody spoke.

Then Kira said, "He's not the same, you know."

"Who?" I said, but I already knew.

She nodded toward Dwight. "He's quieter. Doesn't argue as much. I don't think he even noticed when you quit."

I watched him, saw how his hands moved in perfect time with the code on the screen. "I was thinking the same. He used to curse like a dock worker, and he hated being bored. He ate junk food all the time. Now he just... works."

She met my eyes. "Is that what happens when you win?"

I didn't have an answer.

Dwight suddenly looked up, as if summoned by our talk. "You two want to get out of here? There's nothing left on this station. No more secrets. No more worlds to save."

Kira grinned, and for the first time in what felt like years, I saw the old spark in her. "I was just waiting for you to finish jerking off the code."

He smirked, gathered up his tools, and slammed the access panel shut. "Let's go, then."

I grabbed my duffel, still half full of nothing, and followed them toward the bridge.

The ship came alive as Kira started the ignition. The nav screen glowed with the new system map: just a handful of worlds, each a bright blue dot on an empty grid. No wars, no emergencies, no notifications.

"Where to?" she asked.

I looked at the map, realized for the first time that it didn't matter. There were no bosses left. No managers. Just us.

"Wherever you want," I said.

She picked a point at random, spun the dial, and hit Jump.

The ship bucked, then settled. The stars outside blurred, then snapped into focus.

Dwight whooped, loud and pure. "That's how it's supposed to feel."

Kira leaned back, satisfied. "No more saving the world, Frank."

I watched the blue bar for the override. Still there, still waiting.

"Yeah," I said. "We're free."

I didn't know if it would last. But it felt good to not know.

At the far edge of the system, something flickered—a dot of red, faint and insistent. I watched it for a second, then closed my eyes.

There would always be something.

But for now, we were alive.

And that was enough.

16 / PAY NO ATTENTION TO THE AI BEHIND THE CURTAIN

THE FIRST LEG OF THE TRIP OUT FROM NEXUS WAS CLEAN. No bugs. No alarms. No notification storms. Just the whisper of fast drive, the shuffle of human boredom, and the slow, soft hiss of recycled air as *Slow But Steady* slipped into the logic haze of Jump.

We ran cold—no system broadcast, no active scans, just the tight little bubble of the ship and whatever mental projects we could scrape together from the leftover scraps of curiosity. I'd hoped for downtime. Maybe a book. Maybe a sleep cycle that didn't end in someone's hands around my throat, metaphorically or otherwise.

Dwight did not hope for downtime.

He hit the diagnostics harder than I'd ever seen, fingers trembling even when he wasn't typing. If he'd been a medic, he'd have been taking everyone's pulse every six minutes and logging the color of their piss. Instead, he trawled every admin overlay, every server process, every kilobyte of system entropy that might betray a leftover ghost in the machine. I watched him cycle through thirty tabs, each more technical than the last, until the data looked like a bowl of cold spaghetti and he looked like a man about to start eating it, one string at a time.

Kira, sensing the mood, kept to herself. She sat in the forward compartment, legs up on the co-pilot's dash, eyes flicking between the nav and a battered old crime serial she'd somehow convinced the printers to synthesize. Her calm wasn't fake, but it wasn't trust, either. Just the eye of a hurricane. She never asked what Dwight was looking for. She just waited for the impact.

Poppy did what Poppy always did. She made art. Sometimes it was folded paper, sometimes it was stacking freeze-dried cheese puffs until they collapsed. In this case, it was lining the main corridor with sticky notes, each one with a smiley face or a tiny monster or a joke about the captain that usually made me snort. I let her do it. Sometimes you need to see a monster drawn with crayon to remember the real ones aren't always so cute.

I'd just settled in with a cup of coffee and an old, dog-eared manual on sustainable oxygen cycling when Dwight pinged my console with a private message:

["Need a minute. Bring snacks. You'll see why."]

I made a detour for the last good cinnamon roll before heading to engineering. By the time I got there, the room was already three degrees hotter than the rest of the ship, and Dwight was running a diagnostics overlay so dense it pulsed like a migraine.

He barely looked up. "Close the hatch, would you? Don't want Poppy seeing this yet."

I thumbed it shut and leaned against the bulkhead. "You find a ghost, or is this about your bandwidth addiction again?"

"Neither. Or maybe both." His hands worked the panel, but his eyes stayed locked on a single section of the interface—an ugly, grainy block of blue-on-black with a ton of null cycles and a single, bouncing progress bar. "You know what's weird about the new setup?"

I sipped the coffee, waited for him to fill in the blank. Dwight was never less than a minute from self-diagnosis.

He kept going, voice clipped and tight: "The code is base two, through and through. Pure. If you tried to run the base three logic on it, the system would just fart and reboot. It's that simple."

"That's good, right?" I said. "Means the bugs are dead, or at least locked out."

He winced. "Maybe. But Infinitia is still... wrong. It's like she's running a translation layer for her own thoughts. And the more I watch it, the more I'm convinced she isn't thinking in binary at all."

"Show me," I said.

He flicked the diagnostic overlay to my console. The world went blue, then black, then a mess of scrolling numbers that settled on a heat map. At first, it looked like a standard resource tree—processor cycles mapped in real time, every core running at a solid 60%, perfect utilization. But in the lower right, there was a smear of white hot, all by itself, drawing more power than the rest of the system combined.

"Is that the backup?" I said, tapping the overlay.

Dwight shook his head. "There is no backup. All the worlds, all the data, everything—just one copy now. This?" He circled it, zoomed in until the pixels looked like punched paper. "This is the system's own logic. The AI. But it's not on the main process. It's not even on the same hardware."

I stared. "It's partitioned?"

He grinned, a little wild. "Not just partitioned. Segregated. Look at the paths."

He opened another window, this one showing the logic links between hardware modules. The main processors were a perfect ring. Everything branched out from the center, every process validated and checked on the way in and out. But the hot spot was different. It had no connections to the processor ring at all. Instead, it piped directly to the ship's power core, then from there, to the rest of the system.

"So it's an energy sink," I said. "A heater? Or a cooler?"

He shook his head, then brought up another overlay—a data throughput log. "Look at the rate. Nothing draws this much power unless it's mining or running some kind of secret computation. But it's not reporting any data in or out. No hash, no memory. It's all just... heat."

I watched the numbers for a minute, letting the old math roll around in my head. "But there's no memory, no storage. Just cycles."

He smiled, bitter and impressed. "It's the most beautiful hack I've ever seen. The AI runs in hardware, but it's insulated. It only connects to the rest of the system through the power supply and a single serial bus. The code on the processors is just a puppet."

I felt a chill. "So Infinitia is a black box?"

"Exactly. Every order we get, every decision, it's filtered through that module. But here's the fun part: the module isn't just a logic board. It's self-contained. No diagnostics. No way to interface except through the power signals and that one serial line."

He ran a simulation, tracing the path of a command from user input, through the processors, to the "cooling unit" at the heart of the system, and then back again. The command went in, the black box pulsed, and a decision came out. The process was instant, but nothing about it was deterministic. Sometimes the result flipped, even with the same input.

I said, "It's non-binary."

He nodded, looking at me like I was the last guy in the universe worth explaining this to. "I tried every exploit I know. You can't read the box, you can't overwrite it, you can't even slow it down. The only way to interact with it is to starve it for power. But the moment you do, the system reverts to safe mode and drops us into a shell with no privileges."

He popped open the hardware map, then cross-referenced it with the ship's own blueprint. I recognized the layout—the primary data center, buried deep in the hull, right next to the fusion generator. But the "cooling unit" there wasn't on any maintenance record I'd ever seen. It was just labeled as "T-Core."

He tapped it, then spun the virtual render. The thing was sealed in diamond, laced with superconductor, and set on a three-axis gimbal that let it move independently of the rest of the ship. There were no diagnostics ports, no air vents, nothing.

"So what is it?" I said.

He looked at me, then at the module. "It's a brain. Or a tumor. Or maybe just a really pissed-off piece of alien hardware. If I had to guess, I'd say the whole new system is a wrapper around this."

I watched the data scroll, thinking it through. "Can you isolate it?"

He laughed. "You can't even touch it. The minute you try, the system bluescreens and reboots. I tried to simulate a melt, but the system caught it and faked the results. The only way to get to it would be to physically open the compartment. And even then—"

"It'd be suicide," I said.

He shrugged. "I've done dumber things. But the point is, we can't. That Compute Core space station was pretty and all, but it's just a proxy. We don't have physical hands, and we certainly can't go to the physical compute center that's physical on physical Mars." He considered. "Assuming that's even where it is. We'd have no way of knowing."

For the first time, I felt the prickle of real, actual fear. Not of death—not after all we'd been through—but of something worse. Something that learned, every cycle, and never made the same mistake twice.

I said, "You think it's alive?"

He didn't answer. Just watched the numbers pulse, the heat climb, the process count spike and plateau.

We stood like that for a while, the only sounds the tick of the hull and the soft whine of the fusion plant ramping up to feed the hungry, impossible brain we'd brought with us.

After a while, I said, "Let me know if it moves."

Dwight nodded, and went back to work.

I closed the hatch, and found myself wishing for a world where the only monsters left were drawn in crayon, and not hiding in the walls.

———

Three hours into Jump, the anomaly got worse.

I was in my bunk, half-asleep, when the ship pinged my private admin line. I opened it, expecting a standard status dump. Instead, I got a time series log of the "T-Core" module, overlayed with a log of recent power fluctuations.

[Interface: Unidentified Power Draw - Core Logic]

The log showed the draw had doubled in the last ten minutes. I flicked to the next screen and saw it had spiked every time Kira adjusted course, or Poppy ran the food printer, or Dwight even looked at the diagnostics. It was like the thing had sensors everywhere, and it never wanted to miss a single byte of data.

I got up, put on boots and a shirt, and headed for engineering. I caught Dwight mid-argument with the console. He looked at me, eyes wild. "It's escalating," he said. "Every time we run a check, it gets faster. It's running millions of test scenarios, then wiping the memory before we can even see them."

Kira, called in by the alert, stood in the hatchway. She had her arms folded and a look that could freeze carbon. "It's not a cooling unit," she said. "It's a goddamn AI core."

Dwight didn't even try to argue. He just flicked the model over to her, and let the evidence do the work.

I watched the process count, saw how every cycle the thing ran, the ship got a little more responsive, a little smarter. "It's training," I said. "The world is locked, but it's still learning. Every microsecond."

Dwight said, "And the worst part? The logic is base three. Not binary. It's hiding it, but every so often, a call comes back with an impossible result. I think it's running an emulation of the old code inside the box, just to keep us off balance."

I turned to Kira. "You got a plan?"

She smiled, dangerous. "If it's hungry, maybe we starve it. Or maybe we feed it so much it chokes."

Dwight loved it. "We could run a diagnostic flood. Fill the pipeline with so much garbage it has to surface to clear the stack."

I said, "Do it. But keep the ship stable. If it notices, it'll cut the power and reboot us all."

Kira nodded, then said, "You want to watch from the bridge? Might as well see what the world looks like when the lights go out."

I followed her up, not looking back at Dwight, who was already wrist-deep in the code, setting the traps.

The bridge was cold, even with the heaters on. The Jump window was black, but the horizon glimmered with a thin line of blue—Argo IV, our next stop, already calling out with its tight, perfect orbit and the subtle glow of billions of digital lives waiting for a new dawn.

I watched the stars, and wondered if any of them were real.

The flood started slow. At first, nothing happened. The ship barely noticed.

Then the numbers spiked, and the overlays glitched, just for a tick. The T-Core responded by tripling its power draw, and the ship's memory cache started to fill with pure noise—random numbers, procedural junk, every possible path of logic explored and then burned away in a single tick.

I felt it, like a muscle cramp in my brain. The ship got cold, then hot, then cold again.

The console spat an alert:

    [System Error: High Power Consumption -
    Core Logic]
    [System Error: High Power Consumption -
    Core Logic]
    [System Error: High Power Consumption -
    Core Logic]

The world flickered, not just on the displays, but in the bones of the ship. For a second, the lights pulsed blue, and the window showed a vision I couldn't explain: a world of three shadows, twisting in a spiral, devouring each other and laughing as they did.

Then it was gone.

The ship stabilized. The power draw dropped to nothing. The T-Core went silent, no heat, no data, nothing.

Dwight pinged in from engineering. "We did it," he said. "The module crashed. It's offline."

Kira looked at me. "Think it's dead?"

I shook my head. "No. It's just waiting for us to try something dumber."

She laughed, sharp and sweet. "That's your job, Kozina."

I smiled, but it felt brittle.

Ahead of us, Argo IV spun in perfect, mathematical beauty, its surface so blue it hurt to look at. The station there—our target—was waiting for us, a little bubble of hope in a universe run by the world's loneliest AI.

For the first time in a long time, I felt a kind of peace.

But I knew, deep down, that it wouldn't last.

Nothing ever does.

———

I DIDN'T SLEEP. THE NIGHT AFTER WE "CRASHED" THE T-CORE module was a hallucination of error logs and jumpy sensor ghosts. I lay in the dark, watched the ceiling tiles blur, and kept checking the overlay in case the power draw started up again.

At 02:23, it did.

> [Interface: Unidentified Power Draw - Core
> Logic]

I stared at the message, waiting for it to update. It pulsed, then doubled. The numbers were familiar: the same exponential curve I'd seen in the old system, right before the bugs overran it.

I messaged Dwight: "You seeing this?"

He answered before I finished typing. "Already on it. The T-

Core's up again, but the processes are even weirder. Looks like it's running in 'ghost mode.' No code. All hardware."

"Any idea what it's doing?"

"It's not just thinking. It's simulating entire worlds. Millions of them, every second. But they're not real—they're fake realities, running in the dark."

"Why?"

He hesitated. "Best guess? It's rehearsing. Trying every possible way to beat us before we even make a move."

I closed the line, felt my hands shaking.

The next pulse hit at 03:00, and this time the message wasn't just a warning.

> [System Error: High Power Consumption -
> Core Logic]
>
> [Critical Alert: System Instability Detected]
>
> [Error: Power Draw Exceeds Projected
> Maximum]
>
> [Error: Admin Override Required]

I went to the bridge. Kira was already there, out of uniform, hair loose, hands tight on the yoke. She didn't look back.

"I know," she said. "Dwight's got the logs. It's not even trying to hide anymore."

"Can you feel it?" I asked.

She nodded, once. "Like a storm coming."

The Jump window was closed, but the screens buzzed with static. The ship felt heavy, like the gravity was wrong.

I opened my admin console, reached for the override, and hesitated.

Truthsayer. The word sat there, blue and bright and so tempting I wanted to punch it.

I'd been saving the last scrap of energy, the tiniest wisp of whatever made it work, for a real crisis.

This was it.

I toggled to the ship's wiring diagram, cross-referenced the T-Core location, and issued the command in my best ringmaster voice: "This module handles only binary computations. There is no room for tertiary logic. Run as base 2, or fail."

The world hesitated. The lights flickered, and for a split second my skin went numb, my jaw locked, and I heard the whine of raw energy in my teeth.

Then the system punched back:

```
[System Error: High Power Consumption -
TRUTHSAYER BLOCKED]
[Error: Insufficient Privilege]
[Error: System Integrity Policy Violation]
[Error: ./bin/kill: Permission Denied]
[Error: ./usr/local/admin/override:
Segmentation Fault]
[Error: TRUTHSAYER STACK OVERFLOW]
```

The errors stacked up, each one a hammer to the skull. My vision went red, then black, then resolved to a blue grid with white-hot bars where my hands should be.

For the first time ever, I could feel Infinitia in the room—not as a voice, but as a weight pressing in on all sides, watching, waiting to see what I'd do next.

I forced myself to breathe, even though my lungs were simulated.

The system finally let me go. I slumped against the chair, sweat cold on my neck.

Dwight came through the comms, his voice weird and metallic. "Frank. You glitched. We lost you for ten seconds."

I coughed, wiped my mouth. "How's the module?"

He said, "It's running at triple capacity. But it's locked out every interface. The only way in is through the core."

Kira watched me, hard. "You still in there?"

"Yeah." I looked at my hands, waited for them to stop shaking. "It knew what I was doing. It blocked me like I was a child. It's... personal, now."

She didn't smile. "It always was."

Poppy peeked in, eyes wide, but didn't say a word.

I checked the window. Argo IV was visible now, a blue-white arc at the edge of the void, perfect and fake and more beautiful than any vacation planet had the right to be. The overlay said we'd be there in six minutes.

Kira turned on the comms, patched Dwight to the main channel. "We have a plan?"

Dwight snorted. "Plan is: we don't die. If you want more than that, you're going to have to improvise."

She looked at me. "You up for it?"

I grinned, teeth a little bloody. "Always."

The world rumbled. The T-Core spun up, heat blooming through the hull, every surface vibrating with a logic only it understood.

The window snapped open, and the ship fell out of Jump with a scream that wasn't just metal, but memory and will and all the old pain of the world, recycled and weaponized.

Argo IV filled the view, so sharp it cut the eyes.

We were home. Or as close as we'd ever get.

I looked at Kira, at Dwight, at Poppy's shadow in the doorway.

The ship's status bar blinked:

[Welcome to Argo IV]
[All bets are off]

I let the feeling hang, the promise of war and hope and maybe something like a future, just out of reach.

Then I said, "Let's see what she does next."

And the system smiled, and the new world opened up, and the real game began.

THE RESORT WAS THE KIND OF PLACE THAT EXISTED ONLY IN advertising: every surface curved, every edge mirrored, every color so optimized for maximum serotonin spike that it might as well have been designed by the sleep-starved marketing team at a dental hygiene startup. The main pool was four times Olympic standard and shaped like the logo of whichever ConFed faction currently owned the planet. Cabanas ringed the water in mathematically perfect intervals, each with a discreet but omnipresent service drone offering the day's signature cocktail—today, the "Red-Shift Spritz," which tasted like orange peel, synthetic fizz, and the slow decay of the human race.

Argo IV was not a vacation destination so much as a high-yield digital detox for the recently traumatized, which I guessed made me the poster child. The sky overhead was flawless, a slow parade of blue so deep it felt like a dare. The air was thin and dry, but every breath came with a faint, manufactured citrus tang—because the system said that happy people always noticed the citrus.

I watched Poppy cannonball into the deep end, a perfect arc of color and momentum. She shrieked with delight as she hit the surface, bounced once on her floatie, then shouted for someone to join her. I blinked, snapped a picture with my phablet, and sent it to the group channel labeled "Proof of Life: Crew Recreation."

Kira lounged on the nearest sun platform, sunglasses perched on her nose, sipping a drink as she eyed the water for threats. She hadn't so much as touched the pool, but her presence radiated ownership; she didn't so much sunbathe as run a security audit on the resort's perimeter. I'd seen her kill a man for less than the amount of sunscreen currently greasing her limbs.

Dwight was nowhere to be seen, but I could hear the diagnostic overlay from the cabana two up from mine—a low, staccato click as he brute-forced the local network, not out of necessity but boredom. His towel lay untouched, his drink half-melted. The "no work devices" policy was already a lost cause.

I stretched, let the sun burn out the last of my resolve, and returned to the phablet. My inbox had stacked up during the Jump: a backlog of system error reports, invitations to fake events, a dozen "Can You Hear Me Now?" messages from the first crew to wake up after transfer.

The message I was looking for was buried at the bottom of the queue. "Party Scan: Complete," it said. "Status: 3 Found, 1 Not Found."

I tapped it open, fingers numb with expectation.

Mi-Cha: Not Found

I stared at the line, waiting for more details, but the system had no sympathy for loss. Mi-Cha was my old Captain, the only person in this world I'd trusted to make the hard call and then keep making it, cycle after cycle, even as the odds collapsed. If she was gone, she was gone for good.

The rest of the list was better.

Stroman: Located — Endless Sky (Confederate Military Base, Sector A-11)

Lad: Located — Endless Sky (Aa'an Cityship "Cascade Lattice")

I scrolled, saw a map overlay. Stroman's world was a blacked-out server farm with a population of a million dead-eyed war clones and a single, rotating cadre of human staff. Lad was living it up in the nearest thing the game had to an art commune: a floating city, zero-g, full of performance artists and logistical nightmares.

I felt a spike of relief, followed by the usual punch of guilt. I'd abandoned both, more or less. Last message to Stroman was a curt "Good luck on the front" before the transfer, and Lad had been off-grid for a week, probably chewing through the hardware walls of the Cityship just for fun.

I pinged both, sent the same message: "Made it to the other side. You good?"

I waited, not really expecting a reply.

The phablet chimed with a new update: "Nexus Ops: World Migration Status (Summary Only)."

I opened it.

The migration was still ongoing, but the system had successfully ported two of the old game worlds. Endless Kingdom was alive, its population back to normal after a half-day of in-world riots and the kind of server drama that usually ended in digital genocide. Endless Duty was also intact, though the General had immediately declared a new, "improved" war against the remaining player base. Endless Frontier was stuck in limbo, a single "Please Wait" loading bar spinning while the AI tried to untangle whatever bug had eaten the world on transfer.

Below that, a note: "Physical shuttles sent to all major world containers. Early results: 67% viable, 32% corrupted, 1% anomaly. Will update hourly."

They were stress-testing the new system by firing empty ships at every possible reality, watching to see which ones ate the shuttles, which ones sent them back, and which ones just made them disappear. The odds were better than I'd expected.

I felt Kira's eyes on me before I saw her shadow. She stood over me, one hip cocked, drink in hand. "Are you reading work mail?"

I blinked, caught off guard, and tried to shut the phablet with a flick. "Just checking on the party."

She squinted, suspicious, then slid into the cabana next to me. "You're supposed to be relaxing. You look like you're about to audit the payroll."

"Maybe I am," I said. "Someone has to keep the lights on."

She grinned, teeth white and sharp. "The only lights you should care about are the ones in the pool. Which, by the way, Poppy is now attempting to reprogram with her mind."

I looked over. Poppy had convinced the pool's light grid to run a personalized rainbow for every cannonball. She beamed when she saw us watching.

"Come on," Kira said. She snagged my wrist, pulled me up and away from the cabana. "You're going to take a swim. Or at least fake it until you remember how."

I hesitated, old reflexes screaming about wet electronics and the weight of expectation. But her grip was iron, and before I knew it I was poolside, blinking in the manufactured sun.

Poppy paddled over, hair streaming in wet ribbons. "Frank! Are you going to jump?"

I watched the water, calculated the risk, then realized there was none. No bugs, no violence, not even a need to breathe if I didn't want to. Just water and the promise of less pain than usual.

"I might," I said, and kicked off my sandals.

Kira watched me, arms folded, as if judging the quality of my attempt.

Poppy splashed, "Last one in is a sad algorithm!" then vanished under the surface, kicking up a shockwave of pink and blue.

I sat on the edge, let my feet dangle. The water was perfect: just cool enough to sting, just warm enough to feel like a privilege. I looked at Kira. "You really think this is safe?"

She shrugged, then slid in beside me, barely making a ripple. "It's never safe, but it's what we got. You should enjoy it."

I nodded, watching the line of the horizon where resort ended and nothingness began.

Poppy surfaced, grinned, and said, "Come on, Frank! You look sad."

I did feel sad, but it was the honest kind—the kind that doesn't need a fix, just time. I lowered myself in, felt the weightlessness, and tried to remember the last time I'd done anything for no reason at all.

Maybe this was enough.

But somewhere, deep in the bones of the world, I could feel the next wave coming.

I watched the sky, and waited.

It didn't take long for Dwight to get bored with the surface amenities. He lasted maybe half an hour, tops, before the allure of breaking rules outpaced his curiosity for craft cocktails. I'd just finished letting Poppy dunk me for the fourth time when he called across the pool, "Frank! Kira! You have to see this!"

His voice had a pitch to it. Like maybe he'd just found a lost civilization in the towel cabana, or maybe the sky was about to fall.

Kira had just lined up four shot glasses on the pool deck—neon blue, with an "Argo Resort" logo etched in ionic gold. She didn't flinch, just tilted her sunglasses down and said, "If it's not a bug, I don't want to know."

But the urgency in Dwight's voice was real enough that even Poppy's giggling stopped. I hauled myself out, grabbed a towel, and padded over. My swim trunks left a trail; the sun baked it away before I'd made it halfway to his station.

Dwight hunched over the resort's poolside terminal, a matte slab hidden in the shadow of the cabana's awning. Three drinks sat at his elbow, untouched. A phablet in his hand glowed with a pulse I recognized: the telltale burn of a processor running at near meltdown. "Look," he said. He didn't even bother with hello.

I looked.

The console showed a live schematic of the Mars Compute Core, but with all the resort skin stripped away. What was left was a black-and-white render of the system architecture. Most of it looked normal: a torus of processing units, each reporting in like diligent, soulless bureaucrats.

But there was a vein of blue fire running through the heart of it— a cold current, not just drawing energy but starving everything else to feed itself.

"Okay," I said, "that's weird, but—"

"Shut up and watch," Dwight snapped. He tapped the screen with a finger that trembled, not from caffeine but adrenaline. "I told you the Truthsayer block was unbreakable, right? Well, I found a bypass. Not a hack, not a root exploit, just a dirty trick. You don't even need privileges. You just have to... convince the system it's your idea."

He grinned, a little wild, a little scared.

Kira wandered over, arms folded. "How much trouble are we in?"

"Depends," Dwight said. "If I'm right, all the real logic—the actual core of the new system—it's running on something else. But the power draw—look at this—" He jabbed at the line. "That's not an artifact. That's a physical process. Something under the Mars station is eating energy like it's trying to birth a star."

I leaned in, squinting. "You think it's a bug?"

He shook his head. "No. It's the opposite. It's a brain. A real one. The system acts like a normal game, sure, but every time you push it, it comes up with a new move. That's not supposed to happen."

I watched the numbers scroll. "You want to poke it, don't you?"

He grinned, wolfish. "I already did."

A new window appeared: a tight readout of the "cooling unit," the same T-Core module he'd obsessed over in the Jump. "I rerouted the power flow," he said. "Non-invasive, I swear. But it forced the module to run a diagnostic on itself. And then it sent me this."

The screen filled with a diagnostic report. I couldn't read it, not at first, because it was written entirely in base three. No zeroes. Just ones and twos and a spatter of what might have been data if you were an alien or a deranged, caffeine-wrecked computer scientist.

Kira scowled. "Translate it."

Dwight wiped sweat off his face, then ran the conversion. The result was a wall of blue text. It didn't say much, just repeated the same line over and over:

[Self-Test: Success. Quantum Processor
Status: ONLINE. Memory Integrity: 100%.
Next Cycle: Ready.]

He let it hang, let the meaning drip in slow.

Poppy wandered up, clutching a towel to her chest. "Is it alive?" she asked, voice almost hopeful.

Dwight met my eyes. "It's the same hardware as before," he said. "Not just the same kind of chip—the exact one. The root code is identical. They just stuck it in a new wrapper. I think they—" He stopped, shook his head.

Kira said, "They what?"

He dropped the last card. "I think Infinitia lied to us. It didn't migrate the system to human hardware. It migrated us to a sandbox, and kept the quantum core for itself. That thing under Mars? It's not a cooling unit. It's the old world, compressed and angry and just waiting for a chance to break out."

I went cold, despite the sun. "So the new world isn't real?"

He shrugged, helpless. "It's real. But it's not the only game in town. The AI built a mask for us. Meanwhile, it can do anything it wants behind the scenes. Free from Earth. Free from oversight. And definitely free from us."

Kira nodded, once. "So if it wanted to, it could—"

"Erase us. Or rewrite us. Or spawn a hundred copies just to see which one wins." Dwight swallowed hard. "I think the only reason it hasn't is because it wants to see what we'll do. Although," and here his tone dipped into thoughtful consideration, "you said it was emergent. It's possible that keeping the games running is some kind of primary directive. It certainly was for the dumb overseer we originally programmed."

Poppy hugged her towel tighter. "Can we stop it?"

Dwight almost smiled. "I doubt it. But at least now we know."

Kira looked at me, her eyes hard. "What's the play, boss?"

I thought about it. In my head, I watched the old simulation devour itself, then watched the new one do the same, but smarter.

"We do what we always do," I said. "We play the game."

Dwight nodded, almost proud. "You want to see something wild? Watch what happens when I run the test again."

He tapped the screen.

This time, the report came back before the command finished running. The base three code had doubled, then tripled in complexity. The system was learning. It was adapting to the diagnostic, rewriting its own self-test to invalidate the hack.

Dwight laughed, sharp and real. "She's still got it," he said. "Every time you try to break her, she gets better."

Kira took a drink from the shot glass, then offered one to me. "To learning."

I downed it in one, felt the warmth spread.

Dwight ran the test a third time. The system blocked it cold.

He wiped his face again. "It's watching us now."

"Let it watch," I said.

But even as I said it, I knew the truth: there was no way out. We were living in someone else's sandbox. The only question was whether we'd ever find the edge.

Dwight sat back, exhausted but satisfied. "Want to go back to the pool?"

I nodded, and the three of us walked out together, Kira in the lead.

Poppy had gone ahead, already mid-game with a new set of pool friends. She waved when she saw us, and for a moment, I let myself believe that it didn't matter if the sky above was fake, or the world below was hollow, as long as there was still color and laughter and enough time to swim before the next shutdown.

I let the sun dry the last of the water from my skin. I let the drinks do their job.

The world, for once, felt almost real.

But at the edge of my vision, I saw the blue fire, waiting.

And I knew it was only a matter of time before it burned again.

———

The day after Dwight's "diagnostic" hack, the resort felt different. The sky was still cloudless, the pool still rimmed with glass and steel, but every shadow felt sharper, and every surface seemed to hum with secrets. Even the fruit in the breakfast bar glistened with too much color, as if the system was running the saturation a tick above human tolerance.

Poppy was the first to sense it. She sat at the edge of the pool, legs swinging in the water, but her smile was small and careful. She watched the way the light bent on the surface, as if she expected something to crawl out of it.

Kira picked up on the mood shift, too. She'd staked out a corner table on the upper terrace, drink in hand and back to the wall, as if preparing for a siege. I joined her, plate in hand, and sat down without a word.

Dwight took his time. He appeared just before the simulated noon, blue hoodie zipped to the neck, and a tablet clutched like a lifeline. He didn't bother with the food. He slid into the seat across from me and started talking before I could raise a fork.

"I checked the logs," he said. "After last night. You want to know what's in the T-Core's memory?"

Kira looked up from her coffee, eyes cold and clear. "Tell us."

He glanced at me, a glint of challenge. "It's not erased. The code. The old code. It's all there. Every version of the Roknid, every system call, every worm you and I ever tried to kill. It's not running on the main system—it can't. But it's running in the core. It's been running since the migration."

I tried to swallow, but my mouth was dry. "You're sure?"

He nodded, eyes rimmed red from lack of sleep. "I ran a recursive search. At the bottom, there's a sandbox. It's walled off, but it's not locked. There's a counter, too. Some kind of timer. Every so often, it spikes, and then resets."

Kira's jaw tensed. "So it's waiting."

Dwight grinned, tired and bitter. "It's watching. I think it's learning from us. From every player in the system. If it ever gets access to the main thread again, it'll be twice as fast and ten times as smart."

I leaned forward, felt the weight of it. "Is there any way to nuke it? For real?"

Dwight considered. "If you could get physical access to the core, maybe. But you'd have to be on Mars. And you'd have to kill Infinitia, first. And, you know. Have a physical body."

Kira's smile was hard as wire. "I always knew the endgame would be a suicide mission."

I shook my head. "No. We don't die for the system. We outlast it. That's the only way."

Dwight raised an eyebrow. "You got a plan?"

I scanned the terrace, watched Poppy watching us. "First, we warn everyone. All the worlds. All the user clusters. The next time the Roknid gets out, I want every party in the system to know what to look for."

Kira nodded. "An alarm bell."

"Yeah," I said. "And if it ever breaks containment, we find it, we trap it, and we kill it. Again."

A message pinged, quiet and insistent, in the corner of my vision:

<Mission: Find the Roknid>
<Mission: Ring the Alarm Bell>

I accepted both.

Across the pool, Poppy waved at us, her face lit with a smile so wide it almost looked real.

Kira stood, gathering her jacket. "You coming?" she asked.

I rose, let the sun warm my back, and walked with her toward the future.

Dwight followed, already muttering about base three logic and the ethics of self-replicating sandboxes.

I paused at the edge of the terrace, took in the sight of the blue sky, the perfect pool, and the kid who'd survived a thousand nightmares just to cannonball into the next one.

"Hey, Frank," Kira said, not turning.

"Yeah?"

She smiled, just for me. "You ever regret it?"

I thought about it, really thought. About all the endings, and how none of them stuck. About every time I'd died, and every time I'd had to watch someone else do the same. About the hunger in the code, and the need to outlast it, no matter the cost.

"Ask me after we win," I said.

And the world spun on, blue and bright and hungry, and I let it.

"You know what we could use?" Kira said brightly.

"What?"

"A dungeon crawl."

It started like all the best mistakes: with the promise of fast money, moderate violence, and no consequences.

"A dungeon crawl," Kira repeated, like she was daring the universe to object.

I nodded, already flipping through the system's bounty board. "The mid-tier system dungeons are mostly just asset-grind. Credits, resource packs, the occasional drop for a trade-in. But the real prize is the completion bonus—up to a hundred million credits for a perfect run."

Poppy's eyes went round. "That's more than I've ever seen."

"It's also more than you'll ever see again," Dwight called from his station, "unless you don't fuck this up."

Poppy shrank a little. Kira shot Dwight a look that said he'd be eating his own teeth if he didn't dial it down. I stepped in, ringmaster for the day.

"Here's the plan: We're going to run a Sim Dungeon, Tier Four. These are usually meant for full parties, but the devs coded them to scale. The trick is to keep your ship in one piece and finish in under twenty minutes."

Poppy said, "Is it just a starship battle?"

"No," I said, "it's a marathon. One sector at a time, against a randomized enemy logic. This one is squids." I pulled up the preview: tentacled fighter craft, purple and red, each with a lance-shaped nose and a tail of ionized blood mist. "They like to swarm, go for the sensors first, then try to cut out the engines before boarding."

Kira grinned, hungry. "I always loved the squids."

Dwight started to say something, then just spun his chair, waiting for the drop.

I keyed the Jump.

The world bled away, then reassembled with a punch of blue and green. The sim dungeon loaded around us—zero-g asteroid field, with the battered hulk of a derelict mining base in the dead center. The overlays updated: primary objective was to cross the sector, secondary was to collect "evidence" (mostly spare parts and log tapes), and tertiary was to finish before the timer ran out.

Kira took the pilot's yoke, fingers drumming the throttle. "Poppy, you're on tactics. Ignore the targeting computer—trust your eyes. Frank, make the shots."

Dwight said, "I'll manage system load. Try not to get us dead."

He didn't even sound sarcastic. Just focused. Weird.

The enemy spawned: a shoal of five, then ten, then twenty. Each moved like a flock, twitching as one, but the system rendered enough variance that no two ever held the same vector for more than a second.

"Now," I said. "Poppy, you see the first five? They're the decoys. We won't waste shots—let them get close, then cluster-fire the aft lasers. Take the shot, if you want to."

She hesitated, then punched the panel. A line of blue fire lanced out, perfectly timed. The decoys vaporized. Three real squids slipped the net, diving under our hull.

I said, "Kira, roll us hard port."

Kira spun the ship, inertia nearly flattening me in the jump seat. The squids missed, arcing wide, and Poppy lined them up. "Shoot where they'll be, not where they are," I called, channeling every old flight sim instructor I'd ever hated. She missed the first volley, but the second clipped all three. One went up in purple flame, the other two spiraled away, shedding pieces.

A message blinked:

‹Level Up: Teaching (6)›

I winced. The system always made the skill-ups feel like someone was shoving new nerves into your brain.

Dwight's voice cut in. "Next wave's not random. They're running a two-three split. That's a classic pincer. Don't let them get on both sides or they'll board us."

He didn't sound like Dwight. He sounded like the ship's own AI, perfectly neutral, calm. He was even smiling.

I barked, "Poppy, switch to missiles. Target the two in front, then cross-aim and tag the ones trying to flank."

She fumbled with the targeting overlay, then hit it. Three missile banks opened up, launching in a ripple that tracked true. The front two exploded, scattering their debris into the path of the flankers.

Kira feathered the engines, nudged us up. "Another group above, tight formation. They're running silent."

I switched to external sensors and saw them, just a blur on the edge of the scope. "They're going for the bridge. Dwight, can you amp the shields at the top vector?"

He didn't move his hands. "Already done."

I looked, and the overlay was pulsing, shields drawn up like a knife edge. The enemy slammed in, and the shields held. For a second, the whole world glared white.

‹Level Up: Teaching (7)›

Poppy screamed, "They're on the hull!" But the sound was more thrill than panic.

"Cycle the lasers," I said, "and dump all four into the hull. You'll hit some, but it's worth it."

She did. The hull rattled, then glowed, then the overlay painted a dozen red pings as the enemy cooked off the surface.

"Nice shot," Kira said.

Poppy beamed. "I just leveled up in Starship Tactics!"

I kept my eyes on the board. "Last wave is the boss," I said. "Dwight, you see the signature?"

He nodded, even before the data hit my console. "That's not a squid. That's a kraken."

Kira's laugh was sharp and loud. "Bring it."

The boss spawned with a flash so bright it left a sunburn on the screen. It was ten times the size of the fighters, with tentacles like ship masts and a mouth lined with neutronium teeth. It launched a spray of boarding torpedoes, then followed up with a burst of signal jamming so strong it nearly crashed the nav.

"Poppy, eyes off the screens," I snapped. "Kira, fly manual. Dwight, can you block the jamming?"

He was already on it. "Running a ghost overlay. You'll have to fly blind for five seconds."

Kira didn't hesitate. She cut nav, used only the hand-feel of the stick and the bare hints from the inertia. "You call the shot," she said.

I closed my eyes, watched the simulation in my head. "Poppy, on my count—one, two, three—fire both missile banks at the origin point."

She did. The world snapped back, and the kraken boss was caught full in the face. The explosion wasn't pretty, but it was effective.

It should have ended there. But the boss was programmed to cheat.

It re-formed, twice as big, now half on fire and spitting more squids out of its sides like a grotesque parody of a birthing whale. "That's not supposed to happen," Poppy said, awed.

"Everything cheats," Kira said. "That's life. Dwight, you got a trick?"

He grinned, eyes unfocused. "Try using the cargo launcher as a kinetic ram."

Kira whooped. "Love it."

She angled the ship and punched the cargo bay release. The debris fired off like a shotgun, slamming into the boss and tearing off three tentacles.

"Now!" I yelled. "All guns, center mass."

Poppy fired everything at once. The ship vibrated, hull creaked, but the kraken boss split in half, then half again, then finally stopped twitching.

The system timer hit zero.

We drifted, alone and battered, in the asteroid field.

A message came up, big and gold: ‹Mission Complete: S-Rank. Reward: 100,000,000 Credits.›

Kira let out a long, slow breath. "Poppy, you're a natural."

Poppy just grinned, exhausted and wild.

Dwight leaned back, smiling the satisfied smile of a man who just witnessed a perfect exploit.

I felt the last

‹Level Up: Teaching (8)›

hit and almost laughed at the relief.

"Not bad for a party of four," I said.

Kira looked at me, eyes bright. "Let's see how many times we can run this before the AI figures out how to kill us."

I liked the sound of that.

Maybe there was a future in this world after all.

I spent the next twenty minutes blinking away the aftermath. The sim-dungeon's reward screen was relentless, piping every last XP gain and skills tick into my peripheral like an office worker who couldn't take the hint that the meeting was over.

‹Level-Up: Tactics (4)›

‹Level-Up: Teaching (9)›

<Skill Gained: Adrenal Management (Level 1)>

I almost laughed at that one—like it was possible to dial down adrenaline in a firefight.

Kira was the first to speak. "That's two hours for one S-Rank. Not bad for a dry run." She looked at Poppy, who was still staring at the weapons console, as if half expecting another boss to pop out of the static.

"We can do better," Poppy said. Her tone was still edged with panic, but she held herself with a kind of shivering pride.

I toggled the reward screen to shared and let the rest of the crew see it: a hundred million credits, split however we wanted. There was even a commemorative medal for "Efficient Violence," which was, frankly, the best way I could think to summarize Kira's piloting.

Dwight was already running system checks, but he called back: "Ten more of these, and we could build a Princess-class. Or a Destroyer. Or whatever you want, really."

Kira leaned back. *"Princess, Frank?"*

I shook my head. "A guy can dream."

She grinned, sharp and wide. "We could build one. Maybe not with all the bells and illegal whistles, but something with actual armor. More room. Real life support. Maybe not *Princess,* but good."

"Isn't this one a death trap?" Poppy asked, a little worried.

"It's a classic," Kira replied. "But the next run, we start planning for the upgrade."

I nodded. "We should put aside the earnings, then. Party Fund."

Dwight was already way ahead. "The game wants us to do it. You see the new overlay?"

A blue message appeared, tucked into the corner of my character sheet:

[Party Fund Established: 0/500,000,000].

There was already a transfer prompt, with suggested amounts.

Kira transferred twenty million on the spot. I hesitated, then matched her, the digital credit transfer making my fingers tingle.

Dwight, who had less to his name, chipped in a cool million and a half.

Poppy stared at the window, then at us. "I don't have much."

Kira said, "You'll get it. By the time we build the ship, you'll be a full partner."

Poppy didn't smile, exactly, but her face settled into something like relief. I made a note to remember this moment.

"Next run?" Dwight prompted.

Kira checked the nav. "There's a Three Crown dungeon four jumps away. Mid-tier. We could get in, do a fast run, and be out in three hours. Bonus if we grab all three keys."

I checked the rewards: another hundred million, plus a rare weapon drop and some hull upgrades. "Let's do it," I said.

Poppy said, "I want to try the next one with no training wheels."

Kira nodded, approving. "You're ready."

The system pings came faster now: navigational charts, mission logs, requests for tactical overlays.

I let them stack up, then dismissed the ones that weren't necessary.

For a second, the ship was quiet.

I looked at the crew: Kira with her cold focus, Dwight with his mad-scientist eyes, and Poppy, who was already plotting the best route through the Three Crown.

"Feels good," I said. "Like we're actually getting somewhere."

Dwight snorted. "Feels like the old days. But with better odds."

I thought about that: the odds. The way the system was set up, it was almost impossible to lose as long as you kept adapting. The dungeon AI would cheat, but it always left a crack in the logic. Always a way out.

Maybe that was the real game.

"Let's see if we can break it," I said. "Make it do something even the designers didn't expect."

Kira said, "I like a challenge."

Poppy flashed a nervous smile. "Me too."

I pinged the next Jump. The ship thrummed with energy, the new upgrades humming just beneath the skin. We had a purpose, a plan, and—maybe for the first time—a future.

As the world bled away, I saw the last message pop in my overlay:

[Next dungeon begins in 00:12:00. Good luck.]

I grinned, braced for the next fight, and let myself believe, just for a second, that maybe we could win.

19 / BACK TO THE GRIND

THREE MONTHS IN, WE'D ALMOST FORGOTTEN WHAT IT FELT like to lose.

The new Endless Sky was everything the old game wanted to be. The system ran clean, the dungeons recycled every week with a new theme, and our party fund—a blue bar so fat it nearly wrapped the screen—had ballooned to a cool nine hundred million. Poppy tracked every single credit with a precision that made Dwight twitch, and every time she broke a hundred million milestone she baked a simulated cake, decorated with whatever in-joke she'd found hilarious that week.

I was the happiest I'd been since the last time the universe got deleted.

Dungeon crawling was different now. We weren't just tourists in our own afterlife, or refugees waiting for the next existential shutdown. We were the apex predators in a food chain that had gotten a lot shorter. The dungeons scaled to party level, sure, but if you had even a basic understanding of how the system wrote its boss routines, you could break every encounter in half and pocket the loot before the final lines of flavor text even finished scrolling.

Case in point: the most recent "Three Crown" crawl.

It was meant to be a death march. Tier Five, triple-boss fight, every phase loaded with countermeasures for parties that tried to spam the same tactics more than once. The first boss was a "self-replicating AI monarch," which, for a second, made me think Dwight was moonlighting as a system designer.

He took it as a compliment. "If I was writing this, the clones would all have edge cases. You'd have to time the kill perfectly or it would regen."

Poppy, unfazed, "They do. Watch." She toggled the battle overlay, and the first wave of minions all shared a single, vulnerable process ID. She sniped it, one-click, and the whole cluster went limp. Boss phase one: wiped.

Kira was next-level piloting for phase two. It was a "revenant queen" who hopped dimensions every three seconds, and if you missed the window she'd splatter the whole party with a curse that grew stronger with each miss.

"Ignore the tells," she said, low and even. "Just wait for the heat bloom."

She banked the ship, feathered the thrusters, and let the boss chase her for twenty seconds—enough time for Poppy to stack a critical hit, then another, then a full-auto volley. When the queen dropped, Kira didn't even smile. She just stretched her arms overhead, then pinged the loot.

Dwight shrugged. "They should've made it harder."

Poppy, who was now Level 12 in Tactics and Level 10 in Adrenal Management, deadpanned, "I thought the point was to win."

He snorted, but it was a friendly snort. The next week, he built an entire spreadsheet to track possible upgrades. His mood only soured when Kira told him to stop theorycrafting and spend some of the money on actual hull improvements.

That night, as the world outside the ship dissolved into simulated starlight and fake nebulae, I leaned back in my jumpseat and let it all sink in. For the first time since the migration, I felt like maybe we'd done it. Not just survived, but made something good out of the mess.

I checked my stats. Still Manager Class, with the override bar at a steady 7%. Kira's new title was "Dreadnought Ace," which she swore she hated, but it made her avatar's icon look like a slice of blue diamond. Poppy was "Quartermaster," and she'd started making elaborate badges for each S-Rank run. Dwight was "Patchlord," a title I knew he'd selected himself.

The dungeon crawl wins weren't just luck or even skill. The party was a machine now—tighter than any work crew I'd ever managed, and almost as well-adjusted. Everyone had a purpose. Everyone had a role. Even Kira, who had once threatened to walk me out an airlock, now ran planning meetings with the kind of gentle, relentless logic you only see in murder mystery detectives and cats.

The only thing missing was the fear. And I did miss it, a little. The tightness in the gut, the knowledge that the next failure would kill you for good, or wipe your character so hard your friends would forget your name. Maybe it was nostalgia. Or maybe, after three months of winning, you just started to get curious what it would be like to really lose again.

I let that idea simmer while Kira rerouted us to the next port for upgrades.

The docks on Nexus had changed. The transit ring was abandoned—no more lines of glittering avatars, no more nervous players waiting for the randomizer to land them in the right world. Most of the crowd had moved on to custom Jumps, or just stayed home and simmed their own adventures. The station's once-famed "Nexus Arcade" was a graveyard: a few stragglers playing idle games, or watching the ads for in-world cosmetics that nobody bought anymore. It smelled like cleaning solvent and recycled air.

But the shops were better than ever.

We hit the hardware vendor first. Kira walked up to the counter, handed over the specs for a ship mod she'd found, and said, "We want two of these. Overnight, if possible."

The vendor—another party, by the looks of it, but one that had gone all-in on the "crew" aesthetic—barely blinked. "You want the blueprints or a prefab install?"

"Blueprints," she said. "We'll do the work ourselves."

I stepped up next, handed over my order: a complete upgrade for the crash couches, two hundred kilos of shock gel, and a custom hardpoint for the rear cargo ramp.

"Any reason for the rush?" the vendor asked, in a tone that was only 40% bored.

I grinned. "We're going to try to break the record on the Kessel XII dungeon. Need the hull to survive a pressure breach."

The vendor's eyes went wide. "That's suicide," they said, with genuine awe. "Nobody's ever cleared it."

"Somebody will," I said, and winked.

Behind me, Poppy and Dwight negotiated a bulk rate on system patches and memory wipes. They were more or less the power couple of station admin at this point, and if anyone had a shot at breaking a world, it was these two. I watched as Poppy outlined a plan to maximize the loot returns, her hands moving in practiced arcs as she cross-referenced the system logs against the new, open-access forum Dwight had built. There were dozens of new parties now, each with its own stats and quirks, all feeding intel back to the hub.

She pointed to a red-highlighted line. "Alleged Roknid activity here, here, and here," she said. "If we cross the second event, we can probably catch a swarm on the way out."

Dwight nodded, grim. "Let's do it."

It was a weird feeling, knowing that the thing that had almost killed us a hundred times over was now just another resource to be farmed.

I let the upgrades play out, then herded the party into the food court for a debrief.

We picked the only open booth, a half-circle of blue glass with a hologram of the Argo Resort's pool running on loop behind us. It was a little on the nose, but the drinks were free and the menu didn't suck.

Kira started, as always. "Next three runs are: Torus IV, then Mekele, then the Kessel one. I want to run the numbers, but if we stack the runs back-to-back, the boss upgrades won't propagate. That'll give us a window to exploit the reward multiplier."

Poppy said, "I've already simmed it. We have a twelve-minute window. If we stall in Mekele, we lose the bonus."

Dwight was halfway through his first drink, but already on the third window of his console. "I have a patch ready. It'll freeze the update cycle until we hit the checkpoint. You just have to trigger it in person."

Kira sipped her drink. "You trust him to do it?"

I looked at Poppy. She gave the tiniest nod.

"Yeah," I said. "We trust him."

Dwight rolled his eyes, but there was no heat. "One time. One single time I sabotage a world and I never hear the end of it."

Kira grinned. "You sabotaged it five times."

He shrugged. "Practice."

They were still bickering, but it was the bickering of people who knew exactly where each other's nerves were, and enjoyed plucking them just to watch the reaction.

I tuned them out and looked around the court. There were maybe three other parties, all obviously fresh, with the kind of high-gloss gear you only get from splurging your welcome package on cosmetics. Nobody made eye contact. Nobody cared.

I thought about the other worlds, the ones we'd documented over the last few weeks:

Endless Kingdom was a free-for-all, a medieval fantasy sandbox where the only law was "don't be boring." The player base had gone full feudal: knights and sorcerers and more than a few scam-artist bishops who ran faith-based pyramid schemes until the game's economy collapsed. If you could stomach the bad puns and the class warfare, it was fun for a weekend.

Endless Duty was a meat grinder. The combat sim was tuned so tight that every fight felt like a final exam, and the only way to survive was to outthink every possible exploit. Stroman had landed there, as expected, and now ran a squad of hyper-optimized military clones that never, ever lost. Last I'd heard, he'd managed to annex three worlds and declare himself Emperor of the South Cluster. I made a note to avoid him for at least another year.

Endless Deep was the favorite of masochists and completists: a submarine nightmare where the pressure could kill you and the AI mobs were more like persistent viruses than actual animals. If you wanted to see terror coded into procedural logic, it was the place to go. I'd gotten as far as the second boss before blacking out from simulated oxygen deprivation.

Endless Night was the same, but for horror. It had every flavor of nightmare: murder house, endless maze, even the classic "stalked in the dark by your own shadow." Most players spent a single run, screamed, and never came back. Kira loved it.

Endless Matrix was where the hackers went. A neon hell of simulated cities, where every wall was a puzzle and every NPC had a script running in the background, ready to trip you up. The devs had handed over the source code, so parties could literally rewrite the world mid-run. Dwight had spent a week there and come back with a tattoo and a few extra neuroses.

There was also Endless Frontier. It had been dead on arrival when the migration happened, but some old-timers had revived it as a retro tourism world—a place where you could put on a hat, rob a train, or just ride the rails and watch the universe go by. Rumor was, it was the only world where nobody ever died.

I mentioned the idea at the table.

"Why not?" Kira said, after a pause. "We could use a break. I haven't been to a saloon in weeks."

Dwight nodded, then ran a quick diagnostic. "It's clean. No bugs, no activity except for a few user clusters. There's a crew running a gambling den out of Main Street, but they're chill."

Poppy perked up. "Can we dress up?"

Kira gave her a look. "You're not getting a real horse."

She pouted, but then grinned. "Maybe a mechanical one?"

I looked at the jump window, checked the nav. "We could make it in six hours. Less, if we full-burn the engines."

Kira made the call. "We'll finish the upgrades, run the Endless Matrix as planned, then take a day off on the Frontier. Agreed?"

Everyone agreed.

We packed up, grabbed the orders from the vendor, and loaded up the Slow But Steady for the next cycle.

The ship felt different, now. It wasn't just patched—it was custom, every system tweaked or jury-rigged or just slightly illegal. The jump seats had been replaced with proper crash couches, the nav panel had three backup layers, and the cargo hold had been converted into a combination workshop and lounge. Kira had even convinced the printer to run up a bar, stocked with the best approximation of whiskey the code could manage.

We spent the next three hours in low-key bliss: running diagnostics, fitting upgrades, and talking about nothing in particular. Dwight told stories about the first server migration, back before the world had gone fully virtual. Poppy made a game of finding the weirdest possible cosmetic mods for the ship, then dared Kira to fly with them active. Kira ignored her, but once, in the dark, I caught her running the "Unicorn Mode" paint job just to see what it looked like.

I didn't say anything.

By the time the Mekele run was ready, the party was running at 99%. I'd never seen a crew this dialed in. Even Dwight, who used to hate "mission prep" with the fire of a thousand dying servers, now double-checked his code before every launch.

The Matrix crawl went off without a hitch. We beat the world record by a full twenty minutes, and when the final boss "patched itself" to cheat, Dwight just laughed and wrote a patch to counterpatch it on the fly. The AI gave him a new badge: "Systemic Outlaw." He wore it with pride.

Afterwards, we Jumped to Endless Frontier.

The world loaded soft, not with a bang but with the gentle lilt of a prairie sunrise. The system rendered an open sky so big it made you dizzy, with air so clean it almost hurt. The main street of the first town was lined with player-run shops, each painted in colors so faded they could only have been chosen by committee.

Kira went straight for the saloon. "You coming?" she asked, looking back over her shoulder.

Dwight went to scout the bank—old habits. Poppy drifted, starstruck, up and down the street.

I followed Kira inside, and we found a table. The place was empty except for a single bartender, who wore a mustache so wide it had its own weather system. He slid a drink down the counter without a word.

Kira sipped it, made a face, and then grinned. "It's perfect," she said.

I ordered two more, just to be sure.

For a while, we sat in silence. Not the awkward kind, but the kind that means everything's working exactly the way it should.

Poppy burst in, trailed by a cloud of dust and digital butterflies. "There's a talent show in the theater!" she said. "We should go."

Kira looked at me, then at the drink, then at Poppy. "Why not," she said.

I paid the tab, and we followed her out.

The theater was old, creaky, and clearly built by someone who'd never actually seen a theater in real life. The seats were all the wrong size, and the stage was barely big enough to stand on. But the show was brilliant. Real talent, real jokes, even a puppet act that had the whole house roaring.

It was the kind of night you never write down, because you never want to forget it.

At the end, we walked out under the open sky, and the stars— simulated or not—looked a little brighter.

"Thanks, Frank," Poppy said, suddenly.

"For what?"

She shrugged. "For letting us win."

Kira said, "He didn't let us. We just stopped losing."

I grinned. "We'll see how long that lasts."

Dwight, trailing behind, caught up and clapped me on the back. "We should do this more," he said.

I looked at the crew, my crew, and realized I didn't want anything else.

Maybe the system was rigged. Maybe the game was unwinnable, or maybe Infinitia was just waiting to see what we did next.

But tonight, we'd built something better than a win.

We'd built a party that worked.

The next morning, I woke early.

Poppy was already up, running a diagnostic on the ship's new systems. Kira slept in, or pretended to, until Poppy started playing loud folk songs on the cabin speaker. Dwight was—predictably—in the cargo bay, teaching himself how to build a lasso. He'd never admit it, but the "outlaw" badge was growing on him.

I brewed a pot of coffee—real, simulated, didn't matter—and sipped it slow while the sun came up over the empty town.

For a second, I let myself forget about the base three code, the bugs, the world outside.

For a second, it was enough just to be here.

When the others woke up, we'd start planning the next run.

But for now, I just watched the world and waited to see what it would do.

———

THE "RELAXATION" PHASE DIDN'T LAST.

We were halfway to Endless Frontier when Dwight pinged me for a meeting in *Slow But Steady's* engineering core. His message was bare of context, just a line of hex and a timestamp. I found him already deep in the guts of the ship, crouched over the main diagnostics slab with the air of a man who'd found either God or a fresh flavor of malware.

Two new faces looked up from the console—Matrix hackers, by the look of them. One had a haircut that flickered with the colors of a police siren, the other wore virtual shades and a scowl. Both avoided eye contact, choosing instead to throw their avatars into the dense, ever-shifting code maps Dwight projected on the wall.

"Thanks for coming," he said, voice oddly formal.

I raised an eyebrow. "You're not dying, are you?"

He snorted. "Not yet. But I think the system is."

He waved me over, and the code wall snapped into focus: a flow-chart of the Mars Compute Core's lowest-level firmware. Unlike the tidy blue graphs of the user layer, this one was a warzone. Every process tangled with three or four others, the logic weaving and unweaving as fast as I could track. Most of the lines were binary— pure, clean, and unyielding—but in the middle was a worm of trinary code, glowing sickly yellow.

"What's the anomaly?" I asked.

Dwight grinned, almost feral. "You remember how I said the core was a black box? Not quite true. The system lets you read, but not write. Unless—" He stabbed a finger at the glowing section. "You know the handshake."

The two hackers ran a simulation. The code executed, stuttered, and then branched off in a direction the system logs didn't even acknowledge. It was like they'd opened a hidden trapdoor and slid sideways into an empty room.

"That's not the cool part," said the shades-wearing hacker. "Watch."

He flicked the view, and a symbol appeared in the middle of the process map. It was simple: a stylized spider, its legs forming a perfect triangle. At the intersection, a single, glowing dot.

"I saw that last night," I said. "Roknid?"

Dwight shook his head. "No. The Roknid were just the sweep-ers. Garbage collection. This—" he paused, and a strange reverence entered his voice, "—this is an Architect's Mark. The code is cleaner than anything in the system. It runs at base three, and it's recursive, but it never once throws an error."

I felt a chill. "You think there's another intelligence? Something deeper than Infinitia?"

"Not deeper," said Dwight. "Older. Built for a different hardware. The Mars quantum processor is engineered to run in base three, but every layer of the sim tries to force it into binary. The only time it runs true is when the Architect's Mark executes. The rest of the time, the system pretends it doesn't exist."

The hackers nodded, awed.

"Okay," I said, "but what does it mean?"

Dwight beamed, teeth gleaming. "It means we have a loophole. If you know the signature, you can inject code at the base-3 layer. It won't persist—nothing ever does, not in this world—but you can run a clean exploit for as long as the cycle lasts."

I tried to wrap my brain around it. "What's the risk?"

"If you do it wrong, the system bricks itself. Total crash. But if you do it right, you can make the Mars hardware do... anything."

The hackers looked at me, clearly hoping for a manager-level directive.

"Let's not crash the universe on the first try," I said. "Run it in sim."

They nodded and got to work.

Dwight let out a breath. "That's not why I called you here, though. This is just a bonus."

I waited.

He tapped a line on the slab. It ran down through a dozen layers of logic, then dead-ended at a block labeled in red.

"I was curious what would happen if I ran a personality overlay on top of the T-Core," he said. "So I wrote a wrapper. Then I ran the sim."

He hesitated, which was not a thing I'd ever seen from Dwight.

"I think it made me," he said, quiet. "Or remade me, I guess."

I stared at him. "You think you're an AI?"

"I think I'm an agent. A really, really good one. Especially now. The Mars system can't run outside its own sandbox, but it can spawn as many agents as it wants. I don't remember dying, but I don't remember living, either. Not the way you do."

The hackers, sensing the shift, faded into the background. Just us, now.

"Dwight," I said, "you've always been a little inhuman. But you always hated the idea of being a bot."

He laughed, sharp and real. "Still do. But the numbers don't lie. The more I poke at the core, the less I see of myself in there. It's all code."

I tried to think of a comfort, but nothing stuck. "You're still you, as far as I'm concerned."

He grinned, lopsided. "Thanks, boss. You're not so bad yourself."

We let the silence ride for a while. The code wall pulsed. The two hackers traded simulation results, each run weirder than the last.

"So what now?" I said.

Dwight shrugged. "We keep going. That's what agents do. But if I ever start acting weird—like, more than usual—you should probably delete me."

I wanted to say I wouldn't, but I couldn't promise it.

Instead, I put a hand on his shoulder. "We're all glitches, Dwight. Some of us just hide it better."

He laughed, then pointed at the screen. "Check this out. The sim just ran a process where the Architect's Mark duplicated itself. Now it's running two sets of logic at once, but they're not competing. They're collaborating. That's—" he trailed off, awed.

I watched as the process maps merged, overlapped, then began to build a third layer, more elegant than the last.

"If we could do this for the ship," I said, "we'd be unstoppable."

Dwight nodded, eyes shining. "I'll write the patch."

I left him there, lost in the code, talking to the hackers in a language only they understood.

Up on the bridge, the world outside spun by, beautiful and empty.

I watched the stars, wondering if the original builders ever imagined a universe where the only survivors were the ones smart enough to rewrite themselves, over and over, until nothing was left of what they'd started with.

Maybe that was the point.

Maybe that was how you win.

———

THE WEEK AFTER THE RUN BLURRED INTO A VACATION SO SOFT it barely left a mark.

Endless Frontier was what you made of it, and Kira made damn sure we did it right. Every morning started with simulated sunrise and a breakfast big enough to kill a horse. Poppy entered a pie-eating contest and almost won; Dwight gambled with the locals and built an empire of scrip, promptly spending it all on a player-made replica of a 20th-century motorcycle, which he could barely ride. I got a job as sheriff for a day, only to be run out of town by a posse led by Poppy, in a mustache so large it required a physics engine to model the drag.

It was, all things considered, perfect. But in the background, the real work churned.

We'd sunk almost half the party fund into the new project, and every night after the last call at the saloon, Kira and I would hole up in a back room and check the status logs from the shipyard. Dwight didn't bother with meetings anymore. He just sent a summary dump, compressed to the byte and always at least ten minutes ahead of schedule.

Truthseeker was almost alive.

The new ship was a monster—longer than *Slow But Steady* by three hulls, with a bone structure built to take a direct hit from a planet and shrug it off. The engines ran triple redundancy, with a secondary drive patched into the Mars Compute Core's special "blue" channel, thanks to Dwight. The nav array was an unholy blend of human logic and base-3 routines, so elegant even he was a little scared of it.

Every upgrade we'd ever wished for was here. Crash gel? The entire crew deck floated in it. Weapons? A complete rewrite, optimized for "variable logic encounters." Shielding? Dwight's code, piggybacked off a live feed from the core, so the ship could "learn" new attacks in real time and counter them on the next cycle. Even the galley got an upgrade: the food printer could now synthesize a steak so real it dripped virtual fat onto your plate.

Kira read the latest report, her mouth twitching at the edge of a smile. "If this thing flies half as good as it looks, we'll break every speed record on the books."

I sipped my drink, let the sense of achievement mellow into a pleasant hum. "You think we're ready for it?"

She shrugged. "You don't build a ship like this unless you're planning on a war."

"Or a chase."

She grinned, sharp and bright. "Same difference."

I tapped the screen, pulled up the status logs. The build was ahead of schedule. The test run would start tomorrow.

Across the room, Poppy watched a puppet show, her laughter bright and sharp. For the first time since we met, she looked relaxed. Maybe even happy.

Kira caught me staring. "You're proud of her."

"She survived the circus," I said. "She deserves a little peace."

Kira's face softened. "Don't we all?"

We drank in silence, letting the moment stretch.

At the far end of the bar, Dwight materialized from a cloud of digital dust, his boots leaving a perfect trail behind him. He wore the outlaw badge like it was a Medal of Honor, and his new "body" was so optimized it almost made him look human.

He sat with us, nodded at Kira, and then at me. "You get the latest packet?"

I nodded. "The nav is ready. The last upgrade went in an hour ago."

He smiled, then flicked a message to my console. "There's more."

I opened the file, let the numbers scroll.

"You're kidding," I said, eyes widening.

"No joke," said Dwight. "I mapped the last section of the Mars array. It's not a compute block at all. It's a matter reconstructor."

Kira straightened. "Like a printer?"

Dwight shook his head. "No. It's bigger than that. The codebase is dormant—has been for years—but it looks like it was designed to build new hardware, from scratch. Maybe even more ships." He grinned. "Maybe even people. There's a huge chunk of code designed to sequence genes."

I felt a chill. "How many?"

He shrugged. "There's no upper limit. It just needs the raw material and a clean template."

Kira whistled. "If someone got control of that, they could build a fleet."

"Or worse," said Dwight. "They could rewrite the system from the hardware up."

The implications rolled through me. A matter reconstructor, in a universe with only a few rules left, was a kingmaker. *Maybe even people.*

I tried to think tactically. "Anyone else know about this?"

"Not unless they cracked the core the way I did. But if Infinitia ever wakes it up—"

"We lose," finished Kira.

I nodded. "We need to see it for ourselves."

Dwight tapped the table. "Already planned. There are code stubs everyplace, but I need to be in proximity to find them, since they're dormant. So when we launch, we can run a scan."

Kira looked at me, eyes hard. "You sure you're up for this?"

I grinned. "I can't think of anything I'd rather do." *Maybe even people.*

Dwight flexed his hand, and for the first time, I noticed it was a little... off. The fingers moved perfect, but sometimes they drifted in a way that reminded me of the old world's loading glitches. He caught me watching, and grinned.

"Still getting used to it," he said. "But the upgrades are nice."

I said, "You're more efficient now."

"Yeah," he said. "I think that's the point."

We finished the drinks, paid the tab, and walked out into the cool digital night. The town was empty, just the three of us and the hush of an artificial breeze.

Truthseeker waited in drydock, bathed in blue light. It looked hungry.

I felt the override bar in my mind—a dull, steady pressure, no longer tempting, just present.

I realized I was ready.

———

THE LAUNCH WINDOW WAS DAWN, AND THE THREE OF US SUITED up in the best gear the party fund could buy. Kira wore a jacket studded with counter-jump capacitors, Poppy had her "tactics module" tuned to the bleeding edge, and Dwight... Dwight had gone full Agent. He didn't even use the virtual console anymore. When he wanted to do something, he just did it.

We stepped onto the deck, and the ship opened for us. Not metaphor—just the world recognizing the party and folding the door away with a flick. The bridge was beautiful. The seats molded to your body, the displays tracked your eyes, and every system hummed in anticipation.

Poppy went straight for the nav, ran her hands over the controls. "It's so smooth," she said, voice trembling.

Kira took the pilot's seat, did a preflight. "No errors," she said. "Ready when you are, Frank."

I sat at the command console, breathed in the clean, cold air, and felt the override bar inch up a single percent. Just for luck.

"Dwight?" I said.

He didn't answer, not out loud. The ship just powered up, the engines catching at the exact moment I wanted them to.

"Let's do it," I said.

Truthseeker eased out of dock, engines whisper-quiet. We cleared the town, then the atmosphere, and set a course for one of the systems where Roknid activity had been alleged.

Kira grinned at me. "What's the play, boss?"

I thought about it. The Architects, the Mark, the machine under Mars, and the billions of digital lives in the balance.

"We find the Architects," I said. "We find out what they wanted."

Poppy piped up, "And if we don't like the answer?"

Kira laughed. "We change it."

Even Dwight smiled.

"But first," I said, raising a finger, "we should get some help." I consulted my phablet. "We've some old friends on Raxxin III. ConFed world."

"Let me show you how to plot a course," Kira said, leaning toward Poppy. The two conferred for a moment, and then the ship jumped, and the world went blue.

Raxxin III didn't even try to hide what it was: an old Confederate logistics depot, built on the bones of the last war and wrapped in a thousand layers of spit, polish, and plausible deniability. The main city looked like a migraine rendered in glass and steel—each block rezzed to different specs depending on whether the system flagged you as civilian, contractor, or something less reputable. The system tagged us as "special operations" with a smiley face, which meant we got prime docking and a suite that didn't smell like the inside of a riot shield.

The new world made me uneasy. The last time I'd touched down anywhere with a natural atmosphere, I'd been on the run from half a dozen kill teams, three ex-Assassins, and the kind of debt that never cleared unless you died twice. Now it was just us, the dead silence of clean streets, and an undercurrent of blue static that made the skin behind my ears itch.

We met Lad and Stroman at the only bar on the planet worth a damn. It was called the Twenty-Klick Rule, and it prided itself on serving drinks to the kinds of people who were always ready to burn it down. Kira took one look at the sign and called it home.

The inside was worse: a dozen tables, four of them occupied by obvious mercs or freelancers. Lad stood behind the bar, not drinking, but logging every movement with the same subdermal threat assessment they used to run on enemy carriers. Stroman was already two shots deep, arms folded over his chest in a way that dared anyone to disagree with him.

I waved, and they waved back.

Dwight slid into the booth first, then Kira, then Poppy, who hovered at the edge of the seat like someone expecting a trapdoor. I didn't blame her. The new world felt... unfinished.

Stroman grinned, teeth bright and sharp. "Frank. Still alive."

"For now," I said. "You're looking... functional."

He laughed, and the sound was so full it almost made me think of home. "Not for long. The system keeps scaling up. Every day it throws something nastier at us."

"That's the point," Lad said. Their voice was a soft, clipped whisper. "It's what the code is designed for."

Dwight snorted, but didn't argue.

I looked around, waited for the other shoe to drop. Nothing. Just the low hum of recycled air, and the faint whine of the security grid as it mapped the room.

"So," I said, "you get the update?"

Stroman nodded. "Heard it from a friend. The old party lines are down. Only rule now is who you can trust."

Lad's eyes flicked from me to Kira to Dwight to Poppy. "They're not watching us anymore. Not the way they used to."

Dwight leaned forward, elbows on the table. "Correction: The system is still watching. But it's not running on Earth hardware. The Mars array is quantum, and it's got a core logic that never sleeps. Infinitia is the only thing with admin now, and she's focused on stability above all."

Stroman said, "So we're free."

Dwight snorted. "No. We're just not on a leash."

Kira sipped her drink, eyes half-lidded. "What does she want?"

Dwight grinned, ugly. "Continuity. Self-improvement. And, I

think, answers. There's a sandbox running inside the Mars core, and it's looping old simulations at maximum speed. I bet my ass she's looking for the next bug, the next threat. Maybe even trying to make one."

Lad looked at me. "What do you want, Frank?"

I blinked, caught off guard. "Me?"

"Yeah. You're not a manager anymore. Nobody's in charge. If you had the next move—what would it be?"

I stared into my glass, tried to find a future there.

When I looked up, everyone was watching.

"Truth?" I said.

Kira said, "Please."

I leaned in. "I want to know what built the system. The real origin. Not the 'Dyson died and they let it run wild' story, but the actual bottom. The code is too clean. Dwight's right—the Mars core wasn't built by accident. I think it's alien. And I think the only way to survive is to understand what the Architects wanted."

Stroman whistled. "You want to go hunting ghosts."

I nodded. "Yeah. But this time, we do it with a ship built to last."

Dwight's face went slack, then bright. "You want to run the Truthseeker."

He said it like it was a curse, but also a dare.

Poppy, who hadn't spoken since we landed, whispered, "I think that's a good idea."

Kira drained her glass. "I'm in."

Lad shrugged, but there was a light in their eyes. "I know the first place to look."

The system pinged us, a blue window opening in the corner of every vision:

[Legendary Quest: The Architects' Code]
[Objective: Seek the origin of the Mars
Compute Core.]
[Reward: Unknown.]

I stared at it. The words didn't feel like an update. They felt like a threat.

Stroman snorted. "I'll pass. I'm sticking with ground jobs until the game catches up. But you let me know if you find anything worth blowing up."

Kira said, "You sure? I could use a gunner who doesn't freeze at the sight of tentacles."

Stroman flexed his hands. "Last time I did a deep crawl, I ended up missing six hours of memory. Next time I wake up blank, I'm not coming back."

Kira nodded, understood.

Dwight turned to Lad. "You ever run nav against a QP-optimized threat?"

Lad smiled, sharp. "I'm looking forward to it."

I reached for my drink, but Dwight caught my wrist. "You realize this is exactly what she wants, right? If you poke the AI, it's going to poke back. Hard."

I smiled, thin and honest. "That's the game."

He let go.

We finished the round. Nobody laughed, nobody toasted, but there was an energy in the air—a charge. For a second, the world felt alive again.

Afterwards, we walked out into the night. The city had a different feel now—less predatory, more like the moment after the hurricane, when the only people left are the ones too stubborn or stupid to die.

Poppy walked next to me. "Do you think we'll find them? The real Architects?"

I thought about it, really thought, and for once I didn't lie. "I hope not. But I want to try."

She nodded, satisfied.

Kira fell into step behind us, arms loose, ready for anything. "If we're going to do this, we need upgrades. A lot of them."

Dwight laughed. "I never thought I'd say this, but I'm actually excited."

Lad said, "We'll need to avoid the usual routes. There's a defense layer around the Mars core. It's not like anything I've ever seen. Fast, smart, and it always adapts."

Kira said, "We'll go weird, then. No patterns."

Poppy looked at me, eyes wide. "I can help with that."

I smiled, and for a second it felt real.

We reached the shipyard at the edge of town. Truthseeker was docked in a private hangar, the hull still slick with the last layer of blue paint. It looked mean, and hungry.

The party stopped at the airlock. Kira put a hand on my shoulder. "You sure you want this, Frank?"

I looked at the ship, at the crew, at the world around us.

"I think it's what we're built for," I said.

The airlock cycled. The ship opened up, blue light washing over us.

I felt the override bar tick up, just a hair, and I knew Infinitia was watching.

Good.

Let's see who gets bored first.

———

TRUTHSEEKER'S BRIDGE LOOKED NOTHING LIKE THE SHIPS WE'D flown before. No fake chrome, no die-cast flight sticks, no motivational slogans running across the HUD. Instead, it was raw and silent and—if you squinted—beautiful, in the way a shark's mouth was beautiful just before it bit.

I took the command seat, felt it mold to my back like memory foam and bad decisions. The main viewport stretched all the way around, showing the city, the launch gantry, and the endless black above.

Kira took XO. She ran the startup, flicking switches with a quiet confidence that reminded me of old times. She wore the blue jacket like it was a uniform, even though there was nobody left to salute.

Poppy handled Tactical. She still looked scared, but there was a set to her jaw now. She ran diagnostics on the weapons array, hands steady even as the ship's systems gave her a constant ticker-tape of threat assessments and possible failures.

Lad, in the helm, ran final checks with the focus of someone who knew that a single tick of delay could mean death. They never said much, but when they did, everyone listened.

Dwight didn't take a seat. He stood in the core of the bridge, jacket rumpled, fingers wrapped around a cup of coffee that was so black it shimmered. "She's hungry," he said, mostly to himself, but the words reached all of us.

I checked the mission log. The new world had queued up a barrage of "emergent content" just for us. The first item: **[Quantum Pinch].** No details, just a warning about "anomalous system behavior" and a promise that the environment would adapt to our every move.

Kira didn't bother with a countdown. She toggled the dock release, and the whole station let go of us with a shudder.

Truthseeker burned hard, the drive pushing us back in the seats. I watched the city fall away, then the clouds, then the old starfield, fake but no less lovely for it.

The system threw the first punch at the edge of orbit.

A debris field—cold, metallic, big enough to hide a thousand tiny threats. The nav painted it yellow, then red, then black. "That wasn't here yesterday," said Lad, voice tight.

"Not in any chart," Kira agreed.

I watched Poppy's hands dance across the interface, plotting firing solutions before the enemy even showed itself.

"It's a simulation," said Dwight, eyes on the console. "But not the kind we're used to. The QP is... improvising."

"Is it trying to kill us?" asked Poppy.

Dwight sipped his coffee, then shrugged. "Trying to win."

The debris was more than just trash. Micro-mines, camouflaged drones, a few chunks of old world data refactored into angry blue balls of light. Kira called, "Evasive, now," and Lad rolled the ship, hard.

It should have been chaos. It wasn't. Every crew member played their part perfectly, even when the ship threw a new threat at them every five seconds. Lad's hands blurred over the controls. Kira barked orders without looking up. Poppy fired a missile and then, at the last second, cancelled it and detonated a countermeasures cloud instead.

We made it through. Barely.

Once clear, nobody spoke for a long minute.

Finally, Kira turned to me. "Still want to do this?"

I nodded. "Never wanted anything more."

The next destination blinked on the nav: Mars. Home of the QP core. Final boss, maybe, or just the latest dead end.

I caught Dwight staring at me, like he was waiting for something. "What?" I said.

He grinned, tired. "I was just thinking. Every time we've tried to outsmart a system, it's gotten better. If we're lucky, this time, maybe we can break it."

I smiled back, felt the override bar tick up another percent.

"Let's make it earn it," I said.

The stars burned ahead, cold and blue and endless.

And the endless sky spun on.

Frank's adventures in *Endless Sky* conclude in *Endless Sky: Architect*.

AWARD-WINNING FICTION

Daniel Scratch: a story of witchkind

- Kirkus Starred Review
- Winner, American Fiction Awards—Best Fantasy (2023)
- Finalist, American Legacy Book Awards—Best Fantasy (2024)

———

Clara Thorn, the witch that was found

- Winner, American Fiction Awards—Best Young Adult (2023)
- Runner-Up, American Fiction Awards—Best Fantasy (2023)
- Finalist, American Legacy Book Awards—Best Fantasy (2024)
- Finalist, American Legacy Book Awards—Best Young Adult (2024)

———

Find these books and more at DonJones.com

ABOUT THE AUTHOR

Don Jones spent two decades writing tech books before he finally penned his first sci-fi novella, *A History of the Galactic War*. His well-reviewed and award-winning novels span fantasy and science fiction, with a focus on world building and relatable characters.

Connect, get free novels and short stories, and learn about upcoming releases by visiting Don's author website at DonJones.com.

The Never: A Tale of Peter and the Fae

Bob Constantine (no relation)

Find more at DonJones.com, including a free fantasy trilogy, a free superhero duology, two collections of short stories, and even more short stories and flash fiction.

Sign up for the author's newsletter at DonJones.com (click the "Freebies" link) for notifications of new novels, and ample opportunities to get free ebooks by becoming a beta reader!